LIFFY
ONE
ALPHA

First published 2023
First Edition

ISBN (eBook): 978-1-7393232-1-9
ISBN (Paperback): 978-1-7393232-0-2

Cover design by Flintlock Covers
Typeset in Athelas by Flintlock Covers
www.flintlockcovers.com

PADRIC J KELLY

LIFFY ONE ALPHA

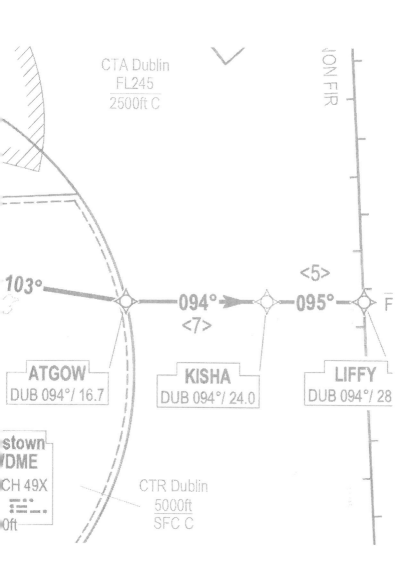

CTA Dublin
FL245
2500ft C

ON FIR

103°

094° ➤

<7>

<5>

095°

F

ATGOW
DUB 094°/ 16.7

KISHA
DUB 094°/ 24.0

LIFFY
DUB 094°/ 28

stown
/DME
CH 49X

0ft

CTR Dublin
5000ft
SFC C

Liffy One Alpha is about relationships, love, greed, the less glamorous side of aviation, and survival when destiny goes drastically awry.

For those intimately acquainted with their Nemesis, and for those yet to experience the phenomenon, welcome aboard.

The Author

To the captain

CHAPTER ONE

B rigid, the majestic, juniper green striped freighter, wings spanning one hundred forty-eight feet, her slender body almost two-hundred-foot from nose to tail, commenced her final descent towards Dublin Airport, trailing fragile ringlets of filthy grey smoke from her four shabby engines. Then, as the altimeters wound down through ten thousand, the turbulence intensified. Six hours earlier, the aircraft had departed Boston for the final leg of a five-day mission, laden with barrels of hazardous chemicals. And with less than ten minutes remaining to touchdown, the four-man crew struggled to maintain concentration. Yet, although well accustomed to fatigue, they had the awareness never to underestimate the associated threats. So, like soldiers in combat, Fergus, Quinn, Enda, and Berko looked out for each other.

Quinn, the first officer, was the pilot flying the aircraft. Convinced he was about to have a breakdown, he burned nervous energy as if it were free, which only hastened the erosion of his weakening backbone—the ensuing months of confusion running riot in his head had brought him to wit's end. So, with no more dithering, after this mission, Quinn would talk to someone trained to fix this sort of thing. He tried unsuccessfully to raise the matter with the rest of the crew on a few occasions. However, this was taboo, and they refused to get drawn in.

Nonetheless, all the soul-searching had brought Quinn to a gut-wrenching reality; he was developing a fear of flying. From the right pilot's seat, clutching the control wheel tighter with every shudder of the airframe, his heart pulsated against the straps of his harness. With sticky, sweaty palms, and devoid of confidence, Quinn eased the graceful Douglas DC8-63 around a monstrous cumulus cloud as they tracked north along the Wicklow coast towards the airport. At times, the morning sunlight would come flooding through gaps in the darkening sky, stinging tired, bloodshot eyes, and yet none of the crew wore sunglasses. Only on rare occasions would they don shades, preferring to offer no hiding place for lying eyes.

This quirky behaviour originated from a funny moment in the hotel's beer garden in Jakarta during a recent mission together. The captain had asked his co-pilot a personal question, and as he began answering, Quinn slipped on his sunglasses, triggering an instant reaction from Fergus. "Take off the shades, ya lying fecker."

It was a blustery late September morning, with storm-force winds wreaking havoc across the British Isles. And not far below, the Irish Sea raged white, with massive walls of breaking waves, ensuring perilous passage for even the toughest seamen. Enda, the engineer, was trying his damnedest to create a little distraction from the thorny weather conditions, which seemed hellbent on displacing the aircraft from its intended flight path.

"Yay, another mission impossible sorted. We're almost home, me lovelies."

Drumsticks in hand, Enda tapped a rhythm on the row

of fuel selector knobs while singing aloud the hit song, Relax, until they all joined in, karaoke style. And, forcing an unconvincing grin, Quinn hummed out of tune a few seconds behind the rest. At twenty-six, Enda was the youngest member of the crew. He could liven up the dullest moment, constantly probing for the craic, whatever the situation. After recently joining the airline, he quickly acquired the technical knowledge to keep up with the best, making him very popular, especially with the captains. That said, Fergus was the only commander to tolerate the young man monkeying around with drumsticks or playing his Walkman while on duty. Somehow, Enda managed to convince Fergus, over a few pints, that music calmed and even helped him concentrate, especially in challenging situations. Enda suddenly stopped singing, and after standing for a moment, trying to steady himself, he lurched to the other side of the flight deck, grabbing hold of Fergus's seat headrest for support. And with his nose pressed against the armoured glass window, he tried in vain to catch a glimpse of Securo, his bijou holiday cottage, tucked away in the mountainous valley below.

"For fecks shake, Enda, will ya get back to your station, lad? The last thing I need is for you to fall over and injure yourself," urged the captain.

Swaying to the unpredictable motion, the engineer flopped awkwardly back onto his seat without question, and tightly buckling his five-point harness, he sang aloud another chorus, this time a little less spirited, after being cautioned by air traffic control about their inaudible radio transmissions.

Fergus covered his ears with the headset, jotting down the recorded weather conditions being broadcasted over the radio. Quinn was on the other radio, talking with air traffic control. Glancing left, he could tell by the expression on the captain's face that all was not well as Fergus dragged the headset from his ears, declaring his frustration aloud.

"That lot in the met office needs a crystal ball, cos they couldn't make an accurate weather forecast, even if their lives depended on it."

"Yeah, but our lives do, skipper. So how bad is it?" queried the co-pilot, not actually wanting to hear the answer.

"Almost the whole of Northern Europe is getting hammered, and even though we checked earlier, this wasn't supposed to be in the script. These damn gales weren't forecasted until later this evening."

Quinn was never a great aircraft handler, and his growing nervous disposition only worsened matters. Lately, he had become aware that the rest of the crew were watching him, concerned that he might make a serious fuck up. He was right; they were. Even with fifteen hundred hours DC8 experience, and a total of more than four thousand in his log book, his landings of late had become borderline scary. During previous attempts, it appeared as if his sole purpose was to test the landing gear to just short of destruction. Enda was listening, waiting for the right moment to offer his input.

"Well, fellas, if it's any consolation, we've got a shit load of fuel. Enough to take us to the south of Spain, if necessary. Yo amo España."

Fergus turned in his seat to face his crew.

"Okay, here's how we're going to play it. First, Quinn, tell air traffic we will make an approach. If that doesn't work out, we might enter a holding pattern until the weather improves or divert. And Quinn, engage the feckin autopilot. Ya better conserve your energy for the landing."

"You've got to be kidding me, skipper. The wind down

4

there is blowing a hoolie, way outside my capabilities. In fact, it's even way outside the aircraft limitations."

"Quinn, you're gonna be flying this one. It's not up for debate. So, you fly. I'll monitor the approach."

Turning his head, pretending he'd noticed something of interest through the left window, a mischievous grin spread across the captains face.

"Enda, try to get more weather reports and keep a close eye on the fuel status. We should almost be in radio range, so I'll call the company on box two. I'll check where they would like us to go if we can't put her down at Dublin."

In the Green Bird Operations Room on the perimeter of Dublin airport, Gerry, the manager, was alone, standing beside the VHF radio with the microphone already in his hand. He was expecting the call from the inbound aircraft and immediately recognised Fergus's voice.

"Hey, Fergie, welcome home. What kept ya? You're running a bit late."

"Gerry, if you think this is late, the next time we talk, I might be phoning you from Spain."

"Jesus, Fergie, don't even joke about that. I've got a crew checking in soon for an early afternoon departure, in your ship."

"Look, Gerry, we'll try a couple of approaches, and if that doesn't work out, Prestwick looks doable. It's also blowing a gale over there, but straight down the runway, and as you well know, it's a wonderfully long runway. That's the best I can offer, boss. I'm not flying a feckin helicopter."

"Cúla Búla, Fergie. I know you'll do your best. Although I'm not sure about the other mad feckers you have with you."

"Enough now, Gerry. Go and sharpen a pencil, or do something useful. Talk later."

Berko, the loadmaster, came forward to the flight deck to

listen to Fergus's approach briefing. For a man in his late sixties, he had an uncanny ability to keep his balance without grabbing hold of something, even in the most turbulent conditions. Although Berko wasn't flight crew, another pair of eyes would always be helpful to try to spot hazards during the landing. Fergus spoke plainly, looking directly into the eyes of his co-pilot.

"Quinn, remember to keep the autopilot engaged until we get lined up for a visual approach. I know it's a big cross-wind. However, visibility is good, and luckily, at the moment, the runway is dry. Without a doubt, there will be windshear, so we'll add an extra twenty knots to the fly speed. Remember, Quinn, keep the wings level, and aim to get the wheels on the beginning of the runway. We'll handle this just like we're having a good day in the simulator. Okay?"

To Fergus's surprise, Quinn didn't protest. Instead, he nodded once before turning to focus on his flight instruments. Fergus called out to the loadmaster without looking back.

"Hey, Berko, you sure those barrels are well tied down?"

"Ja, mein Kapitän, they're as secure as kegs of Guinness in a pub's cellar."

Berko's response brought a timely but short-lived burst of laughter from the edgy crew. The chuckles abruptly ceased after the autopilot disengaged, unable to cope with the savage flight conditions, causing the aircraft to roll and pitch violently. The moment the autopilot let go, Quinn grabbed the control wheel, and cursing aloud, he swiftly managed to dampen the oscillations. Then, approaching ten miles final, Fergus called the airport in sight, prompting Quinn to look ahead through the windscreen as he struggled to keep the aircraft aligned with the runway centre line.

"You're doing grand, lad, just don't over control. You know it only makes things worse."

While Fergus encouraged his co-pilot, the monotone voice from the control tower over the speaker, repeatedly relaying the wind speed and direction, only added to the flight deck tension.

"300 degrees, 35 gusting 45 knots..."

"Hey, tower, no more wind calls. We know it's windy. You're making us even more nervous," pleaded Fergus, failing at an attempt to be humorous.

"Roger that, Green Bird. We have you in sight, approaching seven miles. You are cleared to land."

Quinn was engrossed, fighting to keep the aircraft on course, and if there were any doubts, he was doing an equally good job of concealing them from the rest of the crew. Wrestling the colossal machine, he skilfully overcame the elements until one hundred feet above the landing threshold. Then, to compensate for the gusting crosswind, Quinn pressed down hard on the rudder peddle to steer the nose of the aircraft and align it with the runway centreline.

"Speed, speed, go-around."

Fergus screamed aloud, first to notice the airspeed had dropped dangerously low. Instinctively, Quinn rammed the thrust levers fully forward, and, for a long moment, time stood still, before they plummeted down, the left main wheels of the mighty freighter making heavy contact with the tarmac. The aircraft bounced once, launching twenty feet back into the sky, as positive g-forces wedged the crew ponderously in their seats. As the airspeed gradually recovered from the thrust of the screaming engines, little by little, they gained altitude, climbing gingerly away from an inevitable catastrophe.

"Green Bird, do you wish to declare an emergency?"

Before responding to the controller, Fergus glanced over

his shoulder at Enda, holding his thumbs up, his Sony Walkman headset covering his right ear.

"Negative, tower, not unless you find a piece of our landing gear on the runway. Will inform you of our intentions shortly."

After entering a high-altitude holding pattern, in a less turbulent area over the coast, Quinn spoke, almost in a whisper, after re-engaging the autopilot.

"Fergie, can you take control, please? I'm heading aft to stretch my legs."

Leaning against the cargo netting next to the small toilet cubical, Berko was becoming embarrassed by the sound of retching. And when Quinn emerged, drying his face with a paper towel, he pointed his finger at the loadmaster.

"I don't want to hear any shit, Berko. Please, fuck off."

"Quinn, you're getting me all wrong. I've seen many scary approaches over the years, and I can tell you that you did a fine job back there."

Quinn was shocked, arms folded defensively and with a look of confusion.

"It wasn't your fault, Quinn. I've never seen a better-executed go-around in my life."

Speechless and bewildered, the co-pilot returned to his seat without reply and began to buckle himself in.

"Would ya like to take control, Quinn?"

"No thanks, Fergie. My flying is done for today unless you keel over and die."

"Very well then, but you listen to me. No matter who would have flown that approach, they couldn't have done better. That was serious windshear, and you flew us safely clear. Well done, lad."

A silent, reflective mood enveloped the flight deck until Berko, balancing a tray of coffee mugs and biscuits, announced his arrival.

"Right, fellas, get that into ya. What's the plan, skipper?"

"Well, the way I see it, we have three options. We could have another go. Although, I'm not too keen on that one. We could divert to Prestwick or try to land on the other runway, the short one. While you were away, Quinn, I made some calculations. Aer Lingus 737's are landing on it. We're bigger, and we'll be flying faster than a 737, but with the wind blowing straight down the centre line, it'll make it just about doable."

They were all quietly considering the options when Enda spoke up.

"Let's do it then, skipper."

"And what about you, Quinn?"

"Yes, it's a good plan, Fergie."

"Berko?"

"Ah, Jaysus, Fergie, do ya need to ask?"

After Quinn relayed their intentions to the control tower, a calming female voice replied over the radio.

"Green Bird, you are cleared for the approach and landing runway 29."

Once again, enduring the storm's rage, Fergus applied all his skill to get the aircraft close to the runway threshold. Then, timing the thrust reduction to perfection, the captain firmly planted the wheels onto the beginning of the touchdown zone. Within a split second, Fergus had the thrust reversers at maximum, and both pilots squeezed progressively heavier on the brake pedals while pushing fully forward on the controls to assist the heavy braking. The immense airframe shuddered in agony, trying to resist the deacceleration, until it finally succumbed, stopping with less than one hundred meters of tarmac remaining. Again, right on cue, the controller didn't waste time offering her observations.

"Hey, Green Bird, welcome home. That was impressive. You're the only DC8 to have landed on that runway, ever."

Neither of the pilots replied to what might have been a rebuke, and as they began to taxi back to the ramp, Quinn turned to Fergus.

"Jesus, Fergie, that was outstanding. But, hey, I'm sorry about earlier; I think I've lost it."

Enda leaned forward over Quinn's left shoulder.

"For fucks sake, Quinn, ya never feckin had it to lose."

Before the co-pilot could respond, Fergus intervened, flapping his hands, and gesturing calmly.

"Now, children, behave. Sure, isn't that why we have two drivers upfront? Although, lad, you still owe me a pint. In fact, Quinn, you'll shortly be buying us all lots of pints."

The loadmaster stood in the galley, leaning into the flight deck, rubbing his lower back.

"Hey, skipper, I hope those chemical containers are built as strong as this aircraft. Cos if they're not, we'll all be in serious trouble after that landing."

Berko pretended to act concerned, repeatedly winking at Enda, until the young engineer couldn't resist teasing as he pressed his oxygen mask against his face.

"Yeah, it's your fault, skipper. We're all gonna be gassed to death."

By the time the laughter and back-slapping had stopped, the four friends had again sealed their inseparable bond. And although Quinn joined in, trying to have the craic, it did little to help him shake off an overwhelming sense of awkwardness.

CHAPTER TWO

I n the Green Bird company office, Gerry, the Operations Manager, checked through the reams of official paperwork that typically accumulated during a mission. Gerry's meticulous input was a critical part of the overall success of each contract. Acutely aware of the difficulties they had faced over the previous three years, 1985 was going to be even trickier, with foreign competitors creating severe challenges for the small, independent freight airline. And as a result, he knew how to file the official documentation that always managed to reflect regulation-compliant missions, even though, in reality, they could never financially afford to be compliant. The combination of his dry, sharp sense of humour, and his ability to tread the thin line between management, crew, and the authorities, made him invaluable to the overall success of the airline.

Enda, Fergus, Quinn, and Berko sauntered in single file into the Operations Room. Gerry peered over the rim of his spectacles from his desk at the now familiar sight of broken men, obviously weary, most of it self-induced.

He sighed as a slight grin spread and whispered, "Would

I let my family fly with those mad fuckers? Never, not a chance in hell."

Then, raising his voice to be heard, Gerry offered his usual greeting to the crew.

"Jaysis, what have you lot been up to? You look awful."

"Hey, mister smart arse, you've just arrived after a full night's sleep. Have you any idea how long it's been since we lay in a cosy soft bed?" snapped Enda. Gerry glared back at him but didn't reply.

Thirty minutes later, with all the post-flight duties completed, the crew were dead-set on enjoying every one of their ten days off, but not before a little post-mission socialising. So, Enda went in Berko's car, and the pilots drove the short journey in Fergus's ageing Toyota to The Coachman's Inn, and, as the car pulled away, Quinn cursed aloud while clumsily trying to fasten his seat.

"What a shit fecking design. Can I tell you a secret, Fergie?"

"Of course, Quinn, but ya know me, I'll tell everyone."

Quinn continued in earnest, discarding the teasing remark.

"Well, the other day, I was on the bog having a crap and, without realising it, I felt around the toilet seat for the buckle of me harness to strap meself in."

Fergus burst out laughing.

"And did you find it, ya dozy gobshite?"

"It's not feckin funny. I think I need a long holiday or something."

Quinn protested with a tone of frustration and a hint of self-pity.

"We all do, lad, me included."

CHAPTER THREE

Although their preferred place of worship had not officially opened, no objection was raised by Dave, the head barman at The Coachman's, who had arrived at the pub a few minutes earlier.

"Four creamy black ones," ordered Berko, rubbing his hands together.

In a gesture of goodwill towards four of his best customers, the barman held each glass to the light before sliding it under the tap. Then, and without rushing, he produced four of the best-looking pints on the planet. Enda held his hand up for attention just before taking his first mouthful.

"Fellas, can we plan to pack it in around eleven? Remember the shit we got into the last time we dropped in here... for the one?"

Swallowing three-quarters of his pint in one gulp before replying, Berko ran the back of his hand across his mouth, holding a mischievous grin.

"Now, Enda, me lad, would that be AM or PM?"

So, with deliberate intent, the four crewmen, characters, comrades, and inseparable friends, settled down to discuss every known topic under the sun. Quinn homed in on Fergus, knowing that he was the best listener. Once again, he tried to introduce the taboo subject, but Fergus wasn't having any of it. So, like a priest hearing a boring confession, he offered little to stimulate the conversation.

"I see. Yes, I understand. It all sounds very serious."

They were the only words Fergus spoke over the next thirty minutes, and ironically, from the way they were dressed, they could all have passed as clergy. In aviation circles, it was considered a sin to drink in uniform. So, before arriving at the pub, they removed the airline ribbons and badges, dressing down to white short-sleeved, open-collar shirts, black trousers, and shoes. Now, they all carried equal rank. And then Quinn, in proper form, dampened everyone's mood. He'd changed the subject with Fergus and began babbling about drug smuggling, a real conversation stopper.

"For feck's sake, Quinn, you can be so fucking negative," cried Berko.

"Yeah, he's right, Quinn. That was over six weeks ago, and the authorities have proven nothing," protested Enda, forcing Quinn onto the defensive.

"Fuck off, Enda; you weren't even on the flight. So, I ask again, how the fuck did two thousand kilos of Angel Dust get loaded onto our aircraft without anyone noticing, not even you, Berko?"

Fergus wasn't pleased, feeling the need to calm things down a bit.

"Right, let's not spoil the pints; I'm only going to explain one last time. I was the skipper, so they interrogated me the hardest before finally accepting that the crew and me knew nothing about it. Anyway, it wasn't like it was that other stuff. I think they call it PCP. It was only a growth promoter for cattle.

It appears that it had been going on undetected for years. They had it well organised at both ends, with regular deliveries between Chicago and Dublin. Nobody could have known we were going to divert into Shannon that day. Meaning, the usual ground crew wasn't there when we landed. However, customs were. I can let ya in on a bit of new scandal. It seems that the fecker, the station manager in Chicago, the one who was supposedly independently wealthy, well, he isn't. He was a Provo sympathiser, a big fundraiser for the cause. He coordinated the racket, and now he's done a runner."

Everyone sat dumbfounded, gazing at the wise old owl, wanting to hear more, when the barman shouted across the counter.

"Four creamy ones, lads?"

The banter resumed in earnest as the men began to de-stress under the imaginary cloak that bound them together, in their cosy little corner of the near-empty pub. That is, until just before midnight, when the barman was becoming desperate.

"Ah, lads, have you no homes to go to? The Gardaí are outside. For feck's sake, I'll lose me feckin licence."

Swaying a little, Fergus delivered with surprising clarity the few words he knew he'd need at some point before the end of that day.

"Davie, call Tumper."

Dave placed a steadying hand on Fergus's outstretched arm. "Fergie, I'll do just that. I'll call Tumper to come and get ya. He'll be the only one to get you boyos out of here tonight."

* * *

15

Tumper was sprawled out on his sofa, watching a documentary rerun about the Irish Civil War, when the phone rang.

"Tumper, it's Dave at the Coach. Can you come and get the lads, please, and hurry? They're all pissed?"

"Jesus, Davie, not again."

For a man in his late fifties, Tumper hadn't aged well. He stood about six foot six and weighed around sixteen stone, a tall man who kept himself private, and those who didn't know about his earlier activities considered him the personification of a gentle giant. Although it had never been proven by the authorities, both north and south of the border, he was suspected of being one of the most active and ruthless commanders in the IRA. No one understood, nor did they dare to uncover the reason for his apparent change of heart. Tumper had changed, of that there was no doubt. Perhaps the killing, maiming, and torture, especially when he recalled the few innocent ones, must have caught up with him. And, as he grew older, the righteous cause could no longer offer his conscience sanctuary.

Nowadays, he kept a low profile, content with his minibus taxi service, making a modest living, and adapting well to a quiet existence with his closest companion, a Beagle named Semtrick. Tumper was Enda's father's best friend, and shortly before his premature passing, when Enda was only twelve years old, Tumper gave a deathbed pledge to his pal, promising to look out for Enda as if he was his son.

Tumper ran the crew transport service for Green Bird while frequently extending it as a taxi for some crew, especially for Enda. He had parked his minibus near the rear entrance to the Coachman's and was just about to enter when a Garda, his cap pushed high on his forehead, emerged through the pub's back door.

"Good evening, Mister Dunne. Working late, are we?" asked the Garda.

Tumper didn't reply, as he marched through the entrance, forcing the policeman to take a quick sidestep to avoid a collision. Inside, he glanced around the pub, half expecting trouble, but all was quiet. The last four remaining patrons were huddled together on a couch close to the bar. It looked as if they'd been dropped from a height. Their limbs appeared intertwined, creating a puzzle-like sculpture that no one could dismantle without causing physical injury. Tumper shook his head as he looked across the barroom towards Dave.

"Any damage, Davie?"

Dave shook his head and smiled.

"Na, no damage."

The skilled taximan rescued the crewmen, one by one, lifting them like rag dolls, dangling each in turn across his shoulders, before gently laying them on the back seats of the minibus. Then, just before Tumper departed on the long home delivery, he leaned back, finger gesturing towards the naughty inattentive and half-comatose passengers.

"Stay there, and not a single feckin word till I get ya home."

CHAPTER FOUR

The twins, Amy, and Carol, exaggerated each step as they marched down the long pathway of the family cottage to the front gate, where the school bus collected them each morning. Just inside the entrance, a man was curled up, lying on the grass beside a bush. The girls weren't expecting to find him sleeping in the garden, so Amy ran back to the house full of excitement.

"Mammy, daddy's home! Mammy, mammy, come quick, dad's home."

Carol stood over her father, bewildered, and strangely bemused by the tranquil expression on Quinn's face. An open hand, pillow-like, supported his head, and his other arm was wrapped around his flight case. Every couple of seconds, he snored heavily, dribbling saliva from his half-open mouth, and under different circumstances, it could have been a hilarious scene. Quinn's wife, Jenny, was soon on the scene, with bright-eyed and excited Amy close on her heels.

The family were again united as the big green school bus rumbled to a stop, honking its horn. Jenny ushered the twins out through the gate, trying to remain calm, while strategically positioning herself between the bus and her husband's body, to preserve some dignity.

"Off ya go, girls. You'll see your daddy when you get home from school."

And, as the bus departed, gazing through the rear window, their mother appeared to be saying something as she looked down at their father; her chin cupped in the palm of her hands and fingers poked hard against her cheeks.

"Ya feckin eejit, you've been out here all night. You're lucky you didn't freeze to death, you stupid dope."

CHAPTER FIVE

Aoife's eyelids flickered before popping open. She'd been in a deep sleep before she sprung upright in the bed. Her senses wanted her to scream, but her brain couldn't remember how to. Aoife took a deep breath and, remaining perfectly still, her eyes flicked left and right in an uncontrolled spasm. From the corners of the bedroom, the Bose loudspeakers delivered ninety-plus decibels of Robin Williams, alias DJ Adrian Cronauer, giving his rendering of Good Morning Vietnam. Still half asleep and stunned by the noise, she managed to propel herself off the end of the bed and, with outstretched fingers, one of them made contact with the hi-fi on/off button. The instant void of silence was replaced by the thud of her body against the wooden bedroom floor.

"Shit, I'll kill him. You're feckin dead, Enda."

Sitting on the floor while taking time to compose herself, Aoife figured that, the night before, she must have accidentally selected one of Enda's programmable wakeup calls on the powerful sound system.

"I won't be making that mistake again. Where the fuck is he?"

Desperate for a remedy for her throbbing head, she cursed as she stood under the hot rain shower. Then, naked and dripping wet, she dashed erratically through the apartment, room by room, looking for a clue to the puzzle. The search ended abruptly in the dining room, where dinner had been set for two, but only she had turned up. One side of the table was still neatly arranged, and on the other side, next to the burnt-out candle, were the remains of a half-eaten meal and two empty red wine bottles. She tiptoed across the floor to the window overlooking the carpark, three floors below. Tumper's bright yellow taxi showed no activity and was parked in the disabled driver's space. About to scream, Aoife took a deep breath as she raised her shoulders but could only manage a whisper.

"If you're not disabled, you feckin will be when I get my hands on ya."

She slipped on sandals, wrapped herself in her dressing gown, and headed down the emergency exit staircase to where Tumper and the wanted man lay on the back seat of the minibus.

"The bastard!" She bit her lip. "A night on the piss with the lads instead of the romantic welcome home dinner with his woman."

How they managed to get any sleep at all was a complete mystery. Slouched across the bench seat, they had adopted the foetal position, and through the half-open driver's window, the symphonic-like rhythm of their heavy snoring was audible halfway across the carpark. Aoife controlled her initial impulse to revive the sleepers abruptly. Instead, turning on her heels, she headed back towards the apartment's entrance to consider the options. She stood in the lobby, wishing for divine inspiration, as she rested her folded arms on the fire hose reel. Then, suddenly, she smiled while taking a few steps back, letting the words on the sign filter through.

IN CASE OF FIRE.

"Confirmed," she whispered. "I'm on bloody fire."

She tugged at it like she was wrestling a giant python, struggling to drag the heavy rubber hose out through the entrance door. Then, draping it across her delicate shoulders, she steadily pulled, making determined progress towards the minibus, stopping briefly to silence a quizzing neighbour.

"Is there a fire? I'll phone 999."

"Shush now. Can't you see I'm busy dealing with it?"

Aoife slipped the fire hose through the open window, propping it against the front seat headrest, with the shiny brass nozzle pointing towards the rear seats. Experiencing great difficulty containing her excitement, she rubbed her hands above her head while performing a childlike hop-skip jump. Then, returning to the lobby, she grabbed hold of the lever and rotated until it was fully open. Rushing outside to take in the unfolding spectacle, she gazed as the fire hose wriggled a few times, then stiffened. It was like a scene from a movie when the submarine goes too deep and springs a massive leak.

The panic-stricken men in the minibus scrambled for the doors, convinced they'd dozed off and crashed into a river or canal. The side door slid open as Enda pulled hard on the handle, and the men from the sinking vessel struggled free. Expecting to swim to the surface, they fell from the minibus onto the hard, concrete surface. Turning the control valve shut, Aoife felt satisfied that justice had been done as she wandered casually back outside to survey the scene. The red fire engine from a nearby station was approaching fast, its sirens blazing and getting louder. Then, skidding through the carpark gates, it menacingly demanded right of way before coming to a screeching stop next to the minibus. The fire chief and half a dozen yellow-helmeted men leapt from the vehicle, ready for action. With the situation under control, the fire chief commended Aoife for her quick response to what could have been a life-threatening situation. Although, they were still unable to locate the source of any fire.

Aoife shook her head, mimicking an innocent look that didn't work.

"Sorry, lads, false alarm. I must have been mistaken. I was sure I saw smoke coming from the window."

Even the fire crew stayed to help salvage the waterlogged taxi. Tumper managed to hire a portable dehumidifier from the local hardware store and, moaning continually; he supervised proceedings, wrapped in his long woollen Crombie coat.

"Me bus is fucked, me feckin bus is fucked."

Although gradually beginning to mellow, Aoife didn't regret what she'd done for a single moment.

"You've just had a cold one, so what you lads need now is a hot shower, and I'll cook us some breakfast."

Up in the apartment, Tumper had also calmed down a little, continuing to protest his innocence.

"It wasn't my fault. I was just trying to rescue the little fecker from the pub. I couldn't get him out. He kept me up all bloody night, waffling. He thinks he's a feckin drug runner."

Aoife couldn't control the giggles.

"Hey, Tumper, I really did think your taxi was on fire."

Enda gave his girlfriend a knowing grin, deciding it best to keep the banter light-hearted.

"My dearest Aoife. Isn't this the way women like to show how much they really care?"

CHAPTER SIX

Special Operations Division, Langley, were struggling to grade a developing national security threat. The little known but deadly killer, which had already reached epidemic levels in parts of Africa, and with San Francisco as the epicentre, was spreading rapidly across the U.S.A. They wanted to stop and annihilate it, at any cost, and regardless of any secondary health risks for the unfortunate carrier. The Operations Director was in his office speaking by telephone with one of his senior advisers.

"I'm sure you read or heard the news? About the epidemic? A frigging national disaster. Could be a million people infected. Those cocksuckers have even infected the country's blood stockpiles. Can you imagine? Our best brains at the Disease Control Centre in Atlanta are calling it a contagious form of cancer, so we have to stop it; we have to flush them out. Deckleshine, bless his sole, has inadvertently come up with a solution, and although not ideal, crucially, it only targets the filthy carriers."

Doctor Deckleshine was a brilliant scientist. His unsurpassed knowledge in biochemistry could have brought him world fame and fortune. Instead, he opted for a more reclusive lifestyle, shunning a public profile. Nevertheless, the U.S. Special Operations Division needed his expertise, just like they needed many brilliant minds who excelled in every discipline known to man. They knew precisely how to control and manipulate the chosen few. Deckleshine's specialist work was rewarded with an enviable array of normally unobtainable resources, and often he would be selected as lead scientist of top-secret government projects. Minimum interference and state-of-the-art assets were the keys to Deckleshine, including a hi-tech laboratory on a remote air force base in Florida.

Deckleshine wasn't interested in sharing his discoveries with foreign research institutions, even if they could be used for the common good of humanity. He lived a humble existence on the air base with his small, handpicked team of dedicated scientists. Using the latest computer software and intellectual property, most of it not yet available to other researchers, created a massive wealth of untapped knowledge, giving his team the tools to make astonishing and potentially dangerous scientific discoveries.

Like the archaeologist searching for the Holy Grail, Deckleshine had developed an unhealthy obsession. He always began a new project by trying to identify the good versus the evil elements before linking these forces to his biochemistry research. Then, focusing on enhancing the good, the professor would attempt to weaken what he considered bad or evil facets. At the age of four, adopted by well-meaning but despotic guardians, did little to invigorate the impressionable years the hard-to-place child. In particular, during an awful period of oppression, his father's obsession festered with behaviour akin to that of a schizophrenic, religious fanatic. Even through adulthood, Deckleshine often woke from night terrors, vividly recalling the beatings or one of his father's biblical chants.

"Lament your sinful ways, my son. Good will conquer evil."

As a student, master Deckleshine was an academic phenomenon, constantly adored, admired, and occasionally envied by his tutors. Then, studying as an undergraduate at Massachusetts Institute of Technology, the university Dean summoned the young Deckleshine to his office to inform him of his father's accidental death and was shocked by his prize student's cold response.

"Thank you, sir. Will that be all?"

Within days of leaving the university, he was head-hunted by a major pharmaceutical company, which offered him the opportunity to unleash his genius beyond theoretical possibilities. Many years later, in his heavily fortified government laboratory, Deckleshine worked tirelessly on an antiviral elixir in response to a new and challenging danger. During laboratory experiments, infected primates were injected with his latest creation, ShineOn. Unfortunately, although the results were encouraging, it was a very undesirable fix for the virus carrier.

When viewed through a microscope, Deckleshine's creation could be observed attacking and destroying the virus. However, the subject's blood would thin, and as if receiving an overdose of Warfarin, every organ and vessel would rupture, resulting in death. Then, ShineOn and the virus would fade away without a trace after the battle. The nodus was tagged by him in a research papers, calling it; *the sixty second apocalypse.*

Nonetheless, Deckleshine's creation was extraordinary. It could defeat the virus. Although it was harmless to healthy uninfected organisms, it would remain dormant in the blood cells, ready to attack the invader and perform its aggressive cleansing once injected. The initial trials were conducted on guineapigs, then primates, until a frustrated

Deckleshine succumbed to clever, persuasive arguments from government agents, agreeing that conducting tests on a human volunteer would most likely progress their knowledge of the little-known killer, which was running rampant in the male homosexual community.

The professor's sponsors were delighted with the prospect of a real experiment and wasted no time delivering a suitable candidate to Deckleshine's laboratory. In his late twenties, the male appeared ideal for human trials. Unfortunately, Jessie wasn't exactly sure when he became infected by the virus but suspected it was when backpacking across South America, or the party weekend in San Francisco. Either way, after being briefed by a medical team, the man was informed that his life expectancy was short due to infection. So, without hesitation, he accepted the government agent's offer of better than half a chance of a cure. However, before the pact was sealed, the agent added a stipulation.

"Now, you listen to me, boy. We'll be shaving that hippy mop of hair and beard. Can't have you carrying any other hidden infections, contaminating our germ-free research laboratory."

Deckleshine spoke in a monotone to the enthusiastic volunteer through the microphone of his airtight astronaut-like suit.

"You do realise you're the first? I've had no major success so far, and if you want to change your mind, even at this late stage, I will understand."

Jessie peered up at him from the cold, stainless-steel table.

"Hey, doc, let's get on with it. I didn't have much of a future, but with your genius, I've got a sporting chance. Isn't that right, doc?"

Deckleshine nodded once.

"I'm going to administer a sedative."

"No, no way. Why would I want a sedative? What is it they say? No pain, no gain. So, no blindfold, doc."

The professor completed a final tour of the operating room, and at the main control panel, he made a few instrument tweaks before returning to his patient. Then after giving a reassuring tug on the brown leather restraining straps, he took a few steps backwards to the exit. And when the professor tapped a code on the keypad, the operating room's toughened glass doors sealed shut instantly.

The electronic apparatus was primed, and Deckleshine, the proxy executioner, was ready to administer the ShineOn cocktail. The professor entered a second code on the keypad, releasing his creation into the veins of the trusting man. A few minutes passed, and except for his heavy breathing, the bald-headed recipient remained motionless. But then, his heart began to race, rapid beats visually intensified on his bare chest, and his clenched fists sprung open, hands now gripping the edges of the steel table.

* * *

The assembly of men and women, dressed chiefly in military or medical attire, had gathered in a conference room at CIA headquarters, Langley. A few men in dark suits sat up front, fixated on the giant monitor screening the experimental trials, many hundreds of miles away. Mesmerised, they watched as Deckleshine and the young, frightened man held eye contact through the toughened Plexiglas, with only a couple of metres separating them.

There was a moment of intense anticipation as Deckleshine's creation began to circulate through the subject's veins, to cleanse the evil within. If there was a god, the young man's first bloody cough should have been his last. The leather restraints held fast as Jessie tried to struggle free, and then his whole body tensed, forcing his head back, exposing the protruding veins in his neck. As every blood-carrying vessel ruptured, the blood leaked, as if his skin was porous, and oozed from every orifice. It dripped from the table like a dark-red liquid dye, spreading splash-like patterns across the polished grey concrete floor. His eyes bulged from their sockets as the chronic haemorrhagic-like fever peaked. The fifty/fifty odds were optimistic. It took exactly one minute and twenty-eight seconds to empty what remained of Jessie's life.

Deckleshine, or any of his accomplices, could have reached for the guarded switch that controlled the lethal backup cocktail designed to quickly end the young man's suffering. But no one did. Neither Deckleshine nor his team expressed surprise or emotion, and as he recalled his offer of a sedative, he noted that there wouldn't be a choice in the future.

Some men in suits became nauseated by the images, shuffling uneasily in their seats until a junior officer responded correctly to a nod from his superior and marched swiftly forward to switch the monitor off. The encrypted Teletext message was short and to the point. During one of his rare moments of confusion, Deckleshine read it over and over again.

'Professor, your trial run was viewed by us with great interest. As a result, priority funding and resources are available. Continue your remarkable work. Concentrate on developing an airborne variant of your magnificent creation. END.'

CHAPTER SEVEN

Quinn's head was pounding as he gingerly navigated the pathway from his cosy corner in the garden to the back door of the cottage, and, standing in the doorway; he watched as Jenny sipped her cup of tea.

"Any chance of a cappuccino, Jen?" asked Quinn, trying to sound casual.

"Are you bloody serious?"

After preparing an instant coffee, he moved closer to face his wife.

"Lately, I've been thinking a lot, Jen, and I've decided I'm going to make things better for you and the girls. It's not too late, you know. It really isn't."

Jenny let out a sigh.

"I've heard it all before, Quinn. You're never sober long enough to think. Jesus, look at yourself. You're a feckin mess."

"I know, I know. Please, listen. I've got ten days off, so tomorrow morning, I'm going to call the company and demand the lot, including the other two weeks' leave from last year."

"Then what, Quinn? Two weeks with the lads on the piss in the local?"

"No, no, you don't understand, Jen. I'm really going to make things better. You, me, and the girls are heading off on a real family holiday. No booze, well, maybe just the odd glass of wine. I swear it."

"You look like shit, Quinn. Ya smell even worse, and you're a disgrace to your daughters."

"Jenny, please, I'm serious this time."

"Go shower, sleep it off, and later, if you can still remember what you're suggesting, we'll talk about it then."

Quinn reached for her hand.

"I'm not sleepy just yet, so if I make meself squeaky clean, will you come and snuggle me in? I've missed ya."

Stepping closer, he eased her against him, wrapping his arms playfully around her waist. Jenny punched him softly in the stomach.

"How the fuck? After all the heartaches, can you still manage to draw me in for more?"

"Because you love me, isn't that why?"

"Go wash yourself, Quinn, and maybe I'll come up to tuck you in. But I'm warning you, don't just try to fuck me. Now, more than ever, I need to feel that you care. Are you still capable of making love to me?"

As Quinn, the man with a plan, stood under the shower, washing away yesterday's grime, he cried, overcome with confused emotions. He knew Jenny was right; he was a mess. Not only unfit to be a father, Quinn shouldn't be flying aeroplanes. But, from now on, he would make it up to them. He was going to fix things, for sure, this time.

31

CHAPTER EIGHT

I n an outbuilding of the abandoned timber sawmill in Brazzaville's bacongo quarter, the Special Forces' Officer, dressed in camouflaged combats, could no longer contain his composure. Slowly raising himself off the chair, he assumed an aggressive posture, funnelling his anger towards the American military adviser sitting opposite. The thud of his fist on the wooden table raised fine dust particles into the air, exposing light beams that radiated through tiny gaps in the dilapidated corrugated steel roofing.

"You promised us support," he screamed.

The Texan's eyelids twitched rapidly on noticing his colleague's hand fidgeting on the safety strap of his holstered 9mm pistol.

"We never stop giving and promised you nothing, you thankless black Comanche. One more outburst like that, and I swear, I'll put you out of your misery. Now, sit the fuck down. Do it, do it now."

The tense standoff didn't last as the African's mean-looking posture crumbled, and although he did as ordered, the tense situation persisted. The Officer took a moment to compose himself, and when he spoke again, his voice was calmer, almost pleading.

"My men are dying. We need modern weapons to defend ourselves. You supply arms to our neighbour across the river, so why not us? You bring only words. How can we trust you? Your words will not kill our enemies. Maybe it's time you go home, American, and only return to bring us weapons, bullets, not words."

The opportunist American was skilful and well-trained to take advantage of such moments. He lit a cigarette, and blowing a long plume of smoke high into the air, it vanished in the dim light; reappearing moments later exposed by blades of bright sunlight.

"I take your point, chief. So, what if I could solve your hardware problem? You know how it works. We'll be expecting a lot in return. In fact, chief, this could be your lucky day. There just might be something brewing. As I understand it, we're planning to carry out an off the record operation in a remote area of rainforest, a few klicks south of the Cameroon border. I believe it's connected with medical research."

The African's grin was demonic.

"Take a good look around our land, American. Tell me what you want, and if the others haven't already stolen it, it's yours."

CHAPTER NINE

Had they entered a competition for the happy family of the year award, they would have won it outright. Quinn, Jenny, and the siblings sat at the dining table fantasising about destinations for their holiday of a lifetime. Quinn raised his wine glass while cheerfully announcing to the twins that the holidays had already begun, and he would personally inform the school principal in the morning. Then, noticing a slight concern on Jenny's face, he reckoned it was because the twins would miss school, or maybe he should ease back a bit on the wine, so he decided to probe a little.

"Jen, did you know that Italians drink a bottle of wine every day?"

"Really, so what?" she replied.

"They're a happy people, Jen, and, generally speaking, they live a long life."

Jenny raised her empty glass in Quinn's direction.

"Perhaps they share a bottle, my love."

Later that night, the phone rang as they sat on the sofa, flicking through pages of old travel brochures. Jenny walked to the corner of the sitting room to answer the call.

"Hello, little house on the prairie."

She could sense her expectations slipping away when she heard the familiar voice.

"Is that you, Jenny? It's Gerry here, in Operations. Is Quinn there?"

Jenny tensed, glancing at her husband, sitting with an arm wrapped around each of his daughters, creating the perfect family pose.

"Why do you want to talk to him, Gerry?"

"We need him for a flight in the morning. He'll only be gone for three days, maybe four at the most."

She squeezed, white-knuckled, on the receiver.

"He only arrived home today, Gerry. Please, get someone else."

"There is no one else, Jenny. We need him. We need his whole crew, including Fergie."

"I need him too, you bastard. My daughters need their father."

Quinn turned the television volume down, trying to figure out who was calling.

"Who is it, Jen?"

"It's that asshole, Gerry."

Slightly surprised by Jenny's irate outburst, Quinn crossed the room to where she stood, swinging the receiver by its cable.

"Hey, Gerry, what's up, pal?"

His family huddled on the sofa, listening as their man quarrelled and tried to reason until he finally lost the fight.

"Okay, tomorrow morning at seven."

By the time Quinn hung up the phone, Jenny had left the room, and the twins were halfway up the stairs.

"Where're you going, girls?"

It was Amy, the smallest of the twins, who answered, "It's bedtime, Daddy, and we have school tomorrow."

CHAPTER TEN

Gerry was in his element, proud that he'd managed to persuade the workers, against their will, to trash their personal lives once again; to rally for the company cause, which was, as always, to fulfil another financially lucrative contract.

It had been a long time since they'd secured such a profitable job from one of their most treasured American clients. They paid well above the going hourly rate and always on time, as long as their precious freight was delivered as demanded, with minimal official declarations. However, this particular contract was a bit strange, because it was to provide routine emergency medical supplies to Africa.

Gerry loved firing up a brand-new mission, and finally, at around 7am, the first crew member arrived, still trying to come to terms with the feeling of being conned into agreeing to take the assignment.

"You bollox, I doubt if I'll have any family to return to. So, where the fuck are we going anyway?" asked Quinn.

"I'll explain later when everyone's here," replied the manager.

Gerry couldn't stay still for a moment. He hurried about the office, offering useless suggestions to the weary crew, trying to kick-start their brains and get the show on the road.

"Fergie, have you got all the paperwork? And don't forget the overfly permission licences and the cargo manifest..."

Fergus had just arrived and was already becoming agitated.

"Please, Gerry, calm down."

"Fergie, don't forget to check the maps and the fuel. Fergie, can I get you another coffee?"

"Enough, Gerry, stop."

The manager then turned his attention to Berko.

"Have you got the latest cargo manifest?"

"Yes, Gerry."

"And Enda, have you...?"

Gerry stopped in mid-sentence.

"Fergie, where the fuck is Enda?"

The words were no sooner out of Gerry's mouth when the approaching low-pitched rumbling drifted into earshot. Gerry's head tipped back, his eyes looking up; maybe he'd seen something of interest on the ceiling as his lips moved ever so slightly. "Jesus" was the only audible word, suggesting he must have been in prayer with the Almighty.

Enda carefully guided his Harley Davidson through the staff carpark. He liked to position his much-loved steel companion in the most secure resting place, right outside the Operations Room, under the window, in full view of the security camera that monitored the area below. However, the noise was so intrusive that windows and doors slammed shut in the adjacent offices while phone calls were put on hold.

Fergus's coffee developed ripples, and everyone pressed

their hands to their ears for relief from the deafening sound. Enda sat tall in the saddle, and with the thumb of his left hand, he gestured towards a few admiring fellow bikers. Then, his right hand made three defiant short throttle twists, before the beast's engine finally came to a rumbling stop. With his left boot extended against the side stand, he leaned the motorcycle, stepped off, and slowly removed his gauntlet. With only the sharp, irregular ticking of the engine's hot metal, as it began to contract and cool down, all was once again calm. The Operations Manager was not impressed. Strutting into the office, Enda didn't rush to remove his helmet as the barrage of verbal abuse echoed across the room, until Quinn finally managed to raise his voice above Gerry's.

"Give it a rest, Gerry. You're making a bigger racket than the feckin bike did."

After the bickering slowly faded, Enda removed his helmet and turned to Fergus.

"Sorry I'm late, skipper. It's a long, sad story. Have ya decided how much juice we'll need?"

Fergus smiled.

"Well, now, young man, it says here on the flight plan we need fifty-three and a half tonnes, but that's not enough for me. So, we'll fill her up. How does that sound as a command decision?"

Enda chuckled as Fergus called out to the loadmaster.

"Hey, Berko, full tanks. Will that work on the weight and balance sheet?"

"I'll make it work," was the response.

The fuel quantity on the flight plan typically indicated the minimum required fuel but was rarely acceptable to the captain. The company accountant preferred if the crews took the minimum; as long as it was legal, any extra fuel load would usually create a significant weight and cost penalty. Fortunately, for this crew, the accountants didn't have the final say. When he joined Green Bird, Fergus established a clear understanding with management regarding fuel; that decision would always be his. No experienced crew would fly around Africa in a thirsty four-engine freighter, nervously glancing at the fuel gauges every few minutes. It took very little to screw up the best of plans; maybe an unexpected technical issue or diversion owing to shitty weather. Airborne over Africa was the wrong place to have regrets about an earlier fuel decision. Fergus called the extra top-up 'comfort juice,' comparing it with blood. He'd often offer the younger pilots' words of caution; when the quantity gets too low, you're fucked.

Enda and Berko were first to head out to the aircraft to begin preparations for the departure. Today's payload was relatively light. However, by volume, the cargo area was chock-a-block. Berko noticed that most of the packages were of an unusually high-build spec. In particular, there was a single padlocked wooden crate with thick rope handles, labelled Construction Equipment, and the three special cartons, which made him take note to draw Fergus's attention to them when he boarded.

With some useless input from Gerry, Fergus and Quinn had almost completed flight planning the mission. The captain was satisfied that they would soon be ready to be on their way to begin their onboard pre-flight duties, but not before having a chat with their attentive operation coordinator.

"Well now, Gerry, you know I'm not happy about taking passengers on this trip. Explain why they're needed, and run the story by us again. By the way, which aircraft are we taking?"

"Right then, just for my two favourite pilots, I'll explain as best I can. They arrived late last night onboard a freighter, carrying additional and what they called essential supplies from an American disaster relief group based in Florida. They talked over the phone with Berko, and their personal stuff has already been loaded onto your aircraft, along with the freight. Earlier this morning, I picked them up from the hotel, organised their airport passes, and now I think they're out on the ramp, waiting beside Brigid, best ship in the fleet. You'll see for yourself, a gorgeous couple, full of enthusiasm. Oh, by the way. The satchel is stuffed with extra cash, you'll be able to buy all the fuel in Africa if ya want."

Gerry continued, working hard to make the story sound plausible.

"I received a telex from their superior. He said not to be fooled by the appearance of the petite, baby-faced woman. These guys, he said, are well-trained and know how to take care of themselves. However, due to a small bit of unrest near your destination, in northern Congo, they've been instructed to stay with the consignment until it reaches the designated medical centre. They want to avoid at all costs having the consignment seized by any of the rebel groups operating in the area."

"What fucking rebels? What the fuck are you on about Gerry? I didn't sign up for this shit."

"Relax, Quinn, please. I've already checked it out with our man at the Department of Foreign Affairs," assured Gerry in a breezy manner, which suggested to the crew that he hadn't.

"He satisfied me there's no cause for concern. Where you're heading, the government is stable, they still control the army, and they'll be delighted, even grateful, to see you. Just think of the hundreds, maybe thousands of sick people you'll save, including children, by delivering that stuff in that aircraft."

With his outstretched hand, Gerry gestured toward the airport's cargo ramp.

"Fucking rebels, Jesus..." Quinn mumbled.

"You'll be heroes. You just have to fly in, drop off the consignment and passengers, refuel, and fly back. It's that simple."

Fergus turned to Quinn, but not a single word was spoken; the look on their faces said it all. They'd been stitched up again. Fergus wasn't pleased and responded with uncharacteristic words of warning.

"You better have briefed them well, Gerry, cos if there's any hassle, they could end up needing some of what we're carrying. We won't have time to babysit, so I hope their boss is right about them being able to care for themselves."

Not wishing to dwell on the matter any longer, Fergus gently placed a hand on Quinn's shoulder.

"Okay, big man, let's go."

On the cargo apron, Enda was teasing the last few hundred litres of comfort juice from the bowser into the aircraft's massive, almost full fuel tanks. Then, after the ground crew had securely loaded the freight, the screw jacks began to turn as Berko energised the hydraulic pumps, pulling the enormous main cargo door securely shut. The loadmaster paused, deep in thought, scratching his head. He couldn't remember what it was he wanted to tell Fergus.

The captain felt unusually anxious as he approached the aircraft. Quinn was even more nervous, suppressing the urge to simply turn and walk away. They both knew that irrespective of everyone's input and good intentions, the pilots, particularly the captain, were ultimately responsible. It was his job to return the imposing four-engine aircraft and all onboard safely back home. Quinn was first up the steep, narrow gangway, which led to the galley through the main forward door and casually inspected the rows of stacked cartons before entering the flight deck. Fergus strolled over to the two figures wearing yellow vests on the ramp, standing next to the nose wheels.

"You must be the captain? I'm Haily," said the smiling young woman, offering her outstretched hand.

"And this is Pepe, my colleague."

They were of slim build, athletic types, with tanned faces, wearing dark-green lensed Ray-Ban sunglasses, and in contrast to his crew cut, her pixie cut was a bit more stylish. Given the weather was dull and overcast, Fergus thought it rude, preferring they remove the sunglasses, but neither of them did.

She did most of the talking and appeared to be the senior of the two, while Pepe stood like a soldier put at ease, raised chin out, hands crossed behind his back, and legs wide apart. They radiated an eagerness to get underway. However, the interview wasn't over yet. Fergus was a shrewd judge of character and, at sixty-three, not only had he decades of airline experience, he believed he was good at sussing out the fakers.

"Yes, I'm the captain, and I'd like you to call me by my first name, Fergus. Although, once you board my aircraft, I would appreciate your respecting the chain of command. Have either of you ever served in the military?"

The passengers looked at each other and didn't reply as Fergus continued.

"If ya were, I'm sure you'll understand what I mean."

"We won't be any trouble. You'll hardly even notice we're onboard, captain," replied the young woman, straining to hold the look of innocence on her face.

"Very well then, let's board, and I'll introduce you to the rest of the crew."

Fergus began to feel a bit more comfortable and was even looking forward to the prospect of a few yarns from across the pond, stories that could help pass the time during the long flight. Before the crew settled in at their stations, everyone gathered in the forward galley to offer their American guests a warm welcome.

The moment the passengers were out of earshot, Enda whispered to Fergus and Quinn. "What's with the eye shades? It's almost feckin dark. They're going to bump into something."

The pilots and the engineer coordinated the complex start sequence, and as they each accelerated from the ground air compressor, the fuel ignited, exploding the powerful engines into life. Enda wasn't happy with Quinn's performance and began teasing his friend.

"Hey, Quinn, have ya already had a few sneaky ones this morning? Cos, you're half a feckin sleep! It would help if you kept an eye on those temperature gauges. Look, number two is running hot."

Already aware of the situation and holding a look of concern on his face until he was sure Quinn registered it, muttering something spiritual, the captain reached to straighten the St. Brigid's cross, dangling by a string from the landing gear lever.

"Yes, I mean no. But, of course, I haven't had a few sneaky ones. Anyone can make a mistake, so back off, mister smart arse."

On the apron, one of the Green Bird ground crew kept visual contact with the pilots. Standing well back from the engine's sucking in massive volumes of air, he relayed over the intercom if all was normal during each start sequence. And trying to keep a safe distance from the savage motors made the cable of his headset stretch to its limits. The four engines rotated smoothly at idle while each of the crew silently completed the after-start sequence. They positioned levers, flicked switches, checked instruments, and then stood by for the challenge from the captain.

"Before taxi checklist."

Quinn read aloud the checklist, and as each item was scrutinised, it wasn't unusual for the crew to sometimes identify errors with the setup of the aircraft's systems. Although, today, there were more mistakes than usual. Whenever the checklist picked up something irregular, Fergus would release a cry of concern.

"Ah, for fuck's sake, lads, pay attention. It's just as well our passengers aren't up here to see this bloody circus."

When the setup was finally completed correctly, they were ready to taxi. Fergus spread his fingers like a piano player, resting them on the four thrust levers. Then, glancing over his shoulder towards Enda, he received thumbs up.

"Yep, skipper, we're good to go."

Through his side window, the captain gave a polite salute to the ground crew, released the parking brake and, with a short burst of breakaway thrust, they began to advance slowly towards the departure runway. Fergus loved taxiing the DC8; it always gave him a distinct pleasure, almost equalling the flying. The relatively low flight deck noise and smooth suspension gave the feel of being in a big luxury car, gliding along a newly laid tarmac motorway.

The voice of the ground controller came over the speaker.

"Green Bird Zero Eight, are you ready to copy your clearance?"

"Yes, sir, go ahead," replied Quinn.

"Green Bird Zero Eight, you are cleared to destination Ouésso, flight plan route, via the Liffy One Alpha. Climb and maintain six thousand feet and squawk 2763. Read back, please."

Quinn read the clearance back to confirm he understood, and while holding short of the departure runway, he switched to the tower frequency for further instructions.

"Green Bird Zero Eight. Wind 250 at 10 knots. You are cleared to enter and take off runway 23. When airborne, change to radar on 125.6."

Once again, Quinn acknowledged the clearance. Then, as the crew felt the rush of adrenalin, they tensed a little, precisely coordinating their actions in order to survive another launch and get the old lady safely into the sky.

CHAPTER ELEVEN

I n the Green Bird office, Gerry was alone sitting at his
desk in. Something wasn't right about this mission, and
he wanted to clarify a few details with the airline's boss.
Hesitating momentarily, he selected speaker on the desk
phone, tapping the first of ten pre-programmed numbers.

"Morning, Boss. Sorry for bothering you this early. We
need to discuss a few things."

"Sure, Gerry, no problem. What's the matter?"

"It's this whole mission that's the matter. There're
already taxiing for take-off. So, I just hope we didn't go too
far this time."

"Go too far? What do ya mean, Gerry?"

"The yanks, the ones travelling with them. No fucking
way are they Red Cross, aid workers. Much too slick and
clever to do that sort of work. And they ask far too many
questions."

"Gerry, I'm not following you. What are you saying?"

"I met the pair, and we spoke for a while. I'm telling you,
there's something spooky about them. I've dealt with
hundreds of aid workers in the past, and I'm certain this is
not their day job. Fuck, I even felt edgy turning my back on

them when I walked away. I think they're military. So, I'm suggesting we get a message to the crew to be extra careful, and when they return, we could at least pay them a bonus. We could call it a loyalty bonus."

The airline boss let out a deep, audible sigh.

"I'll bet they've taken loads of extra fuel again. So, as far as I'm concerned, they've already used up their bonus. Gerry, you know what they're like. Great operators, but still a bunch of cowboys and pissheads, with no regard for authority."

Gerry was just about to respond in the pisshead's defence until he realised how pointless that would be, so he didn't bother.

"You're the Operations Manager, so act like one. Wise up and do your job."

Gerry could hardly contain himself.

"That's my point. That's what I'm trying to do. And the thing that's bothering me most is about those fucking Balubas on the rampage. And another thing, I've told the lads that our foreign affairs fella said it was grand, when you said it wasn't even necessary to contact him."

"You worry too much, Gerry. You've always been the same. You'd make the lads nervous if they knew you cared so much."

"Yeah, boss, you're probably right."

"It's a standard and very lucrative contract, and we need it. But, think, man, what could go terribly wrong with an aircraft operated by a bunch of paddies transporting medical supplies to Africa?" queried the boss.

"Okay, you're right. I'm sorry I bothered you. I'll probably see ya tomorrow."

CHAPTER TWELVE

Deckleshine was a small-framed, timid man. Nevertheless, to judge him by his stature would be a mistake, as he could be a formidable adversary should anyone try to undermine his genius. Even though most of his correspondence with Langley was highly confidential, requiring a delete or shred after reading, Deckleshine rarely complied. The daily nit-picking exasperated him, because it focused mainly on in-house security and seldom dealt with his research. Moreover, he didn't like being distracted from his seamless thought process in the only area that interested him, scientific discovery.

However, he was also aware that a small part of his brilliant mind was deficient. He knew he was naïve, which occasionally dwarfed his genius, making him appear like a simpleton. For this reason, the professor kept records. He took precautions, just in case he might need to defend himself in the future, after being coerced to discard established protocols, leaving him vulnerable to prosecution. After his day's work, Deckleshine enjoyed the quiet evenings at home. Habitually, he would listen to his favourite music while attempting to prepare an edible meal, most of which usually ended up in the waste bin. On one of these evenings, while browsing through his stash of copied confidential state documents, he considered the wording of a recent telex.

'Professor, your trial run was viewed by us with great interest- priority funding and resources available- continue your remarkable work- concentrate on developing an airborne variant of your magnificent creation. END.'

There was one part of the message he hadn't thought much about until now, and it struck him as odd. *Concentrate on developing an airborne variant of your magnificent creation.* He had no doubt that Langley knew ShineOn was faulty, so why request an airborne variant? However, it also occurred to him that he had never thought to simply ask.

The following morning, from his office at the research centre, Deckleshine decided to contact his handler requesting clarification. He wrote that he must have misunderstood something, querying why they would need a faulty variant, let alone an airborne one. Previously, he'd tried to record telephone conversations with the agency, but on every occasion, the line became garbled, and the attempt would fail. But, this time, he was going to get it all in writing. Some hours later, while he leisurely strolled along a corridor, reading a medical journal, the sudden ringing of the wall-mounted telephone gave him a startle.

"Professor Deckleshine, good morning. It's Langley."

There was a coolness in the greeting, and it made him feel uncomfortable. He glanced up and down the empty corridor, wondering how Langley knew he would pick up the phone.

"Your recent telex has raised some concerns for me and my superiors. Do we not treat you well? Aren't you aware of the terms of your contract? Professor, you've ruffled a few feathers with your inappropriate questions."

"I'm sorry, sir, I just…"

The voice dismissed Deckleshine's attempt to reason.

"Yes, yes, we get it. And because this is obviously very important to you, we've decided to send two of our people down to clarify matters. So, please make yourself available tomorrow evening. And don't worry, professor, the meeting won't take up much of your valuable time."

Professor Deckleshine had considered the uses they might have for his latest creation, yet none of them made any sense. He compared notes from early evening until late that night and meticulously trawled through plausible theories from the comfort of his brown suede recliner. Finally, it was just before daybreak when he settled on the most credible one. Even the teaspoon of powder caffeine in his cup of Earl Grey could no longer ward off the need for sleep. He'd intended to get an early night in preparation for the visitors. Now, at almost seven in the morning, and just before his head fell hard onto the pillow, he mistakenly switched the alarm off while resetting his wakeup.

The squadron of F-16 Falcons roared, as each, in turn, engaged the afterburners during take-off, emitting the equivalent noise and vibration of a significant explosion, which echoed well beyond the airbase perimeter. Deckleshine squinted at the alarm clock's oversized digits, radiating 13:37.

"Jesus sweet Christ!" he cried.

Leaping out of bed, dashing to the blipping answerphone on the table in the hallway, he pressed play.

"Good morning, professor. Be advised about an update on the meeting. Our people managed to catch an earlier flight and will arrive around one or two in the afternoon. I hope we can chat again after you guys clear the air."

Deckleshine quickly dressed in yesterday's clothing, taking a brief moment to splash water on his blushing face before running his wet fingers through his scruffy hair. Then, slamming the hall door shut behind him, he charged along the footpath towards the carpark. It was 13:46, and after an edgy five-minute dash across the base, he arrived at the research centre's carpark, expecting the usual difficulty in finding the elusive parking space, but not today. He'd forgotten it was a public holiday, and the three-storey building appeared deserted, except for the lone security guard at the main entrance.

The guard behind the plate-glass door watched stern-faced as the professor fumbled through the lengthy entry process, which involved swiping his identity card, iris, and fingerprint recognition.

"Good morning. Anyone looking for me or any messages?"

"Nope, all quiet here, doc."

"Excellent. I'm expecting visitors. Please inform me when they arrive."

From his office desk on the third floor, it wasn't long before he noticed movement on the multi-display CCTV monitor as the people pulled up right next to his car, in the two-hundred parking space facility. Wishing to greet them personally, he rushed down the stairs to the entrance and, to his surprise, they were already inside.

"Ah, professor, I'm agent Bluey, and this is my dear colleague, agent Sable. She will be assisting me today."

Deckleshine liked her soft handshake, and as he moved closer, trying to read their identification badges, he had to endure the pain of Bluey's almost crushing hand grip.

"Professor, before we get down to business, would you please give us a tour of your wonderful facility?"

Deckleshine was proud of his research centre and beamed with delight at the agent's request. He did most of the talking during the grand tour of the entire building while the visitors listened attentively, which encouraged the professor to go a lot deeper into detail than they had wished. The tour ended in the centre's large, windowless amphitheatre-like room on the lower ground floor. The focal point was the operating table, where most of the research work concluded in experimental trials.

"Wow," the agents declared in unison as they stepped slowly down the centre aisle of the dimly lit basement theatre.

"You remember this place, agent Sable?" asked her colleague.

"Yep, I sure do," she replied.

Deckleshine looked bewildered.

"I don't recall meeting either of you before today. When did you visit the centre?"

"Yep, professor, we sort of did make a visit. It was the day you introduced that unfortunate young man to ShineOn. Fascinating stuff, although it was a bit messy."

A broad grin pulled across Bluey's face as he pointed his finger at the CCTV camera on the wall.

The professor felt obliged to defend his research.

"I came under considerable pressure to carry out the trials, and yes, the outcome was indeed unfortunate for the young volunteer. However, he knew the risk he was taking. And because of his sacrifice, we continue to make significant progress."

"Hey, professor, let's not get all tetchy. Fact is, we and our superiors think you're doing an incredible job. So, this brings us nicely back to the reason for today's visit."

Bluey picked up two aluminium stools and, placing one on either side of the long-polished steel table, gestured for Deckleshine to be seated. Sable stood next to a mobile trolley displaying an array of surgical instruments while slowly running her fingertips across each cold stainless-steel object. Then, aware of being watched, she exaggerated the gentle caresses, much to the muted annoyance of the man about to be interviewed.

"Right then, professor, in your own words, tell us why you think we called this meeting?"

"Yes, sir, I will be happy to do that. Although please, don't take any offence if what I say sounds a bit far-fetched. I'm just trying to understand."

"Offence? Did you hear that, agent Sable?" said Bluey, making no effort to conceal the mocking nature of his taunt.

Unable to resist the urge to pick up one of the surgical instruments for a closer inspection, Sable waited until she was sure the seated men were watching.

"And what's this for, professor"?

"It's used to hold organs or tissue apart during surgery. It's called a Retractor," replied Deckleshine.

Directing his attention back to agent Bluey, the professor began to offer his version of the most likely reason for an airborne variant of ShineOn.

"Well, agent Bluey, I can only assume you're planning a mass vaccination programme…"

Except for the occasional interruption by Sable regarding surgical instruments and their uses, the professor delivered an articulated account of his theory in a soft, almost apologetic voice. As he spoke, he wondered why he hadn't noticed the curly wire extending from their earpieces or where the microphones might be concealed. When the talking ended, the men sat perfectly still, eyeing each other as if preparing to make a bet in a card game.

"Professor Deckleshine, wow. Have you ever considered writing a novel? That was truly fascinating. Did you discuss your theory with anyone else, because I'd be very interested in becoming your literary agent?"

"No, I haven't discussed it with anyone. I only pieced it all together last night."

"Okay, professor. On a serious note. You know we can't have you wandering around dreaming up conspiracy theories, making me and our bosses nervous. Anyway, even if you were right, and I emphasise if... well, so what. Aren't we all on the same side? Is that not the case? We're here to give for the good of our country and to willingly sacrifice our lives, if necessary."

Deckleshine was becoming unnerved. He thought about how his naivety would get him into trouble again as the agent continued, his frustration intensifying.

"You must embrace American patriotism and use your god-given scientifically brilliant mind to protect our flag and people."

Bluey was almost shouting. He shuffled in his chair, occasionally coughing heavily into his clenched fist.

"Jesus, sometimes I get too emotional."

On her way back to join the men, Sable picked up another instrument.

"And what's this for?"

She wasn't expecting a reply as she carefully held the blade with her thumb and index finger, allowing the scalpel to swing like a pendulum. Deckleshine's arms were outstretched on the table, and leaning forward placing his hands on top of the professor's, Bluey maliciously applied light downward pressure. Sable stood next to Deckleshine, her shoulder touching his, as she stared across at her partner.

"Professor Deckleshine, it's come to Jesus' time. We need you to convince us that there will be no more conspiracy theories, or questions on matters that don't concern you."

Bluey was becoming hostile, his eyes squinting, and the tone of his voice became menacing.

"Do you understand the gravity of the situation? Haven't you heard it's not uncommon for people with brilliant minds, just like you, to simply overload and even cause themselves harm?"

"Yes, sir, I totally understand, and I wish to assure you there will be no more pointless, naïve comments or queries from me, ever again."

Deckleshine felt nauseated. Sensing the acidy vomit churn at the back of his tongue, he fought back the urge to throw up. "Please, accept my sincere apology. I appreciate all you have done for me, and I only wish to get back to my work and help defend our great country."

Bluey appeared to be considering the emotional plea, when he became distracted, and began fiddling with his earpiece. Suddenly, the dial-less blue phone started ringing. The professor attempted to slide his hands off the table to answer the phone, but felt resistance as Bluey gave a controlling, tight squeeze.

The agent stood and, as he walked the few steps to the phone, he glanced over his shoulder.

"It's for me."

Bluey listened, then briefly replied before dropping the receiver back onto the cradle.

"I do concur."

When he returned to the table, his voice was calmer, and he even appeared to be trying to conjure up a smile.

"Well, Professor Deckleshine, it would appear that our business is concluded. It's been a pleasure meeting you, although I doubt we'll ever meet again. We can make our own way out."

Agent Sable gently laid the scalpel on the bare steel operating table; her heavy sigh possibly indicated relief at not having to perform the rest of her duty. Deckleshine watched from the dome as the agents ascended the narrow aisle, triggering an alarm as they departed through the reinforced double-door emergency exit.

Before returning to his office, the professor first needed to visit the restroom. He pressed the palms of his sweaty hands on the washbasin and, locking his arms straight, leaned his head forward until his nose almost touched the mirror. As the shock of the encounter began to sink in, he took a deep breath, holding it for as long as he could, searching his bloodshot, tired eyes for answers. Then, relaxing his taut body, he slowly eased himself back from the mirror, and removing the miniature Panasonic dictaphone from the inside pocket of his jacket, he placed it on the edge of the basin. After holding the rewind trigger until it clicked to a stop, he pressed play. A part of him wished the recording of the encounter had failed. Hands now shaking uncontrollably, the traumatised scientist listened, struggling to fathom the reality that they were about to kill him, and that a few convincing words of fake remorse had saved him.

CHAPTER THIRTEEN

F ergus applied a small amount of differential thrust on the engines to help steer the machine through a ninety-degree turn, positioning the aircraft perfectly on the runway's centreline. Berko and the two passengers occupied the jump seats in the forward galley listening through the open door as the crew responded in sequence to Quinn reading aloud the before-take-off checklist. The captain applied brake pressure while advancing the thrust levers until the engines screamed and the airframe shuddered, making him press even harder on the pedals, preventing the beast's struggle to break free. Enda sat facing forward between the pilots, carefully making final engine tweaks, maintaining the thrust a fraction below the desired setting, therefore avoiding an overheat. Then, calling aloud, "Thrust set, engines stable," Enda signalled the captain to release the brakes.

The Douglas DC8 initially inched slowly forward, then progressively accelerated from the beginning to just before the end of the runway. Her nose wheels gradually lifted, followed by the rest of the aircraft and, maintaining a shallow angle, she barely cleared the approach lights at the far end of the reciprocal runway. The engines thundered harmoniously, competing to win the maximum decibel award while trying to perform an unachievable task, and combined with the four long trails of black smoke, made her appear to be in agony.

Enda concentrated hard on maintaining the engines at a delicate balance between maximum thrust and meltdown, while Quinn uttered the all-important words of encouragement.

"We're looking good, lads, we're looking good."

After retracting the landing gear, the clean, sleek lines of the ageing goddess disappeared into the base of low-level clouds, gaining height faster and faster. She now climbed rapidly away from the earth below. Within a minute, they had reached an airspeed of 250 knots, and Fergus smoothly eased further back on the control column, coaxing his beloved machine to continue to defy gravity. Swallowed by a thick blanket of cloud, for any plane spotters, the thunderous noise, and the black trails of smoke from the engines were the only confirmation that she ever really existed. Then, as they accelerated and continued their climb to the planned cruising level of thirty-seven thousand feet, leaving their earthly worries behind, the crew's edginess began to ease.

Berko had neatly stacked the two hundred and sixteen heavy-duty cardboard cartons from one end of the main cargo deck to the other. Then, as lots of space was available below deck, he loaded the heavy wooden crate into the lower belly compartment. The cartons all appeared identical at a glance, with each of the three cubic metre containers labelled with arrows pointing upwards, and marked 'This Way Up' and 'Maximum Weight,' plus the now obligatory barcode.

The loadmaster had laid them three abreast at the

bottom, stacking them pyramid-style until they almost touched the roof panelling. He arranged the cartons to create narrow passageways, allowing just enough space to pass on either side, from the front to the rear of the cargo bay. And, to make sure it didn't shift during the flight, the whole arrangement was secured by rope netting and ratchet straps. During any encounter with turbulence, Berko would disregard his safety to inspect the cargo, shuffling along the aisles, pulling, and tugging on the securing apparatus, with a contented look on his face, satisfied that he must be one of the finest loadmasters in the industry.

Pepe stood in the forward galley, watching with amusement as Berko repeated his routine. Then, taking one last drag of his cigarette, he dropped it into the almost full disposable coffee cup.

"Octopus piss," declared the temperamental passenger, discarding it through the steel swing lid of the bin. Pepe removed an electronic device from his pocket and, bending down and balancing on one knee, swiped it across the barcode of the first carton in the row.

"What the fuck is this?"

The screen of the small electronic scanner revealed the contents of the box: Chloroquine, Amoxicillin, Zink Sulphate, Penicillin, Morphine, and Ibuprofen. After scanning a couple more cartons, the contents were exactly the same. Pepe made his way along the narrow passageway with a sense of urgency, randomly checking another few cartons. Again, however, the device registered similar results, adding to his growing frustration.

Turning back, Pepe hurried towards the flight deck, pausing to compose himself before entering. The engineer and pilots were seated at their stations, engaged in conversation with Haily, who was sitting cross-legged on the jump seat. They were at their planned cruise level and had already overflown the Irish Sea, southwest of Lands' End, tracking towards The Bay of Biscay. The chatter upfront was, for the most part, light and friendly. However, Haily never stopped probing, asking technical questions about the aircraft, just like somebody might if planning to pursue a career in aviation.

"Excuse me, Haily. Don't mean to interrupt. We need to talk."

Following her colleague, they sidestepped along the cargo, grabbing hold of the netting to steady themselves. Pepe abruptly stopped and turned to face her, spreading his feet for balance.

"ShineOn. It's not here."

"What exactly do you mean? Not here?"

"Do you remember during the cargo loading, we spoke with the loadmaster and gave him clear instructions about where to stack the three cartons containing the ShineOn canisters? Well, I don't think that motherfucker was listening."

After Haily had scanned a few rows of boxes, she turned to Pepe.

"Are you sure we're reading the barcodes correctly?"

"I'm certain," replied Pepe.

"Then, we'll just have to check them all."

"We can't get at most of the frigging labels. They simply aren't accessible. But, hey, let me find Berko. I'll meet you back in the forward galley in a few minutes," said Pepe.

The aerodynamics made the back of the aircraft a lot noisier than the front. Pepe stood outside the engaged aft toilet, lightly tapping the door with his index finger. On getting no response, he hit harder with his knuckles, triggering bellowing from the cubical that startled him.

"What the fuck do you want? Is the aircraft on fucking

fire? If not, can you please fuck off, and let a man have a dump in peace."

"No, Berko, we're not on fire, and I'm sorry for disturbing you. Is there any chance we can meet in the forward galley, when you're done? We'd like to ask you a few questions about our cargo."

"Questions, what feckin questions?"

"Talk later," replied Pepe.

Although Berko was in his late sixties, much to the satisfaction of his ego, he didn't look it. He could have easily passed as being ten years younger. The loadmaster was a short, muscular man. His dark hair was indeed dyed, and he had the faintest bald patch on his otherwise thick well-groomed shiny mop. His deep-set brown eyes communicated well with his brain, giving him a cognitive skill not usual for a man of his years. However, what characterised him most were his shoes. He had procured at least a dozen pairs of handmade Italian leather brogues. They varied in colour, and were always polished to an outstanding brilliance. It gave him great pleasure when meeting people for the first time, knowing that it usually wouldn't take long for them to comment on his well-shod feet, making him feel like someone special.

Berko had spent most of his career in the RAF's Heavy Transport Division. Then, after retiring from the military, he returned to Dublin and lived alone in a well-to-do south city suburb. He'd been with the company for more than fifteen years and loved the travel opportunities the job offered. Rumour was, he had a girlfriend in every port across the globe. Although the behaviour of one of them, who relieved him of $70K of the company's cash in a hotel room, didn't seem very girlfriend-like. It was customary to appoint the loadmaster as purser, responsible for large amounts of money, because offering credit cards for unscheduled maintenance or to buy fuel was rarely an option at remote outstations. No one knew why he didn't get sacked for his costly indiscretion. Most suspected that he must have had a few stories, or even photos of his employer entrapped by similar improprieties, and anyway, the loss was covered by the company's insurance policy.

Sometime later, Berko returned to the galley, where Haily and Pepe sat patiently waiting.

"Did ya want to talk to me about something?" asked Berko.

Pepe began to speak but was interrupted by Haily.

"I'll handle this. Do you recall on the ramp in Dublin, during loading, how I specifically requested, in fact, I demanded that the three special cartons we handed over to you be placed up here, at the front of the cargo bay?"

"Yes, I do," replied Berko, arms now folded.

Pepe and Haily responded in unison. "And, where are they now?"

"They're in the forward lower bellyhold," replied Berko.

Pepe and Haily were again almost in unison, their voices raised to a shout.

"What forward bellyhold?"

The door to the flight deck was open and, with the headsets draped around their necks, the crew were aware of the commotion, so Fergus asked Enda to investigate.

"Are we getting a bit edgy? A touch of altitude sickness, perhaps?" said Enda, trying to be humorous.

Haily pointed at Berko.

"This fricking idiot..."

Before she could finish speaking, Enda interrupted. "Now, madam, we'll have no more of that. You apologise immediately to the loadmaster, or you'll find yourself confined to the back of the aircraft for the rest of the flight."

Haily's facial expression radiated disappointment.

"I'm sorry, it's just that of all the cargo, those three cartons were the most precious, and we were ordered, I mean told, not to let them out of sight."

Berko could see the disappointment on the Americans' faces, and becoming sympathetic, he acknowledged his error, offering reassurances about how he loaded the cartons securely next to the rope-handled wooden crate.

"Have we access to the bellyhold from up here?" asked Pepe.

"Nope. Anyway, you wouldn't want to be down there because the lower cargo heating system is unserviceable, and I guess it's about minus fifty degrees Celsius," replied Enda.

Pepe and Haily looked at each other, and while trying to recall the cartons' insulation qualities, they hoped there wasn't a temperature limitation for the precious consignment.

Enda returned to the flight deck and stood between the pilots.

"Looks like we've got a pair of drama queens onboard, although I think it's all settled down now. You should have seen their faces when I told them how cold it was in the bellyhold."

Berko soon arrived, and after closing the flight deck door behind him, he stood by Fergus's left shoulder to announce his discovery to the crew.

"I really don't like that pair," said Berko, looking for any sign of agreement on the faces of his friends.

"We've all flown with aid workers before, and pretty much without exception, they'd be almost pissed by now. But not this pair."

Enda was the first to respond. "For fuck's sake, Berko, they can't all be pissheads like you. Sorry, I mean us."

"So, what about the weapons then?" asked Berko.

Fergus looked up at Berko. "What weapons?"

"Well, when I had the chance, I went to the lockers and took a peek inside their rucksacks. They both have Glock semi-automatic pistols, and a couple of nasty-looking knives."

"Was there any ammo? Are they loaded?" asked the captain.

"I didn't have much time, but from what I could see, there was no ammo, and the magazines were empty."

Quinn put his arms out in front of him, waving his hands slowly up and down

gesturing calmness.

"Okay, okay, let's slow this down a bit. Think about it, lads. They're yanks. All yanks have guns, and they're heading to work in one of the dodgiest places in Africa. So maybe we should have guns too."

Fergus wasn't convinced.

"Yep, I get that. But, still, they should have told us. So, Berko, get the pair up here, please."

With everyone up front, the flight deck should have felt cosy, but instead, it began to feel crowded. Fergus handed Quinn control of the aircraft before turning in his seat to face the Americans. The passengers already knew what was coming yet showed no obvious concern, knowing that no matter how much the crew objected, it would be of little consequence.

"It's being brought to my attention that you brought concealed weapons onboard my aircraft. Is this true?"

Haily's reply was far from the truth.

"I wouldn't say concealed. Your company was informed, and they were even on the cargo manifest, to the best of my knowledge."

She threw a slitty-eyed glance towards Berko as the captain continued.

"Well, none of us knew, and it certainly wasn't on the cargo manifest. So, where's the ammunition?"

"It's in the bellyhold, cold-soaked to minus fifty frigging degrees," replied Pepe.

"Right," said Fergus. "We're making good progress and should arrive at our destination ahead of schedule in about five hours from now. So, in the meantime, I don't want to see either of you on this flight deck again. I don't like it when my passengers make me nervous. So, from now on, you can both consider requests from any of my crew as orders, and you better comply, or I'll have the authorities deal with you when we land. Am I making myself clear?"

Chastised and eyes lowered, the pair nodded slightly before departing the flight deck for the last time.

"Jaysis, Fergie, I haven't seen ya as pissed off as this in a long time," said Berko.

Fergus, facing forward again in his seat and resting his right hand on the thrust levers, spoke softly to Quinn.

"I have control, lad."

Ahead of the aircraft, there was barely a trace of a cloud in the sky, and below, the terrain changed dramatically as they overflew southern Spain. Then, crossing the Mediterranean Sea, high above Alicante, they maintained course, tracking north of Oran and into Algerian airspace. The contrast between the hectic European and North African airspace was striking. For the remainder of the journey across the African continent, there would be long periods of ghostly radio silence from the speakers, creating a sense of desolation. It wasn't long before the vast Algerian Sahara lay behind them, and in the distance, the oasis town of In Salah, shimmered in a heat haze. Quinn was deep in thought as he gazed down, trying to imagine life below.

"Camels," he whispered. "Camels and belly dancers."

Squinting a little, Quinn was first to recognise the outline of the Hoggar Mountains, which meant they were getting close to Niger, the halfway point. And although the brouhaha was over, there was still a fidgety onboard. The passengers no longer conversed with the crew except to give snappy replies to questions asked. Berko advised the couple where they could find additional catering at the other end of the aircraft and suggested they help themselves. Haily didn't even raise her eyes, as Pepe acknowledged, leaving Berko to think she was admiring his shoes.

"Yep, buddy, we'll help ourselves."

When Berko entered the flight deck, he could sense the gloomy atmosphere. But, keeping true to character, he decided to cheer things up.

"I'm sure it's obvious to you that I have fuck-all to do except scratch my bollox. So, as you're all busy getting this bus to Congo, I've decided, as usual, to be chef de partie. So, please, I've already fired up the oven. Allow me to present today's menu."

As dictated by the rules, the captain and co-pilot had to choose different meals, to lessen the possibility of both of them getting food poisoning. Enda had a mischievous smile, giggling uncontrollably as he tried to explain.

"Berko, anything will do for me. A surprise, please. But before you start prepping, can you wash your hands, and no more bollox scratching until we've all been fed, me auld flower."

That was all it took; they needed a bit of the craic. It lifted their spirits, just like after a graveyard service when a few of the congregation would retire to the pub to celebrate the passing.

Berko prepared each meal in turn, starting with the captains. Fergus had the Winter Spa with salad, and for his main course, he opted for the Lemon Sole with spinach and mashed potatoes. Quinn went for the Tomato, Cucumber and Avocado starter, then Fillet Steak with pepper sauce and roast potatoes for his main. Enda wasn't hungry, so he just had the Tuna Poke and Mango salad. And if that wasn't enough, there were trolleys stacked in the galley with the finest selection of fresh sandwiches and calorie-loaded desserts.

"Hey, chef, what are you having?" asked Enda.

Berko replied, waving the half-eaten chicken leg towards the inquisitive engineer.

"Mind your own feckin business. Listen, just in case we don't get catered for the journey back, I'll try to keep what's left on ice."

"Does anyone remember those charter flights we used to do for Air France? Fuck it; they'd always serve wine with the flight crew meals. An old tradition, it seems, very fucking civilised. Hey, Quinn, did ya ever indulge yourself with a sip or two?" asked Fergus.

"Let's not start that shit again. Do you lot think I'm a feckin alcoholic?"

Quinn glanced over his shoulder at Enda, then threw a dagger look at Fergus before continuing.

"First, it was him this morning, and now you. So, back off, lads, it's no longer funny."

His sudden outburst made the flight deck feel crowded again.

After they'd finished their meals, the co-pilot went aft to help Berko tidy the galley.

"Are you okay? Ya look a bit flushed?" asked Berko.

"Ah, it's nothing; I'm grand," replied Quinn

Berko seemed to be preoccupied with the earlier episode

"It'll be fine, my friend. Although, you know what,

Quinn? I think those feckers in the back have us all feeling a bit uneasy."

After taking a longer break than usual, they were approaching Niger when the co-pilot settled back into his seat, so Fergus asked Quinn to contact Niamey air traffic control and request a climb to thirty-nine thousand feet. The controller sounded remarkably upbeat and, granting an immediate climb, requested the aircraft's registration, destination, endurance, souls onboard, and overfly permission reference code. Quinn read back as instructed, just as he had previously done on entering Algerian air space. The aircraft had begun to level off at their new cruise altitude when Enda called out to Fergus.

"I didn't want to cause any alarm, skipper, but I've been watching a situation develop, and either we've got a faulty fuel gauge, or it's a leak. I really can't be sure yet."

The captain handed over control of the aircraft to Quinn and turned around in his seat to be further briefed by his young engineer.

"Tell me more," said Fergus.

"Well, skipper, I've been checking the gauges and making some rough calculations. The number two engine appears to be burning about twice as much fuel as the others. Will we run the fuel leak checklist, skipper?"

Fergus paused for a short time to consider the situation before answering.

"Okay, let's say it is a leak. My guess is we won't have many options."

The captain was deep in thought, his situational awareness on overdrive.

"I suppose we could land in Kano or Cameroon, or even turn back to get the repairs done in Europe, because I doubt if we can continue to Ouésso. But, even if we made it, we'll be committed to land there. We'll have no chance of reaching our alternate airport at Brazzaville, or anywhere else, for that matter."

No one had anything to add. The skipper had summarised it perfectly while their brains were catching up with his.

"Right, Enda, let's find out. First, run the Suspected Fuel Leak in Flight checklist."

Berko gathered a few cushions to make himself a cosy corner and was about to settle down for a nap when he heard Quinn's voice over the intercom.

"Berko, come to the flight deck, immediately."

Haily and Pepe also heard the unusual announcement, and called after the loadmaster as he hurried past.

"What's the problem?" bawled Haily.

"I don't know."

When Berko stepped through the flight deck door, Fergus and Enda were troubleshooting and had almost completed the relatively short checklist while Quinn did the flying.

"Looks like we've got a fuel leak, all right, and I hope it's not coming from the engine. Berko, go back and look through the left rear door window. Report back what you see, and Berko, hurry, please," said Enda.

It wasn't long before the loadmaster returned, failing badly to sound upbeat.

"Yep, it's pissing out near the number two engine. You should see the vapour trail. Anyone looking up would think we're dumping fuel. I hope the fuck it doesn't ignite."

Fergus knew he needed to make a decision, and quickly.

"Quinn, we must shut that engine down without further delay. Request descent to thirty-three thousand feet. To stay up here, we need all four engines. Once we go down a few thousand, we should be okay. Enda, check the three-engine performance manual."

Moments later, when queried by Air Traffic Control about the reason for the descent, they decided not to draw attention to their situation, advising the controller that the manoeuvre was an operational descent to avoid turbulence.

After the engine was shut down and the checklists completed, they levelled off at the highest sustainable altitude, feeling more at ease after Berko confirmed that the fuel vapour trail was gone. All the crew had to do now was narrow down the options and pick the best one and, after considering the pros and cons, they appeared to have reached a decision. However, at the rear of the aircraft, the passengers had changed clothing, adding a new dimension to their troubles. Now dressed in paramilitary style, the agents had changed into dark blue cotton jumpsuits, trousers tucked into short black boots, and lightweight body armour with long side pockets containing pistol magazines. Moving quickly along the cargo, they reached the flight deck and listened through the slightly ajar door.

"So, we think we should put her down in Kano. Are we all agreed then?" asked the captain.

CHAPTER FOURTEEN

Quinn was about to request the diversion from ATC when the passengers burst through the flight deck door, unsettling the crew with their untimely interruption. Everyone's initial instinct was to stand and confront the intruders, but no one dared.

Instead, loud voices intermingled with cries of aggravation.

"What the fuck."

"Get the fuck out of here."

"Who the fuck do you think you are?"

"That's it, you've gone too far," bawled the astonished crew until the woman screamed back.

"We're not diverting anywhere," ordered Haily.

Stunned by her audacity, she produced the pistol tucked inside her leather belt before Fergus had time to articulate a sentence. Ejecting the empty magazine, Haily ripped open the Velcro pocket running down the side of her body armour to retrieve another one. With a slap from the palm of her hand, the new magazine snapped home, priming the weapon with seventeen rounds of live ammunition. The Red Cross emblem on the plastic identification card still draped around her neck looked out of place, no longer exemplifying a symbol of hope.

Except for his less hurried pace, Pepe stood in the doorway, mimicking his colleague's actions. Then, simultaneously, they released their grip on the slides, and the weapons made a second crisp metallic sound as the magazines released a nine-millimetre bullet into the chambers. Then, once again, the flight deck became crowded as the captain and his crew tried to come to terms with the new chain of command.

CHAPTER FIFTEEN

Troops from the Congolese army's most elite platoons spread out, forming an impenetrable cordon around Ouésso airport, while their commanding officer waited impatiently for the Americans to arrive at the entrance to the control tower.

When the yanks finally showed up, they were dressed like modern bankers, attired in quality tailor-made suits, with open buttoned-down shirt collars and polished leather shoes; they couldn't have looked more conspicuous. By the time the agency had caught up with them, they'd been finalising some foreign policy business in neighbouring Zaire. After the short river crossing from Kinshasa to Brazzaville in a chartered helicopter, a government turboprop aircraft flew them north to Ouésso. To be ready for a quick departure, the Americans demanded the Antonov An-24 captain park on the taxiway near the beginning of the runway. The two pilots were under strict orders to remain with the aircraft until their passengers returned, and, to be sure there were no misunderstandings, the American in the white shirt spoke again to the senior pilot.

"Captain, under no circumstances will you or any of

your crew leave the aircraft. You are to keep a listening watch on the tower frequency, and only if you hear me or my colleague call over the radio AN24 Shine will you respond. Is that clear, captain?"

"Oui, yes sir, I understand," replied the captain in a strong French accent.

Earlier that day, the soldiers had departed their base at Owando in a four-vehicle convoy. Except for their well-worn jungle combats and machetes, the rest of their kit was brand new. And proudly clutching their polished AKM assault rifle, in addition, they were all armed with leather-holstered Walther PPK 38 semi-automatic pistols. The two BTR-60 and two ZSU-23-4 vehicles looked like they had just come off the production line. Ten soldiers occupied each amphibious troop carrier, and their commanding officer sat in the lead vehicle with two anti-aircraft ZSU's following closely behind. The title 'Elite' was not awarded because of their soldiering excellence, but more likely gained because of their willingness to execute orders with devotion and, when deemed necessary, in the most savage ways imaginable. The incentive was quite simple. Of all the divisions of the Congolese armed forces, including the Navy and Air Force, they were the only ones being paid regularly.

All hand-picked, their numbers totalled no more than a thousand, so deployment was always very selective and usually concluded in bloodshed. However, today's mission was unlikely to become violent, as their presence was only required to ensure the safe delivery of cargo from an inbound aircraft to a remote jungle destination. Up in the airport's control tower, the lone air traffic controller was numb with anxiety after recognising the regiment's insignia. The lieutenant could sense his fear, and proud of the agita-tion his presence was having on the fretting man, he repeatedly tapped his fingers on the panga machete's dark wooden handle hanging by his side.

From the elevated tower, the forecasted thunderstorms to the north were becoming visible above the treeline. As this year's usually predictable weather pattern wasn't cooperating, temperatures in the shade were over thirty degrees centigrade, and the air's humidity was almost totally saturated. The thunderstorms were abnormally ferocious during the previous weeks, persisting for most of the day.

Standing about one hundred and sixty feet high, the control tower was accessed from a ground-level armoured door, and inside, a rusting steel spiral staircase wound all the way up until its handrail protruded above floor level in the centre of the vast control room. The array of outward-tilting, dark-tinted glass panels, stacks of radio receivers and transmitters, including a monochrome radar display, gave the room the look of a place of great importance. And near the stairs stood a large glass-topped metal table and six plastic chairs, with not a single one matching. When the two Americans arrived up the staircase, they looked exhausted, and grabbing a chair each, they shuffled uncomfortably in their seats. The Texan could see the air traffic controllers' distress and tried to put him at ease.

"It's okay, man; no harm will come to you. Just sit back, relax, and do as you're told. Where's the air-conditioning?"

The man didn't answer, gesturing with a glance towards the twelve-inch fan on the wall, oscillating to a rhythmic squeak. Sitting in his seat, fiddling with the microphone cable, the controller was petrified and didn't take his eyes off the lieutenant who was standing, fingers intertwined behind his back, towering over the Americans.

"What are your names?" asked the officer.

"I'm Mister White, and this is my dear colleague, Mister Pink. And what's your name, sir?"

The officer held a faint grin, remaining silent while he studied the men, one dressed in white and the Texan in a pink shirt, he considered his favourite colour.

"You may call me Lieutenant Cramoisy."

His grin widened to a laugh, revealing the gap in his chipped front tooth.

Mister White was eager to broaden the conversation.

"Whatever happened to the other guy? I mean the Special Ops soldier who we originally met in Brazzaville. We had a little get-together a few weeks ago."

The Texan interrupted. "Yep, in fact, we were expecting to meet him again today. A very passionate man, although, unfortunately, he could also be a little ungrateful."

"He's dead," replied the lieutenant.

"Fuck, must be tough being a soldier around here," said Mister White.

"It had nothing to do with soldiering, killed by a hit-and-run. We've been interviewing people from the town near where it happened. Their tongues are beginning to loosen, and we expect to have the perpetrator soon."

He tapped a finger on the panga. as he continued.

"You mentioned he was ungrateful, and I hope this won't make me sound the same, but can you tell me why you only supply us with Russian and not American weapons?"

The men in suits took their time to consider his question until Mister White, not wishing to hold his head up any longer, leaned back until the rear legs supported his weight.

"Firstly, there's nothing much wrong with Russian weapons. Have you ever been on the receiving end of an AK47? Hey, man, you remember the Viet Cong."

He glanced solemnly at his colleague before letting his seat fall forward with a thud. Then, with head slightly tilted, he gazed down at his shoes and continued.

"So, lieutenant, you'd prefer the US-branded gear?

Haven't we already given you the Walther PPK? Aren't you getting a freighter load of quality medical supplies? We have a special close relationship with your cousins across the river in Zaire. Because of that, they've been receiving copious amounts of our American weaponry for quite some time. However, you guys here on this side of the river haven't convinced us of your loyalty. Even so, we're still willing to part with some of our adversary's hardware. We've been stockpiling locally for years, especially for occasions like this. To be frank, from time to time, we'll test your allegiance with little tasks. In fact, tasks much like the one that brought us here today. Then, depending on the outcome... well, need I say more?"

Mister White again leaned back in his chair, smirking up at the attentive soldier.

"Does that help answer your question, Lieutenant Cramoisy?"

Reticent and without reply, the officer abruptly turned his back on the seated men.

From their strategic positions on the airport's perimeter, the soldiers' camouflaged uniforms blended well with the habitat. After synchronising the communications equipment between the four support vehicles, the mobile radio soldier arrived and pressed the intercom button next to the door that led to the control tower. The noise from the gong striking the rusty metal dome made everyone cringe. Then, acknowledging a nod from the lieutenant, the air traffic controller put the receiver with the built-in electric lock release button to his ear.

"It's your radio operator, Lieutenant."

As the new arrival struggled to make haste, with the twenty-four-kilo backpack supporting a complete KY38/PRC77 radio kit, the radio's five-foot whip-antenna slapped against the steel rail as it ascended the stairwell.

Exhausted, the soldier sat sideways and heavily onto the chair chosen by the pointing finger of his commander. With a little more than two hours remaining before the expected arrival of the freighter, the welcoming preparations were almost complete.

CHAPTER SIXTEEN

Quinn was thinking back to when his judgement would become impaired after drinking multiple pints of Guinness, and all women began to look beautiful. Might Haily, under those circumstances, also appear to be a beautiful woman? He tried to view Haily from a sexual perspective. Her dominance possibly aroused in him some untimely and totally senseless desire, until his mind drifted to the image of a mating praying mantis, which grounded his thoughts. Attempting to ease the tension, he asked a mistimed question.

"Anyone knows which hotel we're staying in tonight?"

Quinn wasn't expecting a reply and was surprised when Haily tried to address the query.

"Let me be clear, gentlemen, we are not terrorists. We are intelligence agents engaged in critical government business, and if it weren't for mister nosy in the corner, we wouldn't be having this conversation. So, do not test our resolve if you don't wish to spend tonight in a hospital or worse. Be smart, cooperate."

Berko made a few inaudible remarks, as if not entirely

understanding the gravity of the situation. However, the captain did, and quickly intervened.

"Right, lads, you heard the woman. Let's get this delivery over with, so we can go home."

Berko was leaning against the back of Quinn's seat, with his right foot raised and resting on the edge of the pedestal frame. He couldn't take his eyes off the Americans. Maybe something was missing in his military training, because Berko appeared to doubt whether their weapons were actually loaded.

"So, Missy, what do you think would happen if you discharged that weapon up here?"

Releasing the hammer under control with her thumb, Haily continued to point the pistol at Berko's chest. She moved closer, forcing him to lean away until his back was stiff against the seat. Then, fixated on the weapon, he gazed nervously down at the gun.

"Well, mister know-all, as a former soldier, I'm sure you have heard of the hollow-point bullet? Whether you have or not, it doesn't matter, as you're just about to be introduced to one. You may recall, it's designed to explode on impact. Or, to put it another way, normally, it shouldn't pass all the way through and damage the aircraft. But, on the other hand."

It was instantaneous, and nobody saw it coming as she pulled the Gerber Mark II from the sheath strapped to her right boot. Then, with a stabbing motion, Haily brought the blade down onto the middle of Berko's raised shoe. She appeared to want to minimise the damage, resisting from running the knife through the sole. Berko felt the cold steel of the gun's barrel being shoved under his chin, and as his head went back, it forced his mouth shut, muffling the shriek. Resisting the urge to twist the knife, Haily taunted while slowly retracting the blade from his foot.

"I never liked those frigging shoes anyway."

Aa if surprised by her aggression, showing an uncharacteristic gesture of compassion, she slid the blade under the shoelace, slicing it apart, making it easier for him to remove the shoe. Haily took a few steps back from the loadmaster, leaving him wide-eyed with shock and, returning the knife to its sheath, she screwed up her eyes cat-like, giving him another look of contempt. When Pepe shouted an order for someone to get the first-aid kit, the captain appeared to be angrier with the victim than the assailant.

"Are you trying to get us all killed, lad? Enda, help them get that foot bandaged up. Search those feckin boxes in the back if you need more stuff."

After demonstrating how ruthless she could be, Haily had made her point, which only helped to unnerve the crew further. They knew how dangerous it would be to offer physical resistance. However, attempting to subvert the American agent's progress was still an option. Fergus reached over for the clipboard resting on Quinn's lap, and before handing it back, he drew two short diagonal lines on the flight plan.

Quinn took a moment to examine what Fergus had done and, glancing back over, slightly nodded, acknowledging that he understood. Pepe was preparing Berko a painkilling cocktail when Fergus beckoned Haily to move closer for the briefing. Before the captain began, Quinn keyed the mic to check in with Kano air traffic control to relay their details, including the alphanumerical code required to overfly Nigeria.

"Roger that," replied the controller.

The agents were eager to understand how the crew were going to deal with the remainder of the flight and listened attentively to the captain.

"We've got a couple of hours to go, and I reckon, providing there are no more surprises, we should be on the ground at Ouésso with about ten minutes of fuel remaining. Fifteen, if we're lucky."

"That's not so bad, is it?" she said.

The captain turned a bit more in his seat to face Haily, wanting to be sure his message was getting through.

"Not so bad! Well, maybe it wouldn't be if we were down there in a tour bus, but we're up in an aeroplane. So, unless you pair have parachutes, which wouldn't surprise me, yes, it is bad, madam. This could have a dreadful outcome for us all," cautioned the captain.

Passing a few kilometres east of Kano, and while everyone quietly reflected on the latest predictions, the same air traffic controller called over the radio.

"Green Bird Zero Eight from Kano control, do you read?"

"Go ahead, Kano, this is Green Bird Zero Eight," replied Quinn.

"Your overfly reference code EIQTR567Q has been rejected by my computer. Please transmit the correct code."

Quinn glanced over at Fergus before reading back the same information from the flight plan, noticing that the earlier politeness in the controller's voice had faded away.

"Green Bird Zero Eight, I say again, your overfly licence is invalid. You violate Nigerian airspace. Turn right, heading 240 degrees, and descend to flight level 100. Expect radar vectors. You must land your aircraft at Kano airport."

"What the fuck are you two doing? What the frigging hell is going on? Disregard that instruction, and maintain our present course," screamed Haily.

After a few minutes, the controller once again called over the radio.

"Green Bird Zero Eight, my radar indicates you are not obeying my command. Therefore, you must comply immediately."

Haily reached over and grabbed the clipboard from Quinn. She frantically flicked through the six pages of the flight plan, searching for anything that might appear irregular.

There was now frustration, even a hint of anger, in the controller's voice.

"Green Bird Zero Eight, you continue to disregard my commands at your peril. I have scrambled two Sepcat Jaguar fighters. You must obey their instructions when they intercept you in about eight minutes. Then, prepare to be escorted down to land at Kano airport. Do you understand, over?"

Except for the pilots, everyone listened in amazement to the unfolding drama while Quinn did his utmost to distract Haily.

"They'll shoot us down, you know."

Haily's finger came to rest on the alphanumeric code. She snatched the hand mike from Quinn, and keyed the transmit button.

"Kano from Green Bird Zero Eight, do you read."

"Go ahead," replied the controller.

"Kano, I believe we may have transmitted the wrong information. Please copy the revised code."

Haily read aloud the revised code, EIOTR567O, in a slow, deliberate voice. Then, after releasing the transmit button, a tense minute's silence ensued.

"Green Bird Zero Eight from Kano control. Madam, may I advise you are transiting a politically sensitive area. Your overfly permission is now validated. Please, be more attentive in future. You will shortly enter Cameroon airspace, so contact Douala control. Have a nice day."

Haily took a few steps back from the pilots, pointing at the pen strokes Fergus had made on the flight plan; the EIOTR567O was now EIQTR567Q.

"That was clever, that was very clever. Was your load-master not enough? Do you think I wouldn't put a bullet through one of your heads? It only takes one pilot to land this machine."

"Hey, take it easy, partner. Put the gun down."

As Pepe pleaded with the incensed woman, the captain struggled to maintain his composure.

"Normally, you would be right. One of us could land it. But on three engines and with low fuel levels, you need us both. You need all my crew."

Berko could hear most of the conversation, which was beginning to make him feel even more vulnerable. He wasn't flight crew, and, as loadmaster, his services were no longer required until their return flight. If they ever returned. He wasn't sure if the Ibuprofen or his adrenaline lessened the pain, but he had a bad feeling she wasn't finished with him yet.

"This is not over. You can be assured of that. We'll discuss this when we land, you bunch of morons." Shoving the pistol inside her leather belt, Haily drank thirstily from the water bottle until it was empty. Then, after crushing it bullishly, she threw the plastic container, bouncing it off the flight deck window.

Although Enda was struggling to rationalise their predicament, one thing was clear; his friends would be depending on him. His engineering skills were going to be tested like never before, way beyond the most challenging simulated training session. No one dies in the simulator. If they are to have any chance of survival, his ability to pump every drop of usable fuel from the aircraft's tanks will dictate the outcome.

CHAPTER SEVENTEEN

From the elevated vantage point in the control tower, the effect of the distant gust-front could be seen before being felt as it advanced from a northerly direction and darkest section of the sky. The top of the massive Afrormosia in the storm's path swayed violently as the wind increased from almost calm to fifty feet per second. With every short-circuit, lightning bolts splintered, as if trying to jab the forest into submission. Then, streaking wildly across the canopy, the gusting spasms of wind arrived as if sent to test the well-built control tower's integrity; the tempest rampaged, doing its utmost to blow it down. Except for the radio operator, everyone stood watching in awe as nature awakened, making the tower howl and creak under extreme pressure. A sheet of corrugated steel roofing slapped erratically on the massive nearby storage shed until, finally, the fasteners let go as it was ripped away, sending it spinning aimlessly like a leaf in the darkening sky.

"Better be still standing after this blows through. We plan to use that hangar to store the medical supplies."

"Well, lieutenant, that'll be your problem. We're only

making the delivery. But, more importantly, the runways water drainage better be effective," replied the Texan.

From the swollen grey cumulous nimbus, a few rain-drops splattered on the windows before it began to pelt down, reducing visibility to almost zero. It was as though the sky had been gathering every scrap of noise for the occasion, freed in seconds by gigantic lightning spasms, and overhead a river-less waterfall came flooding down. Then, not content with its magnificent display of force, the thunderstorm unleashed wave after wave of hailstones, and when a section of the runway once again became visible, it was white. The multiple layers of what could easily have been mistaken for Ping-Pong balls, bouncing after impact, eventually coming to rest before gradually melting away.

In the elevated room with panoramic views not appreciated by all, speech became inaudible. Resembling heavy cannon fire, each reactive thunderclap returned a dozen rumbling echo's, making the building and everything in it tremble from the aftershocks.

Lieutenant Cramoisy, noticing that the Americans looked perturbed, responded to each clap of thunder by waving his arms above his head, like a deranged orchestra conductor, while repeatedly bellowing at the top of his voice, "Magnifique." Then, abruptly, almost as quickly as it commenced, the hostilities began to subside after nearly thirty minutes of battering. The men returned to their seats, and the Texan spoke to no one in particular.

"Fuck, and I thought I'd seen some big ones. Let's hope the inbound doesn't encounter one like that during the landing."

Unable to resist, the lieutenant poked fun at the foreigners.

"That shouldn't be a problem for your American pilots."

CHAPTER EIGHTEEN

The aircraft's weather radar was obsolete. It was installed during the DC8's manufacture, and should have been replaced long ago. After surviving numerous encounters with severe weather, which, according to the radar display screen, didn't exist, most captains had written it up in the technical log as unserviceable. Still, the avionics report always returned the same remark: test carried out satisfactory, no faults found. The reluctance to replace it was undoubtedly dictated by cost. Enda recalled a particularly heated exchange with Gerry in the operations room, when he pleaded to get the radar replaced. Still, Gerry dismissed the idea, arguing to replace the aircraft would probably cost less.

Overflying Bertoua, and shortly before requesting descent, Quinn contacted Douala air traffic for the latest weather conditions at their destination. Although Ouésso was still out of radio range, with less than three hundred and fifty kilometres to go, the flight was nearing its end. In a peculiar English idiolect, the controller read aloud the only weather report available and, as it was more than three hours old, it was useless. Moreover, except for one showing the airport layout, there were no instrument approach charts for Ouésso, making a visual landing the only possibility.

That said, there was a non-directional beacon near the airport's centre, which, if serviceable and tracked by the needle of the onboard automatic direction finder, would help guide the aircraft towards the runway. The instrument had a compass card and a single pointer needle that pivoted from the centre, resembling the face of an old windup alarm clock, with only the minute needle. The crew dreaded the prospect of relying on this basic instrument for the approach, knowing that early visual contact with the runway would be the only sure way of completing a safe landing. But, because of their low fuel status, they also knew they would only get one shot at it. Fortunately for everyone on board, the man at the controls was considered in Irish aviation circles to be an exceptional pilot.

Fergus scribbled a few notes on the clipboard while Enda adjusted his seat to get close to the pilots in preparation for the captain's final briefing.

"Right, lads, this should be a doddle. So, let's review the main points, and if ya think I've missed anything, speak up."

While Berko sat in the forward galley, resting his heavily bandaged foot on a seat cushion, the American agents moved closer in the busy flight deck, attentively listening, ensuring the pilots weren't getting up to any more tricks.

"Please, can you move back a bit and give us space," said Enda.

To the engineer's surprise, the agents obliged, and Fergus continued with the briefing.

"Okay, on the good points, and I can only think of one, we'll have at least an hour's daylight left when we arrive."

"Skipper, are you kidding? We won't need the extra

daylight if we don't get her down on the first attempt," said Quinn, his pessimism only aggravating the already stressful situation.

The captain turned stony-faced for a moment, before his smile returned.

"We will get her down on the first attempt. Now then, let's consider the tricky bits. We'll be landing in a southerly direction, and the runway is short. This place is almost twelve hundred feet above sea level, so be careful when resetting the altimeters. Remember, we can't use full flaps on three engines, so our landing speed will be higher than usual. Not ideal, lads, on a short piece of tarmac. Finally, if for any reason I fuck it up, and we need to go around, I'll attempt a teardrop reversal onto the other end of the runway. The wind was reported to be almost calm, so that at least shouldn't be a factor. If all that's not enough, I guess you saw the remark on the weather report about thunderstorms forecasted in the vicinity of the airport. So, that's about it. Any questions, suggestions?"

This time, it wasn't only Quinn, as all present looked tense, unable to resist throwing repeated glances towards the weather radar's blank display. Until now, they didn't get the opportunity to check the system, as there were no cloud build-ups along their route. Either way, at this stage, it no longer mattered whether it was serviceable or not.

Enda turned his head and looked up at Haily.

"You were planning to shoot one of them. Well, who's the moron now?"

The palm of her hand fell hard against Enda's face, instantly drawing a trickle of blood from his lower lip. The engineer dragged the back of his blood-smeared fingers across his mouth and sneered.

"It was worth it, bitch."

Pepe, fist-cocked high, was about to punch Enda's face when the captain intervened.

"Enough, for fuck's sake, enough."

Pepe hesitated and, relaxing his taut muscles, lowered his clenched fist.

Fergus spoke softly to his co-pilot, hoping he would take the offer as a vote of confidence.

"Quinn, if you wish, you can fly the approach. You're a better pilot than you give yourself credit for."

The grateful co-pilot reached over and gently brushed his hand across the top of the captain's balding head.

"No way, skipper, you're the wizard. If you can't get us down, then nobody can."

"Okay then, call Douala and request descent, please."

Quinn had taken advantage of the earlier brief melee. Not even his friends noticed him removing the aircraft's short-handled crash axe from the side panel of the engineer's station. Although he fumbled a little to avoid drawing attention, he didn't look down as he stuffed it into his flight case next to his seat. Hurtling inbound, with about one hundred and twenty kilometres to run, they veered left and right, trying to avoid the enormous storm clouds. Then, as they rapidly descended through nineteen thousand feet, Douala control advised them to contact Ouésso tower for further clearance. Peering ahead through the windscreens, four massive thunderstorm cells loitered in the vicinity of their destination, with one of the anvil-shaped Cumulous Nimbus cloud tops appearing to punch through the troposphere. Any captain facing such a menacing display of nature would, after taking in the wow moment, order a timely U-turn or divert to somewhere less scary. However, this crew could do neither.

After repeated calls, Quinn had almost given up trying

to make contact with the tower when a calm, professional-like voice finally came over the speaker.

"Good evening, Green Bird Zero Eight. We have been expecting you. Please state your position, ETA, souls onboard, and endurance."

Quinn keyed his mike. "Good evening, Ouésso tower. We are northwest of the airport, descending through sixteen thousand feet. ETA in about thirteen minutes, six souls onboard."

Pausing for a moment, he glanced back to see Enda flashing a hand of fingers five times.

"Endurance twenty-five minutes. Please, forward your latest weather and runway conditions."

The response from the tower was immediate.

"Green Bird, that would mean you expect to land with twelve minutes of fuel remaining. Confirm, sir, is that correct, twelve minutes?" asked the controller.

"Affirm, sir, that's what I said. Now, forward your field weather conditions, immediately."

Quinn's voice was abrasive and strained.

The lieutenant and the Americans gathered around the seated air traffic controller. Mister White had written a short note on a tissue paper before placing it on the table before the anxious man. Even though the message was written in typical aero-drome weather format, it did not reflect the actual storm conditions at the airfield. The controller got to his feet and read the contradictory note to himself. Then, noticing the hesitation, Cramoisy yanked the Walter PPK from its holster and tapped the gun's barrel against the Bakelite microphone, encouraging the preceptive man to begin transmitting the significantly modified weather conditions to the inbound aircraft.

"Good visibility in light rain, cloud base overcast at about eight hundred feet, temperature 34 degrees- dew point 29 degrees. Set altimeters to One Zero Zero Six."

Quinn fiddled with his earlobe, and feeling greatly relieved, he advised the controller that they would land on the southerly runway.

"Bollox, I don't get it. Apart from the cloud base being a bit low, it sounds like a reasonably good day down there. Strange though. For fucks sake, look at that weather ahead. We're going to get trashed on the way in, but at least the direction finder needle appears to be tracking true," said the captain. His voice raised with a tone of confusion.

After Fergus had advised everyone to tighten their seat harness until the straps hurt, the agents were about to return to the forward galley when Enda asked them to check that the loadmaster was well strapped in, and was surprised when Pepe even offered to sit next to the wounded man.

"Lads, I will be head down, focused on the flight instruments. I'll try to guide her towards the runway, so I'll need you both looking outside. That's a low fucking cloud base, and we have to make visual contact with the runway pronto. Remember, we don't have a plan B."

Enda adjusted his headphones and pressed the play button on his Walkman. His pals from the Solomon Islands were thinking of calling their band Deep Forest and the song Night Bird. But, as the normally beautiful, bewitching musical chant filtered into his psychic, it became contrastingly eerie.

The captain manoeuvred the freighter, trying to remain clear of clouds for as long as he could, until, no longer able to avoid one of the massive clouds, the flight deck darkened almost instantaneously. Their hopes and lives were about to be entrusted to a single instrument, the small pointer needle behind the glass. The first lightning strike on the fuselage made a deafening whip-like noise before exiting the tail, causing the heartbeats of everyone on board to falter. And with no time to check for damage, everyone stayed focused on their task, wishing the aircraft ever closer to the runway.

Except for the soldier with the radio in the control tower, the four men donned tatty raincoats before proceeding onto the flimsy wooden platform, which offered exterior passage around the top of the building. Positioning themselves facing north, they stood ill at ease, hoping to catch a glimpse of the aircraft carrying their precious cargo.

Quinn made repeated calls in vain for a weather update from the control tower. As the soldier sat motionless below the speaker on the wall, he listened, trying to imagine what the foreigners looked like. Once again, the autopilot could no longer cope, and after the final disengagement, Fergus was hands-on but doubted if he still had control of the aircraft. The torrential rain and gusting wind pounded his machine, dangerously stressing it beyond its design limits. Moreover, the severe weather appeared to be carrying out an untimely integrity test on the steel rivets that fastened the wings to the fuselage. Enda couldn't help noticing the sweat trickling down the co-pilots face, and squeezing his pal's shoulder, it prompted Quinn to glance briefly back at his young friend with a wink. To get the best downward angle of visibility out through his windshield, Quinn applied an old simulator practice by selecting the height lever on his seats to maximum up.

Fergus struggled to control the fly speed. Usually, a smooth handler, but today, abrupt engine thrust changes were necessary to target the flaps and landing gear speed. What made this captain special was his ability to anticipate, to always have that extra bit of skill in reserve. Encouragingly, the tip of the navigation needle appeared to confirm they were on track. Descending well below what would be considered safe, they should break through the clouds and see the airport at any moment.

Straining their eyes and struggling to spot the runway had Enda and Quinn totally absorbed until Fergus, still maintaining situational awareness, calmly called aloud, "Quinn, how about the landing checklist?"

By the time the co-pilot had completed a shortened version of the checklist, they were passing four hundred feet, with sections of green canopy becoming visual, streaking past not far below. But still no runway. The torrential rain made forward visibility almost impossible, and Plan A was being washed away. Becoming trapped, and unable to descend any further, for fear of hitting the treetops, the captain levelled off to the scream of Quinn pointing to the right.

"There, Fergie, over there!"

Arriving too far left of the runway, even for the maestro, it was too late to attempt a landing. The men on the control tower platform could hear the engines, and when they eventually saw the approaching aircraft screaming towards them, they became frozen with terror. Quinn and Enda were still looking towards the runway, so didn't see what the captain saw dead ahead. At one hundred fifty knots, desperate to climb the underpowered aircraft, Fergus rammed the throttles forward, while simultaneously applying a boot full of right rudder and aileron to counter the thrust asymmetry.

"Ah, fuck," were the only words from his mouth, as the captain aggressively manoeuvred in a vain attempt to avoid impacting the tall building. The number one engine, outboard of the left wing, was producing maximum thrust when it made contact with the top of the control tower. Then, before it separated from the aircraft, the astonished Americans were snatched from the platform by the motor's ferocious suction, and emitting an orange blowtorch-like flame, a column of dark reddish detritus billowed from the exhaust. The remaining two spectators scrambled to get back inside, but were instantly butchered by shards of hot titanium compressor blades, ricocheting like bullets in all directions as the engine disintegrated

Feeling the splatter of warm raindrops on his face, the lone survivor in the tower gazed in shock at the grey clouds through the vast aperture above him. He was still seated in the same spot, with a small jagged piece of metal protruding from his left shoulder, oozing a trickle of blood that ran down his jungle combats.

After separating from the wing, what remained of the two-tonne engine tumbled violently through the air before crashing down; the rain-sodden earth offered little resistance as it sank deep before finally coming to rest in a smouldering pile of twisted steel.

Most of the soldiers guarding the perimeter dived at the ground for cover, pointing their weapons skyward, believing they must be under attack, as the stench of burnt flesh drifted across the airfield. Even in nearby Ouésso town, rumours quickly spread about a military invasion by Mobutu.

The noise generated during the demolition added to the freighter's roaring engines developing full power and harmonised well with every boom of thunder from the forest. Onboard the stricken airliner, the crew struggled to maintain composure, desperately striving to carry out emergency procedures. Even though they had all been trained to cope with life-threatening situations, no training could have prepared them for this. Enda and Quinn worked together to complete checklists while Fergus fought and trimmed, trying to gain altitude from the output of the two remaining engines.

The captain called out in near despair, making sure his engineer could hear him.

"Get every drop of fuel from the tanks, lad. We don't have much time."

Wrestling to maintain control, Fergus climbed the aircraft wings level, and as they gained a few hundred feet, it took them back up into the clouds. With the possibility of turning back now gone, the stark reality of crashing into the jungle was all that remained. Sudden impact with high ground was becoming more likely, and might even have been the most merciful conclusion for all on board. Then, gradually, the dimly lit flight deck became brighter as the clouds began to dissipate. Stunned by the sudden improvement in visibility, which was now clear to the horizon, it brought a little optimism to the beleaguered crew. The sun hung low to the west, and forging its way through the dense rainforest, the outline of the snaking Shanga River was unmistakable. In the smooth, clear air, the captains struggle to maintain control of the aircraft was no longer necessary. Even on two engines, he flew the stricken ship with precision, applying gentle control-wheel inputs, although, very soon, none of that would matter.

The Antonov remained parked on the taxiway as ordered, and when the soldiers charged up the steps, they screamed at the captain to get airborne and chase after the crippled freighter.

"I cannot abandon my position. My crew are under strict orders from the Americans not to do anything without receiving the password. We stay until they tell us otherwise. Do you want to fuck with the Americans?" goaded the captain.

All around the airport's perimeter, there was pandemonium. The troops in the vehicles made continuous radio calls in a vain attempt to contact their commanding officer, Lieutenant Cramoisy. The surviving soldier in the control tower could hear noise from the speaker, but the loud buzzing in his ears left him almost deaf. Dazed, he staggered to his feet and, rotating the knob of the radio receiver to the maximum, he keyed the mike.

"He's gone. They're all gone."

"What you mean, man, he's gone?" shrieked a voice over the speaker.

"The plane took them."

Then, wanting to be sure that a return manoeuvre wasn't possible, Haily cocked her pistol, and after tapping it lightly against the captain's right ear, she stepped back a little, aiming the weapon at the back of his head.

"Turn this fucking ship around, right now. You still have a delivery to make."

Quinn replied on behalf of his captain. "Ah, Jaysis, for fuck's sake, you can't be fucking serious."

Pepe seemed confused and pointed his weapon at Quinn.

"Yes, we are frigging serious. Now, do it. Turn this fucker around or..."

Although the agents knew this was not a good time for a standoff, they still tried to intimidate. Fergus squeezed hard on the control wheel, his white knuckles protruding, trying to control his temper.

"Or what?" asked Fergus. No one said a word, so he continued.

"If we turn back, we're all dead. If you shoot him or me, we're all dead. So, if you and your partner put away those guns and sit the fuck down, we might survive this day. If we do, we might even make the delivery, but not to Ouésso."

The agents lowered their pistols, and as the sweat stains spread out on everyone's shirts, the air-conditioning fan could no longer shift the stench of body odour hanging thick in the crowded flight deck air. Benko's shouts for attention from the galley sent Pepe hurrying to investigate, and moments later, the loadmaster limped through the doorway with his arm draped across the American's shoulders.

"Fergie, I know you're considering putting her down on the river. Please, Fergie, not yet. Listen to me first. About six months before leaving the RAF, we flew a low-level reconnaissance sortie out of Kinshasa in a C130 Hercules. It was close to where we are now. We overflew dozens of mining camps on both sides of the Shanga River. I know that was years ago, but nothing much has changed since then."

Everyone listened intently, as if being entertained by a great storyteller.

"Even though most of the camps are probably abandoned by now, I'm certain they all had decent-length airstrips, some long enough to accommodate a C130."

Fergus didn't take long to see the big picture and was almost rushing the words from his mouth. "Okay, here's how we're going to play this. I'm going to fly, keeping the river to our left as a ditching option, and I want the rest of you to try spotting one of those landing strips, except Enda. You keep that fuel flowing. We just have to get her down in one piece. She won't be flying out again. So, if we don't spot something before the fuel runs out, I'll put her down as gently as I can on the river."

The partially crippled aircraft achieved a decent speed even on two engines, leaving Ouésso and the soldiers well behind them. Sensing the minutes quickly passing, Enda pressed rewind and then play, helplessly watching as each amber low-pressure fuel light on the engineer's panel flickered, before illuminating bright. Astonished that the engines hadn't already stopped, Fergus was eyeing up a good spot on the river when Quinn roared with excitement. For all of his failings, one thing never let him down; he had the eyesight of an eagle.

"Yes, over there, Fergie, two o'clock. We can make it. We're almost within gliding range."

The landing strip ran in an east-west direction, making a ninety-degree right turn the shortest route to land, and although the strip looked short, it was probably more survivable than the river. Once again, the captain ordered everyone to tighten their straps and, as Berko and Pepe were about to return to the galley, the captain called out to the American.

"Hey, mister, help him to get out if we survive the landing. He just might have saved our skins, including yours."

The captain spoke his thoughts aloud; faced with attempting to achieve the impossible was weighing heavily on his mind.

"I'm going to stay high in case the motors stop before we land. At least that would still give me a chance to glide her in. Hey, Enda, if by some miracle the engines are still running, I want you to shut them down if it looks like we're going to exit the landing strip. Don't forget to discharge the extinguisher bottles and close all the fuel shutoff valves, as we have to prevent a fire from developing. Then, Quinn, when we land, and if they're available, I'll apply the reversers, so follow me through with your hands on the controls, and remember to press hard with me on the brake pedals."

Even though the captain had made his plan clear, he continued to speak his thoughts aloud, his sharp situational awareness recognising new hazards. The remaining daylight would be sufficient; however, landing to the west would put the sun directly into their eyes. Quinn pointed ahead to a small plume of smoke rising from the forest, guessing it was probably from a local tribe's fire. The smoke was drifting from east to west, which indicated a very undesirable tail-wind landing on the short runway. Fergus began to realise that by taking the slightly longer route, not only would he avoid the tailwind, they might even get the opportunity to make a quick visual assessment of the landing strip.

"New plan" he shouted. "I'm going for the easterly landing."

"But, Fergie, the fuel," cried Quinn.

The captain glanced over his shoulder at Enda, and although only one fuel pump remained operational, he held his thumbs up, gesturing approval.

When Quinn spoke again, there was determination in his tone.

"I'm with you, skipper. You can depend on me."

"Believe me, lad; this is my last one. I'm going to apply for early retirement when we get home," muttered Fergus, unable to conceal the slight quiver in his voice.

Repeatedly flicking the lid of his Zippo open and shut, Pepe's face turned pale after vomiting into a sick bag, making his partner seated opposite unimpressed. Then, as Haily picked at a small piece of flesh at the edge of her thumbnail, it bled, prompting the frown on her face to deepen.

"For god's sake, Pepe, pull yourself together, and let's pray that guy flying this fucked up machine knows what he's doing."

CHAPTER NINETEEN

The platoon sergeant now held the highest rank and was in charge. Arriving with two of his men, he shouldered and banged his fist against the locked control tower door until one of the soldiers stepped forward, firing a short burst from his automatic weapon, the lock disintegrated, and the door flung open with a single kick from the sergeant's boot.

The radio operator was pointing his weapon towards the stairwell in the control tower, and stunned at being threatened by one of his men, the wide-eyed sergeant bellowed a command. "Down your weapon, soldier. Do it, now."

Confused but without hesitating, the soldier flicked the safety on before throwing his assault rifle to the floor. Displaying no surprise or emotion, the sergeant looked at the devastation before reaching for the ringing wall mounted Bakelite phone.

"Ouésso tower, this is Brazzaville centre. Can you hear me? Ouésso tower, I repeat, can you hear me?"

"Yes, I can hear you. I'm the platoon sergeant."

"We have been trying to make contact for over thirty minutes. Has the freighter landed?"

Overburdened while trying to describe the event that led to so many deaths, the sergeant became agitated by the constant questions and interruptions. Then, for a few moments, there was quiet before a calming voice took control of the confused situation.

"This is Colonel Kombo. Your men have a mission to complete, and you will take your orders directly from me. Is that understood, sergeant?"

CHAPTER TWENTY

The landing gear smashed through the treetops, gouging a channel all the way down to the beginning of the forty-foot-wide airstrip, which was barely wide enough to accommodate the enormous main wheels. The concrete section had large cracks sprouting green vegetation along its entire length, and bordering each side was a wide section of soil and rock laterite. Not only were they faced with the high probability of crashing into the dense forest trees ahead, the right-wing would surely make contact with the small brick shed near the end of the concrete strip.

To everyone's amazement, the aircraft touched down gently, and with the engines still developing power, Fergus could apply the much-needed reverses. Then, abruptly, the airframe began to shudder violently on the uneven surface as the effect of the thirty-eight thousand pounds of reverse thrust raised a massive column of red dust around the right wing. In a wasted effort to gain traction, both pilots shoved their control columns fully forward and, pressing down hard on the brake pedals; the force rammed them even tighter into their seats. With a wingspan of almost one hundred fifty feet, the right wing was about to demolish the brick shed. So, unable to further delay the engine's shut-down, Enda reached forward and moved the fuel levers to shutoff.

The exceptional aircraft handling was lost the moment the wing hit the solid structure. The ferocity of the impact slicing away the wing's outer section made the pilot's efforts to maintain directional control useless, and even the crew became passengers onboard the careering bulk of metal. The crippled aircraft veered off the concrete, its new trajectory taking her thirty degrees to starboard. Then, before the right and left main undercarriage dug in, the nose gear had already sunk deep into the soil, spewing up mounds of red dust as it collapsed under the strain. Paradoxically, on exiting the concrete strip, the resistance of the undercarriage dragging through the laterite created enough deceleration to stop them from slamming into the treeline ahead and inevitable carnage.

Like a mortally wounded animal falling to its knees, Brigid, the ageing sky goddess, had reached her final resting place. Grinding to a stop about thirty feet short of the expansive forest trees, the nosecone was partly buried in the earth, and her tail protruded proudly up, almost as high as the forest canopy. Moments later, the red dirt rained down from the massive cloud, bouncing violently against the metal fuselage like hailstones on a car's roof.

Survival instincts fully intact, Pepe was first to secure an escape route. Pushing hard, he rotated the long door handle in the direction of the red-painted arrow, the nose-down body attitude making the heavy door swing open with ease. Then, as a reddish dust cloud surged into the galley, the rubber escape slide swelled instantly with an explosive whoosh. Designed to inflate downwards to bridge the twelve-foot drop, instead, it settled like a life raft, flat and almost level with the bottom of the door.

Haily struggled from her seat harness and rushed to where Pepe stood, the couple almost choking after breathing in a lung full of laterite vapour. The captain, co-pilot, and engineer remained seated, momentarily incapacitated with shock, knowing they had just eluded death. The tanks were empty, and any remaining fuel vapour had most likely been smothered by the dust cloud, making the possibility of a flash fire less likely, with every minute that passed. After unbuckling their seat harnesses, the crew scrutinised each other, checking for any trace of blood or injury, but there was none. With legs like jelly and trying to keep their balance on the sloping floor, they bunched together for support and, weeping uncontrollably, they hugged. Although for the Irish men, their troubles were far from over. Plotting her next move, Haily waited by the escape door, ready to make it clear that she was still in charge.

CHAPTER TWENTY-ONE

"Pepe, get out there, see if you can open that forward cargo door, and try to be quick."

Berko was still strapped into his seat, his outstretched leg on cushions, not knowing whether to laugh or cry, watching as the heroes shuffled clumsily out from the flight deck. Then, stooping down, Fergus gently wrapped his arm around Berko's neck, applying a light squeeze as he drew his head against his hip.

"Okay, you lot, your stupidity just got my colleague and me into a whole lot of shit, and the worst part is, I don't think you fully understand the magnitude of the situation," Haily sneered, as if chastising naughty children.

Berko looked up at her, convinced he had her measure, while his three friends stood flabbergasted, staring wide-eyed at the ungrateful, agitated woman.

"Aren't you ever going to wise up, missy?"

Those were the last words Berko spoke.

Before raising her pistol, Haily's cold eyes explored his. Then, it was over in a split second. The bullet exploded, splintering as it struck his forehead. Metal fragments passed through the back of his skull, splattering bone and brain tissue onto the seat's headrest, and, as shrapnel ricocheted, a piece fractured the opposite door's small glass panel. Overwhelmed by a sense of helplessness, the men gazed in disbelief at Berko's lifeless body as spew gathered at the back of their dry tongues.

"That was an accident. I didn't mean to shoot him, although he was right. Look at the window; definitely not a good idea to discharge a weapon when airborne."

Devoid of emotion, her mocking words were intended to demonstrate control, but for the witnesses to a murder, it signalled the complete opposite.

Pepe ran back and leapt up onto the rubber mat, and with a tug from the woman, he clambered back onboard.

"Goddamnit, buddy, what the fuck happened? What have you done? Hand over your weapon."

"I don't know. I wasn't even aiming at the guy. The gun just went off. Anyway, it'll give these motherfuckers a lesson in discipline."

Flustered, she tried to maintain the façade, but her words fell wanting.

"You evil bitch," screamed the engineer.

Enda lunged towards her in a rage until another deafening noise stopped him dead in his tracks. The gunshot came from Pepe's pistol, fired as a warning. The bullet slammed into the roof, inches above the young man's head. Instinctively, Quinn grabbed Enda's arm and restrained his forward momentum and certain demise.

"Jesus, Haily, try to remember to keep the safety on unless you intend to use it. Here, put your gun away. "

"With that foot wound, I doubt he would have left this place alive. He would have slowed us down. Perhaps I did us all a favour."

Staring defiantly at the killer, the Irish men only wished she could sense the boiling hatred in their blood and souls. After the agents holstered their weapons, confident their captives would no longer offer any resistance, Pepe pulled heavily against the Velcro straps until the escape slide detached from the aircraft. Then, dragging it clear from the bottom of the door, he shinnied back onboard.

"It's going to be dark soon, so listen carefully to my instructions if you want to stay alive." Haily pointed the finger at Quinn, then Enda. "I want you two to get him off this plane, clean up this mess, and bury him. If you've nothing to dig with, dispose of the body over there." She gestured towards the thick green undergrowth.

"Listen," said Fergus, "we don't want any more misery. Let us move him to the rear toilet cubicle. Then, come morning; we can give him a decent burial. Please, if we leave him out there tonight, animals are sure to take him."

"Okay, I can live with that. Although you better wrap him up well, because if I get any bad smells during the night, he's out, you get it?"

Fergus lowered his eyes, unable to offer a reply.

"How much battery power does this machine have?" quizzed Pepe, directing the question at the engineer. "Are you fucking deaf? I asked you a question."

"If I switch the nonessentials off, we should have at least twenty-four hours for lighting," replied Enda, becoming reacquainted with his survival mode.

The agents huddled together, and speaking almost in a whisper, Pepe tried to summarise his thoughts.

"They're probably already looking for us, and there's not much we can do tonight. Unless something flies overhead, the planes radio range will be useless at ground level. From what I could see, opening that lower cargo door will take some effort. So, let's stay put till morning, and if they haven't found us by then, we can use the satellite phone, which is with the rest of our gear, so we really need to get that frigging door open."

Apart from the overspill from the freighters lighting through the windows, it was pitch dark outside. The nocturnal creatures of the jungle all wanted to be heard, releasing unfamiliar sounds of pain or joy that reverberated in the darkness, as though in a heated discussion about the new arrivals to their world. As for the humans, transitioning from the aircraft's air-conditioning to the rainforest's natural steam bath was overwhelming. With mosquitos and other insects already on board, indulging themselves on the foreigner's flesh, it was going to be a long night.

Pepe called Quinn to help close the heavy exit door, but they couldn't. After emptying the contents of two catering trollies, they shoved them out through the open door, creating a makeshift ramp. Quinn leapt down and, pushing against the bottom of the door, Pepe pulled on the handle. As it began to swing closed, Quinn had just enough time to clamber back inside.

Haily had been evaluating the risks and was ready to set the mood for the night.

"So, gentlemen, here's how it's going to be. When you two have finished settling in, your departed friend, you, captain, can sleep on the flight deck. Quinn, find some space along the cargo, and you, boy, you can have the rear galley. Don't congregate. Pepe and I will cosy up right here in the galley. It's probably already occurred to you that unless your people manage to rescue you before ours arrive, you're all screwed. Wait, don't panic; there is hope. Because even if our people get here first, we still might need you to pitch in and help get us out of this shithole. I'm a light sleeper, so if any of you try to escape or cause me grief during the night, we'll execute all three of you. Before you help yourselves to food and water, one last thing. I want you to gather your personal stuff, passports, licences, IDs, and rings and bring them here to me."

After the men obeyed as ordered, Quinn wrapped what was left of Benko's head in tea towels before sliding him off the seat onto a large tarpaulin sheet, tugging at it until he was tightly swaddled. Then, when no one was watching, Enda slipped the loadmaster's insignia ring from his finger and stuffed it in his pocket. They needed to stop frequently, struggling to carry the dead weight up the steep incline to the temporary mortuary, the rear toilet cubicle. And, with their heads lowered in disbelief, they made a silent farewell to their friend, hesitant to close the door.

Except for the agents, no one slept much during the long humid night, tormented by visions of extraordinary moments of horror that invaded their thoughts with foreboding. Enda was awake, sitting in the rear galley, scheming. His twentieth attempt at contriving an escape plan collapsed in bloodshed: his and his friend's blood. Without making a sound, he stepped a few meters into the darkness and slid the concealed roof panel open. Then, knowing what he would find, he removed the dark green satchel, delaying checking it until he returned to the dimly lit rear galley.

When the first morning light began filtering across the crash site, on the planes thick metal skin roof, the faint sound of heavy raindrops generated a white noise throughout the cabin. The only thing that offered any sense of normality to the new day was the soft sound of a flushing toilet, and from the forward galley, Pepe's roar could be heard above everything else.

"Get your asses up here. I mean now."

Before Fergus left the flight deck, he peered through gaps in the mucky windows, where the rain was washing away the reddish dust, recreating images of blood streaming down his close friends' faces in his memory. Then, sliding open a side window, he could see raindrops splashing off the lavish shiny green leaves, and hovering above the surface, everything was layered in a spine-chilling shifting mist.

When Pepe rotated the long handle and shoved, the door swung open to a whoosh of warm moist air that engulfed the interior like a shockwave. In the early morning light, the closeness of the forest made surviving the forced landing even more astonishing. With his fingers clinging onto the doorframe, Pepe leaned his head out to check for any signs of danger and immediately raised the alarm.

"The frigging escape slide is gone." As rainwater trickled down his nose, he tried to scan the treeline in the reduced visibility before easing himself back inside to the shelter of the galley. "We've obviously got company. My guess is a native tribe. I'm also guessing they're not hostile. Otherwise, they would have already had a go at us."

"Yeah, Pepe, let's hope they're more afraid of us than we are of them. Now, you lot, here's what's on today's menu. First, Quinn, get the crash axe and hand it over to me." Hands on hips, she glared at him.

"You don't seriously think we're that stupid, do you? Pepe, chop away a section of that panelling. Try to shape it into something they can dig with. Hey you, Enda, keep a lookout from the galley and callout if the Indians return. We'll be monitoring things from the other side of the aircraft. Also, before we get started, you can change into something more comfortable if you wish. But hurry up, move it."

The agents, quite content with their outfits, remained dressed in their jumpsuits, and although the flak jackets seemed inappropriate for the hot sticky conditions, they stayed on. Except for their shoes, Fergus, Quinn, and Enda discarded their uniforms and dressed like tourists from the limited choice in their overnight bags, which under the circumstances was also inappropriate, but it was all they had. Enda leaned out of the doorway, watching as the workers disappeared under the fuselage to where the upper section of the forward cargo door was visible above the sodden earth.

After scraping away a narrow channel, Pepe could reach the door handle and, disengaging the lock, although it moved, it wouldn't open. So, leaping back to his feet, he pointed at the ground.

"Okay, you two, dig."

Fergus and Quinn knelt at each side of the big door and began scooping away small amounts of laterite and mud with the improvised tools. Not familiar with manual labour, it wasn't long before their hands began to suffer from their efforts. Then, reluctantly, Quinn stood to face Haily with outstretched, bloodied palms.

"We won't last much longer digging like this. Can I get the fire gloves from the aircraft?"

"Go ahead, get them, and while you're at it, fetch a sheet of tarpaulin, something like the one you used to wrap up your friend.

Enda was waiting and, grabbing his arm; he dragged his friend onboard. Not wanting to leave Fergus with what he perceived was a pair of psychos, Quinn was in a hurry to get back, but not before hearing what the young engineer had to say.

"Listen, you won't believe this; I saw them. I even waved to them. There's a bunch of little people with spears and stuff, over there in the forest. Maybe they can help us. When you get the chance, you and Fergie have to make a break for it. I'll be waiting to help you back onboard. I've come up with a way to lock them out. Ya have to trust me."

After spending most of the morning scraping and

digging to clear the area below the cargo door, something prevented it from swinging fully open. Haily was quite slim, and by removing the body armour and lying back on the tarpaulin sheet, the gap was sufficient for her to wriggle through the narrow aperture. Even in the dim light, she could see it was all there and stacked, just like Berko had described.

Haily called out to her anxiously waiting colleague. "They'll never fit under the door, too heavy and too big. Although, good news, I managed to unlock the crate, and after I open the cartons, I'll pass the essentials out through the gap."

Pepe stooped to get below what remained of the severed right wing, which was offering shelter from the easing rainfall. Then, in a conveyer-like motion, the pilots passed each of the heavily wrapped items along to Pepe, who laid them out on the only dry piece of earth beneath the wing. While awkwardly moving the stash through the narrow gap, she hadn't noticed dropping a couple of the cigar-shaped metal canisters, which rolled along the sheet into a shallow muddy puddle. But Quinn did. Timing his moment to perfection, he reached over to where they fell and recovered the canisters, slipping them into his trouser pocket.

After Haily had salvaged the required merchandise, she crawled back out, cursing the filthy state of her uniform. With everyone gathered beneath the wing, Fergus and Quinn shuffled back a little, enough to give them room to stand upright, unnoticed by the agents, who were busy examining the hardware. Although the array of merchandise was impressive, it wasn't representative of what might be required by lifesaving charity aid workers. Amongst the assortment of weapons, including two Uzi mini-machine guns, were flares, ammunition, radio, and GPS navigational equipment. There should also have been twelve small metal canisters.

Quinn and Fergus made a break for it. The plan was to duck under the fuselage, left-wing, then dash for the open door, where Enda would be waiting to help them onboard. Even though the agents didn't get much time to react, Pepe kicked out instinctively, catching Fergus's right ankle and causing him to trip and fall. Quinn kept running; glancing over his shoulder, he saw his friend sprawled out, belly to the ground. Fergus strained to hold his head back, and, as if doing the butterfly stroke, he threw his arms forward over his head, shouting.

"Keep going. Fuck it, Quinn, go."

Enda tugged on the handle, and applying the well-practised technique, with the door in motion, he grabbed hold of Quinn's shirt, dragging him thuggishly onboard. Then, as the door slammed shut, with a shove of the handle, it rotated to lock.

Enda had been making preparations while he was alone on the aircraft. Securing the opposite entry door by jamming the handle with an aluminium catering tray, he quickly anchored the final one, and with the rear exits high off the ground, it rendered all doors impossible to open from the outside. Keeping their heads down, Quinn and Enda crept about, and panicked about their friend's fate, occasionally they would risk a peek out through the aircraft windows. The agents didn't let the captain stand; instead, they each grabbed a foot and rolled him over onto his back after dragging him back under the wing.

Haily's choice of words once again created a sense of the surreal. "Well, captain, you're a very naughty boy. But, as you can see, we're a little bit busy right now, so while you're waiting, may I suggest you do some praying."

Discarding what they didn't need, Haily and Pepe

loaded only essential items into their black canvas rucksacks, occasionally lifting them with one hand to check the weight. Machetes in brown leather sheaths hung loosely from their belts, and as Pepe slung one of the Uzis over his shoulder, Haily tuned the satellite phone and GPS receiver. Langley was expecting the long overdue call, and the encrypted connection was almost as clear as a landline. Uninterrupted for several minutes, she delivered her report, in a clear monotone.

"Standby," demanded a voice.

While waiting, they watched as a tiny black spot on the GPS centred, blinking rhythmically, until an almost featureless map spread across the small screen. Then, hearing faint chatter, she raised the phone to her ear.

"Go ahead, base."

"It is imperative you deliver the cargo without further delay. If local intel is reliable, we've already lost two operatives. This must not escalate into an international incident. One of the amphibian troop carriers left Ouésso some hours ago, heading in your general direction, but bad weather is hampering progress. You will proceed on foot through the jungle, on bearing three-one-five degrees. It's the least dense section of forest and continues for about ten clicks. That will lead you to a trail used mainly by the natives. We will coordinate the rendezvous with the friendlies. They will escort you back to Ouésso, where you will hand over the consignment to the officer in charge. A sergeant is in command of the troop carrier, and he's already been briefed. At Ouésso airport, an Antonov is waiting to transport you to Brazzaville. Unfortunately, we have no helicopter support available."

"Understood, sir, and what about the three-remaining crew?"

"You don't have time to dick about. Forget about them.

We'll deal with that issue later. Even if they managed to survive, who's going to believe them?"

By the time they had packed the remaining items into their rucksacks, the rain had eased to a light drizzle. Visibility was rapidly improving, and the occasional bursts of sunlight piercing the cloudy sky accentuated the steam-like mist swirling above the sodden earth. Fergus stumbled from the shove before they marched him back, stopping a short distance from the locked freighter door. With the aircraft sealed shut, the men inside were having difficulty hearing what Haily was saying, each, in turn, risking a quick look through the small cabin window aft of the left wing.

"We've been ordered to move out and not waste time, so we'll be on our way."

Leaving Fergus facing the closed door, they took a step back, and turning in unison; the agents departed towards the forest. Then, just before disappearing into the dark undergrowth, Haily called heads, tossing up her Peace Silver Dollar, she snatched it from the air as it spun, pausing momentarily, before removing the covering hand. Pepe grinned as a playful frown pulled across her face.

"Tails, you win. He's yours."

Sauntering back to where Fergus was standing, Pepe eased his sunglasses along the bridge of his nose until they covered his eyes, and with both men now facing the aircraft, draping his left arm lazily across the captain's shoulders, he scorned.

"She left it up to me. You Irish should know all about this one. What's that, you call it? Ah, yes, kneecapping, or to put it politely, a punishment shooting."

The captain hadn't noticed the pistol in his right hand, and as Pepe slid his arm from around his shoulder, he shot Fergus through his right calf, dropping him with a scream of agony to the ground. As the gunshot echoed, the forest erupted with loud screaking cries, as if the animals were trying to express their displeasure. Curled up with his knees to his chest, making a slight rocking movement, Fergus moaned, gripping his bloodied leg with both hands.

"I was planning to do both your legs, but I will be merciful. Consider it gratuity for yesterday, captain. That was a nice bit of flying."

Before re-joining his colleague, Pepe fired a single round at the aircraft's dull metal skin. As expected, the bullet disintegrated, leaving an oval-shaped indentation.

"You pair are lucky that we only have hollow-point ammo. Otherwise, your hiding place wouldn't have saved you."

Enda ran down the narrow passageway to the galley, and before he reached the door handle, Quinn wrestled him to the floor, shaking him by the shoulders and shouting in his frightened face, "If you open that door, we'll be next. For the moment, there's nothing we can do for Fergie. Think, lad, to survive this fucking nightmare, we're going to need each other."

Enda knew his friend was right, but refusing to give up the struggle, he punched Quinn in the side of his face, rolling him over from the force. Enda was now on top of Quinn, gripping him by the throat, squeezing as hard as he could, and staring up through inflamed watery eyes; his friend wouldn't fight back. Then, suddenly, becoming aware of what he was doing, Enda got to his feet, and, taking a few steps to the door, he was about to rotate the handle when he hesitated. Quinn was still lying on his back when the engineer offered his outstretched hand, and grabbing hold; his pal staggered a little as he got to his feet.

"Quinn, I'm sorry. I'm really, really sorry. Maybe you're right, but he will need our help real soon, or god knows, he could bleed to death."

"I know, Enda. Fuck it, I know."

Inside the aircraft, the captain's howling was barely audible as he defiantly laboured to shout out a command, determined to protect his crew.

"Keep that feckin door locked."

Watching from a distance, Haily waited for her colleague to return, and arms folded, with her head slightly tilted to one side, a knowing mien stretched from ear to ear.

"You were always a softy. Let's go."

A short time had passed since the shooting, when tapping on the fuselage startled them.

"They're back," said Enda.

With their backs to the main entry door, Enda turned around, first to risk a look through the window. There were four male pygmies, one squatted next to Fergus, and armed with long spears and bows with quivers of arrows; their dark-skinned weathered bodies were sparsely clothed in mulumba wraps. Although bearing weapons, the pygmies displayed no sign of aggression. However, until they understood more about the native's intentions, Quinn knew it would be unwise to unlock the door, opting to slide open the left flight deck window instead.

"We have to help Fergie. I'm not waiting much longer," protested Enda.

Hoping it would be viewed as a goodwill gesture, Quinn tossed food items out through the open window. Then, inquisitively, one of the hunters cautiously approached behind the point of his spear and, scooping up the almost liquefied foil-wrapped chocolate bar, he scurried back to investigate the foreign object with his companions.

Enda pushed on the handle, launching the door open, alerting Quinn, who came dashing from the flight deck to follow. Stepping cautiously down from the aircraft, they made friendly gestures, holding their hands high above their heads. Then, scarcely taking their eyes off the tribesmen, gingerly, they crabbed sideways to where the captain lay. Still squatting over Fergus, the hunter waited until Enda was close enough to touch before retreating to join the rest of his band at the forest edge. Wasting no time, Enda dashed back to get the medical kit from the aircraft, while Quinn knelt and gently cradled his friend's head in his lap.

"Tell me this isn't happening, skipper? What the fuck have they done to you? We've got to stop that bleeding."

"I thought I would get the same treatment as Berko."

The captain's voice was weak, and attempting to straighten his leg, he flinched from the pain.

In his eagerness to help, Enda was about to give his friend an overdose of morphine when Quinn snatched the small plastic bottle from his hand.

"Jesus, take it easy with that stuff. Half that measure will do. We'll wait for it to take effect before we try to doctor him up."

When Fergus could tolerate the pain, with the tail of his shirt brushing the soil, they gently carried him by his arms and legs to a dry patch of earth beneath the left wing. Then, after carefully laying him down, Enda tore away his trouser leg, exposing the wound. Using his canvas trouser belt as a tourniquet, Quinn tightened until the belt dug deep into the flesh above Fergus's knee, reducing the bleeding to a little trickle. From where the bullet exited, Quinn folded the flabby wodge of flesh back into the gaping hole, and covering it with a thick sterile dressing, he firmly wrapped the bandage, ensuring it would hold everything in place.

"Where did you learn to do that?" queried the young engineer.

"I didn't. Must have seen it in a movie or something.

We're gonna have to stitch him up, you know? Can't leave that tourniquet on forever."

After washing the blood from his hands, Quinn returned from the aircraft carrying a few seat cushions. They tried to make their skipper comfortable, but he was already unconscious. Watching over their friend, with a sense of desperation setting in, taking turns, they repeatedly checked Fergus's breathing before resetting the tourniquet.

Enda and Quinn heard a familiar noise high up in the distance. Confused, Quinn even thought it might be the sound of a giant flying insect, but as it got louder, it became more distinct until they knew it was the sound of a light aeroplanes engine.

"Bloody hell, check it out. But, be careful, lad," said Quinn.

The hunters followed, keeping their distance, and from the middle of the airstrip, looking skyward, Enda spun around, almost tripping over himself, trying to spot the plane. Then, frantically waving his arms at the small aircraft descending towards them, he couldn't contain his excitement and screamed aloud, "Jesus, it's a miracle, they found us."

When the Cessna 172 touched down on what remained of the runway, Enda, breaking into a sweat, chased after it until it swung around, forcing the engineer to stop about ten meters from the spinning propeller. The pilot left the engine running and, stepping from the Cessna, he stood by the open door, trying to size up the situation. Finally, he bellowed above the engine's rhythmic throbbing noise.

"I'm Jack Kavanagh. Does anyone need medical assistance? I'm a doctor. Speak up, as I can't stay for long. I've got two very sick people with me."

"You can't stay for long! You've got to be kidding me,"

muttered Enda, moving as close as he dared to the propeller.

Jack reached for a knob below the dashboard and pulled, starving the engine of fuel until it came to a shuddering stop. After exchanging a brief greeting, the men rushed to where Fergus lay, slipping in and out of consciousness. Jack looked around, struggling for words, trying to take in the devastation around the crash site.

"Sweet Jesus, lads, what the fuck happened here?"

Enda and Quinn spoke together, frantically trying to explain.

"Hang on a second, fellas, let's save it for later. I want to check that wound."

After a brief inspection, Jack gathered his thoughts before offering his plan to the anxious men.

"You fellas did good. That should hold things together until I stitch him up later. But listen, sorry, I really must be on my way. Help me lift your friend into the plane. I must also get the others to the clinic as soon as possible. They're very ill, and once I've dropped them off, I'll return to get you both. It looks as if your immediate danger has passed. I'll be back in two, maybe three hours at the most, and when airborne, I'll put out a distress call with your position. If you're lucky, you might even get help before I return."

Jack had beckoned the hunters to come forward, and when they gathered around him like a long-lost friend, they communicated in a dialect of French and Bayaka.

"My pygmy family will stay and keep you safe until I return. It was one of their tribe who alerted me about the crash. Hey, lads, before I leave, are you sure your friend in the aircraft is dead?"

Forced once again to face reality, Enda nodded slowly, first to say yes, before changing the subject.

"Jack, have you room for a few cartons of medical stuff, cos we've got a planeload."

The small Cessna was already well-laden, so they could only squeeze a couple of cartons in. Quinn suddenly held up one of the metal canisters in his hand.

"Take it, Jack. Whatever the fuck is in that tube will very likely be connected with our misfortune."

Jack reached for a biro in the glove box and wrote a six-digit radio frequency on the back of Enda's hand.

"When you hear me arriving overhead, tune into this frequency. Let me know if it's safe to land. Don't look at me like that. I promise, lads, I'll be back before ya know it. But in case something goes wrong and you have to leg it, listen carefully to these simple survival rules. Stay close to the hunters always, be mindful not to offend, and never refuse food and drink offerings; travel light, taking only the essentials, like salt, tape, water purification pills, and basic medicines. The leeches would have a field day, so use duct tape to seal your trouser ends, and pack a change of dry clothing for the nights. The hunters will guide you south, tracking inland, adjacent to the Shanga River. Then, all going well, we would rendezvous near Mossaka in a few days. Lastly, stay off the river to avoid being seen. But that's only if something goes wrong. It won't. I'll be back soon, so cheer up."

Before Jack pulled the door shut, Fergus had come too and straining from the effort; he managed a little humour for the concerned onlookers. "Try not to get yourselves into any more trouble."

Within minutes, the Cessna was climbing above the forest, wings rocking in a wave. As the engine noise faded, the towering, thunderous clouds, visible far beyond the tree-tops, mushroomed. Heads lowered and struggling to be upbeat, the men dragged their weary bodies back to the freighter, followed closely by their minders.

Back onboard, they gathered what was left of the food and water supplies, although from the look of the quickly darkening sky, water was going to be the least of their worries.

Quinn doubted his friend had heard the story, so he sat beside his pal in the galley.

"Did you not recognise him? It was all over the newspapers, the Doctor Jack Reilly scandal. I can't believe it was actually him."

"Yeah, I think you're right, but the details are vague. I didn't want to say anything for fear you might think I was losing my mind. They'll never believe us back home. We crash-land in the middle of Congo to be rescued by a flying doctor, a Paddy!"

As they sat in the dimly lit forward galley, trying to stomach a little food, Enda asked a question.

"So, tell me about Jack? I don't mind if it's a long story. I could do with some distraction."

"Well, it seems our new friend, Jack, is a bit of a character. It must have been almost three years ago when it happened. He was in Paris, waiting to catch a flight, and that's when he wrote it all down. I think he wanted to shake off the press, so he sent his version of events to Private Eye Magazine. He told them everything, in great detail, the whole fucking lot, although he did keep his travel plans a secret. It was as if he wanted to clear the air, or maybe he simply didn't care anymore."

"Go on, Quinn, what happened?"

"After spending most of his medical career working in Ireland, Jack emigrated to head up Birmingham's University Hospital's Department of Tropical Diseases in the UK. He openly acknowledged being confrontational with everyone, including his family. The drinking and drug abuse worsened after she eventually pissed off with the kids. Then, finally, the shit hit the fan one night when he was on the piss in his local pub."

Quinn inspected the inside of the chicken sandwich before biting off a piece.

"It's okay; you can talk with your mouth full," encouraged Enda.

"A friend of his, an intern at the hospital, knew where he was and phoned the pub. The intern was concerned about the discharge of a young girl from the hospital, believing she was misdiagnosed. After Jack asked a few questions, he told the fella that, in his opinion, there was nothing to worry about. Well, two days later, the girl died of Double Pneumonia, and they held Jack responsible for giving a medical opinion while under the influence of alcohol. Found guilty of negligence, the court had no option but to pull his licence for good. That's when things started to nosedive seriously. You know, he even considered suicide."

"The poor fucker. What happened next?"

"Yeah, well, I can't recall all the details, but this bit I do remember. After the court hearing, he went to his apartment, stuffed a few essentials into a backpack, left his keys on the table, and headed off by train and ferry to Gibraltar. Now, here's the bit about Africa, fucking amazing. While travelling by train through France, he was seated alone on a bench seat, flicking through a discarded local newspaper, when he came across a full-page geographical map of Africa. Taking a penknife from his pocket, he shut his eyes and brought the blade down. In that split moment, the outcome of the dice-throwing madness was decided. When he opened his eyes, The Republic of the Congo was the country where the tip of the blade had landed and where he would make his new home. Anyway, that's the short version.

When we get back, I'll see if I can find a copy of the full article."

"Wow, what a story. So, now we know what brought Jack to Africa. He obviously changed his name. It sounds to me like the poor fucker was the fall guy, although I'd really like to know where he got that Cessna and what about this clinic of his," said Enda, picking the raisins from a muffin.

After they'd finished chatting, Quinn went to the flight deck and sat in his pilot's seat. A short time later, Enda joined him, and after making himself comfortable in the captains seat, in almost darkness, they sat quietly together. Neither of them wanted to raise the subject, accepting the harsh reality that, regardless of his good intentions, the approaching storm and rapidly fading light meant Jack wouldn't be arriving any time soon.

"So, tell me, Quinn. What's all this shit about fear of flying?"

"It's not shit, Enda. Do you think it's easy for me to say that?"

The men sat without talking for a while, gazing out through the windscreens as vanes of silver-jagged energy lit up the night, tormenting the naked jungle, implanting more haunting images into their fragile minds.

"Yeah, but it doesn't make any sense. We probably wouldn't be here now if it weren't for you. Now don't go taking that up the wrong way, Quinn. Ya know what I mean. Maybe it's something else you're afraid of."

"What do you mean by that?"

"Look, it's none of my business, but I can recall the moment well. Your words. 'I think she's going to take the twins and leave me.' It was during our last trip to Chicago. You were very drunk at the time."

"You think that's it?"

"Yes, I do, Quinn."

The young engineer waited a while, but his friend remained quiet, not wishing to continue the conversation. Returning to the cabin, Enda rechecked the door handles and searching from every window; he tried to spot their minders, but they were nowhere to be seen. Then, slamming the flight deck window shut, Quinn could feel the airframe vibrate from the distant reverberating thunderclaps.

* * *

During Jack's weather-dodging flight back to his camp, he managed to relay the position of the crashed airliner to Brazzaville air traffic centre. The doctor was well known to the authorities, and while the controller praised the courageous deed, he jotted down the details, handing the paper to the government soldier standing next to him.

CHAPTER TWENTY-TWO

P epe and Haily made slow progress through the dense forest. After hours of zigzagging, owing to GPS signal loss, they finally reached the rendezvous point. With no sign of their transport, after a short satellite linkup, HQ insisted they maintain their position, offering reassurance that the BTR-60 was only a short distance away. Impatiently, they waited next to the narrow-deserted trail until the hefty drone of twin petrol engines gradually subdued the confused chattering forest. Then, venting dark grey smoke from its exhausts, rumbling to a jerking halt next to them, a soldier dressed in jungle combats appeared through a hatch from the roof of the cumbersome-looking eight-wheeler.

"I am the sergeant in charge. The trek here was difficult. Expect a six, maybe seven-hour journey back to Ouésso."

Haily and Pepe clambered onto the machine and slipped in through a side hatch. The sweltering heat and body stench made them retch. Ten heavily armed soldiers were crammed into the claustrophobic space, and the driver sat eagerly awaiting orders in the left front seat. The sergeant eased himself down from the roof hatch to be confronted by the agitated Americans.

"You're not in charge. I am. Now, turn this mother around, and let's move. We don't have all fucking day."

She then pointed up at the roof.

"You see those two hatches? One is for him, and the other is for me. If we remain in here for much longer, we'll suffocate to death."

The soldiers eyed their sergeant with disappointment, without even a fight, allowing the white woman to take over his platoon so easily. After a couple of hours, and with the American's permission, the sergeant ordered a halt for a short break. Haily and Pepe kept to themselves. They sat on the vehicle's armoured roof. As the late evening light began to dim, they inspected their equipment. Haily's fingers searched inside her rucksack before she abruptly upended it, spreading the contents along the roof. Then, lifting one of the small metal canisters, she counted again.

"Pepe, I can only find ten. So, you must have the other two."

"Nope, my dear, we put them all in with your kit."

To avoid having a disagreement, Pepe rechecked his rucksack.

"Fuck, we must have dropped them when we were offloading from the freighter, or worse, those assholes we left behind have them. Either way, this is major shit. We'll have to call it in," snapped Haily, reaching for the sat phone.

After securing a good connection, there was a long pause until a more senior person came on the line. Then, before Haily had even finished explaining, she moved the phone back from her ear, and the angry voice faded, along with the possibility of her long-awaited promotion.

"You can't be serious. This is not good. Remain where you are. Do not proceed any further. I'll call you back," shouted the enraged colleague, thousands of miles away.

Aware of the risk of being ambushed by rebel troops, the

sergeant positioned his men as darkness descended, creating a cordon around the troop carrier. When the call finally came, the agents listened in disbelief as they were ordered to terminate the mission. However, Haily had her own thoughts on how to remedy the situation, and pleaded with them to reconsider. Langley had run a risk assessment, and her idea to continue to Ouésso and then return to the crash site in the Antonov was dismissed outright.

"It's too risky. What if the weather closes in? What then? The Antonov is not suitable. Forget about it. Also, that vehicle you're travelling in is amphibian, which gives you an added advantage."

"Sir, with respect, if you think I'm going to venture into deep water in that Russian-built rust pot, then you're crazy."

"Your disapproval is noted, madam. Now, listen up. Had it not been for your cockup, we wouldn't be having this conversation. Go back and sort out your mess. Now, put the sergeant on."

Haily gestured to the sergeant lurking nearby, and, tossing him the phone, she snarled, "We'll camp here tonight. Then, come first light; we're heading back to the freighter."

Before the satellite conversation had ended, the raised voice of the unsettled sergeant engendered a state of malevolence in the eerie darkness.

"No, sir. I refuse to do that to any of my men."

CHAPTER TWENTY-THREE

On every trip, whether by jeep or Cessna, Jack traded his doctor skills, returning to his camp with new medicines and paraphernalia. Always trying to make improvements, after considerable coaxing, he even persuaded everyone helping out at the clinic to wear white linen wraps and adopt basic hygienic practices. Although this benefited the sick, Jack often wondered if he was going too far, interfering too much in their primitive way of life. But, on the other hand, he knew all too well if these simple tribes' people were going to have a future, they must prepare for the world rapidly closing in around them.

Because of threats from rebel activists, its previous Belgian residents abruptly departed, leaving behind a substantial and well-equipped mining compound, right down to the comfortable quality mattresses on every bed. One of the cosy timber cabins that used to house the contractors now harboured Fergus, and the rain dancing on the rooftop made it feel even cosier. After checking his blood pressure and temperature, Jack stood stern-faced, arms folded, beside the bed.

"You're a fortunate man. He shot you through the upper

calf. The bullet went straight through, taking bits of muscle and tendon with it. Had it severed an archery or hit bone, you would have most likely bled to death. We don't offer blood transfusions here."

"He said he was going to kneecap me, called it a punishment shooting. So, forgive me for finding it hard to consider myself lucky right now," replied Fergus.

"Well, he missed. Anyway, I'm going to sedate you. I still have work to do on that leg. But again, consider yourself lucky. Since arriving in Congo, I've had lots of practice treating gunshot wounds."

"Wait, what about my crew?"

"I'm afraid there's no chance today; the weather's closing in. We'll talk again in the morning, then we'll see. I'm going to administer an anaesthetic because that wound is gonna need a lot of stitching. Now, rest, captain."

Until the weather cleared, Jack could not risk flying the Cessna in the treacherous conditions. But, before retiring for the night, he couldn't wait to check what was in the donated cartons. Reading each label aloud, Jack hadn't expected to find such a wealth of lifesaving medicines. Remembering that the mysterious metal canister was in his jacket, after a brief examination, he placed it on his desk. Jack couldn't recall the last time he was in such a foul mood. Feeling somewhat despondent, he sat back in his chair to consider the day's strange sequence of events, jotting down his unstructured thoughts.

'Remote crash site: DC8 airliner, Irish aircraft, Irish crew, one dead and one injured from gunshot wounds, the American killers depart heading northwest through the forest, two crew still onboard, sophisticated medical supplies, with some placed in metal containers.'

The pelting rain against the corrugated metal roof muted his softly spoken words.

"What the fuck is this all about?"

Later that night, Jack decided to examine the mysterious object more closely, clearing his desk to create more space in his modest laboratory. With a screwcap at one end, it measured about the length of a fountain pen, but thicker, like a cigar tube. Manufactured from high-grade metal, he guessed it was most likely titanium from his knowledge of surgical instruments. The attached label, running along its side, carried the inscription, ShineOn. After unscrewing the metal cap, there was just enough of the small glass tube protruding for him to grip. Sipping it from the shock-proof foam swaddle, he carefully placed the glass tube containing the cloudy yellow liquid on a shelf next to the microscope.

Except by snapping the designed break-section at one end, there was no other obvious way of opening it. Concentrating as he peered through the eyepiece, Jack tweaked the microscope's fine adjustment knob until the image of the liquid was well defined, enough to reveal a live organism. Running his finger down a cell comparison chart, he searched unsuccessfully for a match. Clumsily reaching out for a second chart, he knocked over the tube. Striking the wooden floor at the wrong angle, it fractured, splitting the glass into two pieces. As the potent yellow fluid leaked out, it instantly vaporised, drifting invisibly through the still air.

"Bollox!"

Jack became very perturbed. Until now, the possibility of a connection between the downed airliner and biological weapons was unthinkable. Hurrying to don rubber gloves, he wiped away the few drops of liquid that remained on the floor. But, still not content, and to be sure, he had eliminated all of the risks, and after scrubbing the spill zone, he wrapped everything, including the pieces of glass, and tossed them onto the smouldering campfire. When Jack returned to his hut, the stench of disinfectant lingered in his nostrils. Then, stripped naked from his drenched clothing, he flopped face down, exhausted, onto the bed, drifting almost instantly into a deep sleep.

* * *

Enda and Quinn had another restless night. When morning came, they tried to busy themselves packing their company-issued green duffel bags with the essentials, ready for a quick getaway. Returning from the rear of the aircraft, Enda placed the leather satchel on the table next to Quinn.

"We sure as hell won't be buying fuel with this. Although that said, it might come in handy should we need to trade our way out of here. I think we should divide it three ways. I know Fergie would have approved."

"Why three ways?" asked Quinn.

"Jack's going to be back soon, and I'm sure he could do with a little financial support. He's one of the best. Can ya imagine the good he could do around here with this money?"

Quinn nodded his agreement and, dividing up the wads of one-hundred-dollar bills, Enda laid one envelope on the table and then stuffed one in each duffel bag. They knew it would be difficult to get anyone to believe what had happened, especially if only one of them survived, so they began jotting down their gripping account of events. Then, after they'd finished writing, they swapped notes, concealing them in the side zip pocket of their duffels. Quinn's bag also contained the remaining metal canister, and in his written account, he even speculated on the reason for the catastrophe, noting that it might have something to do with experimental chemical weapons.

The four sentinel pygmies gathered at the forest's edge, watching Enda watch them. He stepped down from the doorway. Approaching to within arm's reach, squatting, he almost managed to equal their height. Enda couldn't guess their ages, and their colourful mulumbas garbs painted in abstract patterns were new to his eyes. Offering the soft chocolate bars in the palm of his hand, they babbled what he hoped were words of elation, and broad smiles spread across their weathered faces. Like a hungry cat, head down in a bowl of milk, fervently they licked every ounce of the melting chocolate from their fingers. Not letting anything go to waste, they hoarded every scrap of silver foil in small leather purses hanging around their necks.

Not feeling at ease about joining the party, Quinn watched from the safety of the galley. Then, as the sun's radiation began to lord over the thin cloud cover and morning mist, Quinn called out, making an effort to portray an air of optimism.

"Hey, lad, I think this could be our lucky day."

Screams awakened Jack. Never before had he heard such terror from the tribespeople. Leaping out of bed, he slipped on a pair of shorts and sprinted towards the clinic. Through the windows, the early morning sunbeams fused with the orange glow of the oil lamps, spreading a foreboding light on the slaughter. Everyone was shrieking uncontrollably. Disregarding his own safety, Jack hurried inside, trying to bring order to the bloody scene.

Although terror-stricken, the tribespeople trusted their leader and obeyed his commands without question. They shepherded the terrified patients who'd survived the attack, some still screaming, to shelter in the surrounding huts. Jack stood inside the doorway of the emptying slaughter-house. After dismissing his initial theory of a large predator attack, he called on all his medical experience to help him understand what had caused such bloodletting. He removed fresh linen from a steel locker, and covering all his exposed skin, he dressed as if preparing for surgery. Then, stepping along the row of blood-drenched corpses, he checks the clipboards hanging from the end of each bed.

Everyone who helped at the makeshift clinic was accustomed to bloody violence, but this was different; they needed reassurance that their leader could protect them from the evil spirits. Learning a new technique from the teacher, Jack showed them how to sanitise the blood-splashed floor and walls. Then, to dispatch the evil spirits, he told them to build a fire, a furnace, deep in the forest and incinerate everything used in the clean-up, including the bodies; everything must be burnt to ashes. Returning to his cabin, with the situation under control, Jack sat at his desk. Then, having no one to express his thoughts with, he spoke the words he was writing aloud.

"Whatever it was, why did it only attack those infected with that new virus, the one western medicine is calling 'gay-related immune deficiency'?"

Jack wanted to remain until the trauma had settled, but now convinced there was a connection between the crashed freighter and the carnage at the clinic, he also knew that the waiting crew must surely be in danger.

The Bayaka hunters poked the sky with their spears, frolicking excitedly as if performing a tribal dance. With faces beaming on hearing the sound of the fast-approaching single-engine aircraft, Quinn and Enda also felt the urge to join in. The engineer rushed back to the freighter and powered up the radio. Jack's voice was calling over the speaker.

"Green Bird, report your status?"

After making an impressively short landing, Jack immediately shut down the engine and hurried to where the crew waited outside the freighter's entrance door. There was the faintest smell of decaying flesh, which further soured the moist warm air.

"You can't leave him in there for much longer. We must bury his body, and soon."

"Hey, that's my fault, Jack. Earlier, I stupidly opened the cubical door, sorry. Jack, can we take him with us? Be good if we could get him home for a decent burial," said Quinn

"Not a chance. It will be difficult enough to get you out of here in one piece. So, forget it. Fellas, this morning, I witnessed a horrible event at the clinic. It was like a slaughterhouse, but don't worry; your captain wasn't harmed. The locals believe it's an evil spirit, a belief so strong it drove even the very sick into the forest, fleeing for safety. I don't think they'll be coming back. The whole episode was weird. Those who died bled to death. Even the way they bled wasn't fucking normal."

As Jack proceeded to describe the incident, his countrymen moved closer and listened attentively.

"Do you think Fergie's gonna be okay?" asked Quinn.

"It's early days yet, but if I can keep infection at bay, he'll survive. Although, he won't be doing much walking for a while. He doesn't appear to be able to grasp how lucky he was."

Quinn interrupted. "This whole thing seems to get weirder by the minute. Hey, Jack, I knew who you were when I first set eyes on you yesterday. The press really milked it. Except for the tan and ponytail, you haven't changed much. Hasn't anyone else recognised you?"

"Maybe they have. I don't know, nor do I care. After arriving in Brazzaville, I changed my name and appearance. Anyway, down here, nobody gives a shit about the outside world."

"Yeah, but hang on a sec. We know a little about your past, but can you tell us the rest of your extraordinary story?" asked Quinn, not quite getting the urgency of the situation.

"Some other time, we can't delay. We must bury your pal. It can't be delayed any longer. Listen, lads, up until now, my world was beginning to settle down. I have a good life. The local tribespeople are my new family. So, let's hope your arrival hasn't fucked all of that up."

"Jack, this wasn't our doing, and I get the feeling you know more than you're saying," said Enda.

"Yes, you're right. I think I understand why this shit is happening. However, this is not the moment. So, we'll save the conspiracy theories for a bar stool and a Guinness. Although, I will say this. Since the first invaders set foot on this land long ago, they robbed, raped, and pillaged, and nothing's changed. I have the feeling some powerful organisation is testing biological weapons, and from what you've told me about your passengers, my guess is the yanks are involved. Do you have any more of those metal canisters? If you do, hand them over to the authorities when you get home."

The crewmen paid attention while Jack drew a simple map displaying the main features of the surrounding terrain, sketching the route they would take after they'd buried Berko's body. The plan was to fly south, towards Brazzaville, and make a short fuel stop at his base on the way. He could then decide whether Fergus would be well enough to travel with them. Quinn stepped forward and handed Jack the large brown envelope.

"Hey, doc, we don't care about your past. But we know you're a good man, so please accept this gift and put it to good use."

Jack looked inside the envelope and became hesitant to accept the offering.

"Fuck, are you bank robbers or what? Should I ask where you got this money from?"

"Don't worry; we're not thieves. It's the cash we were meant to buy fuel with," replied Quinn.

Jack was placing the money in the Cessna's glove box when he recognised a familiar engine sound approaching through the forest and ran to where Quinn and Enda were preparing to bury their friend, in front of the freighter's nosecone.

"We won't have enough time to get airborne before they arrive, so do exactly what I told you earlier."

"What about Berko?" Enda protested.

"I'll take care of him. Now, go."

The pilot and engineer grabbed a duffel bag each and chased after Jack to the forest treeline. Speaking to the hunters in their native Bayaka, Jack pointed his hand toward the Sanga River. Then, with the engine noise getting louder, he hurriedly shook hands with the Irish men, promising to search for them as planned in Mossaka. Then, with another wave of his hand, the two remaining hunters vanished into the shin-tangle. Reaching his aircraft moments before the military arrived, Jack lit a cigarette.

The BTR accelerated out of the forest along the runway's edge. Then, swerving hard right, it came to a halt uncomfortably close to Jack and his plane. Troops piled out of the side hatches. Spreading out, they promptly encircled the Cessna, and from the roof hatch behind the heavy machine gun, the sergeant bellowed down to his driver, "Shut down the engines."

As the noise and cloud of light grey smoke lazily dissipated, the sudden quiet invited the songs of the forest to resume. Sweating profusely, the overweight sergeant clambered down and briskly marched the few steps to stand facing Jack.

"Ah, Priest, my dearest friend. It's been some time since we last met. How are you?"

Jack shook his hand without returning the greeting, and holding the sergeant's stare without blinking; the ruffled soldier levelled his assault rifle at the freighter.

"So, what do we have here, my friend? I hope no one was injured."

Beginning to feel the pressure, poker-faced, Jack kept his cool, declaring that while overflying, he saw the freighter and decided to land to see if anyone needed medical assistance.

"Tell me, Priest, were you able to assist?"

"I found nothing except a large quantity of medical supplies, although it smelt like there might be a body onboard."

"A body? Those damn rebels must have gotten here before you."

Pepe was first to emerge from the troop carrier, followed by Haily, her face buried in her sleeve, coughing heavily as she tried to clear her lungs.

"I'm Haily, and this is my colleague, Pepe. We were sent to assist the military in anti-rebel tactical training. This freighter might have been involved in supplying the rebels, when something obviously went wrong. Did you carry out a search of the aircraft?"

"Nope, as I said, I arrived not long before you did."

Haily placed an open hand on the Cessna's engine, cowling, glancing a knowing look at Pepe.

"Do I detect a bit of an Irish brogue, Mister Priest? I guess the logo on the freighter's tail must make you feel a little homesick," said Pepe, pleased with his attempt at dark humour.

"Listen here, my name is Jack Kavanagh, and I travel this country with impunity. I hold two passports, Irish and British. In the glove compartment, you'll find a permit signed by the president himself," Jack protested defiantly.

Haily blocked Jack's advance towards the aircraft, shouting an order at the sergeant.

"Check it out."

Jack watched as the sergeant rummaged inside the aircraft, and then he found it, jamming the thick envelope inside his combat jacket before returning with the permit. Haily snatched the document from his hand, and as she quickly read over it, she spoke the significant bits aloud.

I, President Denis Sassou Nguesso, grant Mister Jack Kavanagh safe passage... blah blah blah.

"Wow, I'm impressed. However, unfortunately, your permit has just been revoked."

Then, pointing toward the BTR, she stepped up the tempo.

"Okay, Priest, enough of the crap. You probably helped them escape, so I want you to climb up there, where we can keep an eye on you. We've got a few important things to do, and we wouldn't like to see you getting accidentally injured. So, Pepe, just in case they object, I won't call base to request permission. Instead, we'll be hitching a ride out of here with our new pal, Jack. We'll call it in when we get to Ouésso; let them decide his fate. I'm not getting back into that stinking heap of junk."

Pepe looked content, in total admiration of his partner's thought process.

"Yep, sounds good to me, my dear."

Haily and Pepe stood below the freighter's tail, which was jutting up higher than the tree tops, and beckoned towards the sergeant to join them. Then, speaking earnestly, she focused on the soldier, holding the canister out until it almost touched his nose.

"I want you to gather your men and search every inch of that freighter, especially around the belly cargo door, and, just in case you need reminding, you're looking for this. Unfortunately, we mislaid two of them."

As she continued, the sergeant broke off his stare of contempt, fidgeting with his weapons shoulder strap.

"Regarding the tidy-up, I've some good news. You'll only have to sacrifice two, not the five men originally demanded by my superiors."

The soldiers carried Berko's body from the rear cubical to the flight deck and strapped him upright on the engineer's seat. The bloodied tea towels remained pasted against his bowed head and secured with the five-point harness; rigor mortis helped to keep his body upright in the seat. Then, reporting back to the American agents, the intimidated sergeant stood to attention before saluting.

"Nothing, we found nothing. Pay heed to my advice, madam. I suggest you cover your faces before boarding?"

Shortly after their names were called, the chosen ones were ordered to buckle up, one in the first officers and the other strapped into the captains seat. Speaking rapidly in French, the sergeant reassured the compliant soldiers. Then, creating a distraction, shots rang out as the sergeant executed the two, in as many seconds, their lifeless, limp bodies restrained by the tight harness straps. The roguish sergeant hurried from the flight deck to confront the rest of his platoon, now scrambling towards the freighter's entrance. Leaning from the open door, he held his arms up, pistol in hand, screaming down at his men.

"They were traitors. They planned an ambush with their rebel comrades. Their betrayal is no longer a threat. I have protected you. Now, spread out; we must complete our mission."

Before slipping them over their heads, Pepe and Haily sprayed what was left of the deodorant onto the front of their dark grey cotton balaclavas. Then, standing next to the muddy entrance, the agents directed proceedings while the soldiers passed up two five-gallon jerry cans of petrol to the sergeant.

"Give the flight deck a good soaking," ordered Pepe before heading to the BTR, where Jack was sitting on the steel roof, observing the puzzling activity.

"Please, if you're going to torch the freighter, offload the medical supplies."

Rooting through the wooden crate behind the driver's seat, Pepe found the detonator, and hurrying to return to his comrade, he hesitated, eyeballing Jack as if he was going to reply.

"Take it, my dearest. Be careful, it says handle with care. Guess what? That frigging martyr wants us to save the medical supplies."

"Goddamnit, why not. You never know; we might need some of that shit before this is over. Also, while you're at it, see if you can find the smoke hoods. We're going to need them later," replied Haily.

The soldiers closed the belly cargo door and shoved the two catering trolleys through the door into the galley. After completing one final check, Haily ordered everyone away from the aircraft. Steadying herself, she tossed the phosphorous grenade through a gap in the main door. Pepe anxiously watched from the troop carrier as his partner struggled with each step, boots sinking in the muddy earth until finally able to gain traction; Haily clambered along the fuselage until she reached the freighter's tail. Making a beeline for the BTR, she dived behind the armoured beast for cover. Although the explosion wasn't catastrophic, it did have the desired effect, blasting the door wide open. The raging inferno that ensued sent flames licking along the forward fuselage, and as the billowing white smoke darkened to pitch black, it cast a giant shadow over the crash site. Everyone, including the soldiers, watched in awe as each carton full of medicines ignited, generating muffled booms from the front to the rear of the freighter. Bizarrely, the Americans witnessed what might have been had the landing not worked out so well.

"Yeah, I know. I was thinking the same thing." Her telepathic intercept was acknowledged by a nod of his head.

The fire was taking longer than expected to run its course, delaying the final act of the façade and their departure. Then, seeing that the smoke had reduced to a trickle, it was time for Pepe and Haily to make a last visit to the smouldering wreck. Before climbing onboard, they donned orange-coloured smoke hoods, ironically making them look like firefighters.

Loaded with a new film cartridge, Haily tried to control her breathing as she photographed the blackened interior with her Ektralite camera, paying particular attention to the charred bodies on the flight deck. Task complete, the overzealous soldiers jostled the Americans off the aircraft. Slapping one of them across the face for putting a hand too close to her breast, Haily tugged awkwardly at the smoke hood, dragging it from her head. Although the mission hadn't been a total success, pleased with the work, the agents briefly hugged. Then, placing a caring hand on

Pepe's shoulder, Haley was eager to share the cunning plan developing in her burdened mind.

"Before we arrive back in Ouésso, I will write a report. It won't be the most factual report ever written, but assuming the crew don't survive, it will serve our purpose. Missing canisters aside, we might even impress our boss with how we tidied things up. It will read something like this:

While assisting the Congolese military on tactical issues west of the Sanga River, we stumbled across the ill-fated freighter. After recovering some of the dead crew's personal items, we were photographing the site when we came under attack from rebels, forcing us to retreat. Although we got photos of three charred bodies on the flight deck, there was no time to photograph the other three in the galley. Due to the pursuing firefight, which left two government soldiers dead and a number badly injured, it became too risky to investigate further. Finally, I'll recommend that due to the remoteness and danger from rebel attacks, in our opinion, the crash site should not be approached."

As she continued, Pepe draped an arm across her shoulder.

"We'll include a few photos and, for special effect, after blowtorching their personal belongings, we'll gift-wrap the lot. So then, all the old fart, Flush in HQ has to do, is whizz it off to Dublin. It should appease the Irish authorities, the airline, and the bereaved, regarding the shocking accident. It should also keep them from nosing around. As for Jack, we'll chat with him after we land in Ouésso. He knows more than he's telling. Unfortunately, as I see it, neither he nor the freighter crew appears to have a future."

"Well, my love, you're an absolute genius. But do you ever get the feeling this is all getting way out of hand"

"Nonsense"

Seated behind Jack in the Cessna, Pepe sweated

profusely. Haily stood leaning against the wing spar in ecstasy, the spinning propeller washing over her body, offering some relief from the oppressive weather conditions. Then, realising the flight to Ouésso would take some time; she poked her head inside.

"Sorry, boys. My bladder is just about to burst, so you'll have to wait a while longer. Pepe, hand me the Uzi."

She had only taken a few steps when the sergeant called down to her from the troop carrier.

"Where are you going?"

"Never mind, I won't be long."

"You must take one of my men with you. The forest is not safe."

"Take one of your perverts with me? Are you insane? Mister Uzi is all the company I need."

Before drifting out of sight in the undergrowth, she turned around, waving the weapon above her head, flicking a salute for the solitary fretting admirer. Then, feeling the darkening forest closing in around her, she went no further, unzipping her jumpsuit and letting it drop around her ankles. Squatting against a tree trunk, from her t-shirt pocket, she removed the Peace Silver Dollar, tossing it repeatedly. She lost every throw of the coin.

"Wow, I smell terrible. I can't wait to...."

Carelessly snatching, she failed to hold on to the coin, sending it spinning through the air before it fell, striking the head of the serpent, which was coiled protectively around her nest.

Haily's act of accidental aggression received an instant response. As though the snake knew what she was capable of, it acted in self-defence. The five-metre female Rock Python struck like lightning, burying its teeth in her leg, then yanking its head back, it caused her to lose balance. Falling awkwardly to the ground, stunned, Haily was fully aware of what was happening. The serpent had begun coiling its tail around her when she released her first scream of terror. Frantically, she struggled to reach her weapon, but the snake coiled itself repeatedly, trapping her arms by her side, squeezing harder, intensifying the death grip.

Gasping for air, Halie's final breath emptied from her crushed lungs. Her screams turned to a sob as her struggle for life ceased. Resembling the sound of dry splintering branches, her mangled ribs snapped, and the image of Madame Liberty lying close by, faded slowly from her bulging green eyes. Cardiac arrest spared her the final agony, as the muscular reptile changed its bite grip and, with jaws dilated, her head began to disappear inside.

Pondering on how much private time she might need, the men waited, no one daring to disturb her, until, becoming flustered in the back seat, Pepe climbed out of the Cessna and shouldered his Uzi.

"Something's wrong. I'm going to check. Wait here."

Following to where she was last seen entering the forest, he called her name aloud. Moving cautiously through the undergrowth, when confronted by the vision of savagery, it stopped him dead in his tracks. Pepe's first instinct was to shoot the snake, but she was now a part of it. In desperation, spraying bullets into the air while screaming for god's intervention brought everyone stampeding to where he stood. The soldiers didn't hesitate. Careful not to cut its prey, they repeatedly slashed the serpent with machetes until Haily's regurgitated, bloodied head reappeared oozing saliva. Deprived of its kill, the snake retreated into the cover of a thicket and, mortally wounded, slithered silently away.

Jack shoved his way past the soldiers and knelt beside her. Before searching for signs of life, he already knew he wouldn't find any. So, easing himself back to his feet, with mixed emotions, he gazed down at her lifeless, battered young face.

"She's gone. She's dead," declared Jack.

Pepe dropped to his knees, whispering words of grief. He gently cradled her limp body and suddenly lashed out, screaming at the onlookers, his cries of loss making it clear to all that she was more than just a colleague.

"Leave us, leave us, go away. Please, let us be."

As the tears streamed down Pepe's face, tugging at her clothing, he tried to dress her half-naked body. When one of the soldiers reappeared, approaching as close as he dared, he unrolled a black body bag. Then, taking a few steps back, he delivered the message.

"Sergeant say, we take her."

"No, you won't. Don't even come near.

Struggling to contain his composure, Pepe laid her gently down in the body bag and, stunned with grief, robotically, he zipped it closed.

"She's coming with us. Help me carry her to the aeroplane, or so help me, Jack, I'll shoot you dead if you refuse."

Bearing the weight of her petite frame with ease, Pepe glanced over his shoulder, wanting to be sure he hadn't left any of her belongings behind. Unaware that he was about to make an offering to the rainforest spirit, Nkisi; as his boot trampled the silver dollar into the soft earth.

The sergeant waited until the Cessna got airborne, and delivering two sharp kicks to the back of the driver's seat, he bellowed down new orders.

"Move out, direction Owando. We're returning to base."

Jack made one low pass over the wreckage before heading east, planning to follow the Sanga River north to Ouésso. Sensing the pain of his dazed passenger, Jack reached out.

"Pepe, I'm sorry for your loss. She must have meant a lot to you."

"More than you'll ever know."

"Well then, help me understand what drives you to do this sort of shit? Innocent people are dying."

"I'm a soldier. You know the fucking cliché."

"Yeah, but soldiers aren't supposed to commit murder."

Forced to concentrate harder in the worsening weather conditions, Jack tensed, bringing the debate to a timely end. Sheets of rain from the nimbostratus-covered sky reduced visibility, forcing him to fly dangerously low. So, Jack decided to extend the wing flaps, enabling him to safely slow the aircraft down, giving valuable extra reaction time if needed. Weaving his machine left and right to avoid the branches, the tree tops swayed ominously above them. Chasing the winding river, he scanned, until, recognising landmarks, with a sigh of relief, he knew the airport would shortly come into view beyond Ouésso town.

Blaming the damage on severe storm weather, Jack wasn't aware that the authorities had closed the airport. Not receiving a reply to his repeated requests to land no longer mattered, as he was going to land anyway. Touching down too softly on the flooded threshold caused the Cessna to aquaplane, sending it skating halfway down the runway before the tyres found grip. Then, as they cautiously taxied to a stop in the parking area, Pepe unbuckled his seatbelt after making a brief call on the sat phone. Both gazed up wide-eyed through the torrential rain at what used to be the control tower.

The freighter's engine had gouged away most of the roof, taking with it the enormous rotating beacon that once perched on the tower's highest point. From where the Cessna sat parked on the apron, the vertical stabiliser of the Antonov, which remained on the taxiway, was clearly visible. But, apart from the fast-approaching shabby Land-cruiser J40, its blue rotating light flashing, there was no other sign of life.

The men stepped down from the Cessna, standing in the warm rain, as the jeep's brakes squealed it to a skidding stop. Then, rushing over, beaming broad smiles, the policemen stood to attention, facing Jack. They warmly shook his hand in turn, sending Pepe into a tizzy.

"What the fuck do you think you're doing? Cuff this man; he's my prisoner."

Seeing the confusion grow on their faces, Jack held his arms out in front of him.

"It's okay, my friends. For the moment, do as he says."

Whizzing across the airfield, the J40 came to a halt alongside the waiting Antonov. While Pepe discussed his plans with the crew, the police officers carried the body bag onto the aircraft. Then, with everyone back in the jeep, they drove to the nearby police station.

To one side of the large open-plan office was a narrow hallway leading to the holding cells, where the apologetic and embarrassed officer removed the handcuffs before locking Jack inside.

CHAPTER TWENTY-FOUR

The phone in the Green Bird office at Dublin airport never stopped ringing, and fumbling to reassure the very anxious callers, Gerry was running out of excuses.

'I know, but it's only been a few days. Listen, it would appear they have diverted. Communications are impossible over there. You know this is not the first time, so please try to be patient. Yes, I promise I'll contact you as soon as we have news.'

Before switching over to answerphone, Gerry took one last call, and although he didn't know his name, the caller's voice sounded familiar.

"This is Special Operations Langley. With deep regret, I must report the loss of your aircraft."

"We know they're feckin lost, but where? Do you know where they landed?"

"Gerry, I need you to listen. When I say lost, I mean crashed, and everyone, including some of our people, is confirmed dead."

Losing his grip, the receiver slid through his fingers, falling with a thump onto his desk. Then, after slapping his own face, hand trembling, Gerry held it back to his ear.

"Go ahead, please. I'm listening."

CHAPTER TWENTY-FIVE

The rainforest terrified Quinn. Even if every living organism were dead, right down to the last mosquito, it still wouldn't help to relieve his anxiety. After what Jack said earlier, he knew the dense, menacing undergrowth sheltered some very nasty creatures. If there were any brief moments of joy for Quinn, it would be when occasionally spotting patches of blue sky above the forest's impenetrable shroud. The night-time terrified him the most, having to camp alongside the villagers, displaying their primitive ways. Then, when it was time to move on, he would become even more distressed, fighting for every step forward through the dark underworld or squelching his way along a narrow strip of a swampy green abyss.

His pal Enda was the complete opposite, fascinated by nature; his curiosity grew with every day that passed. Embracing his surroundings, he studied the little people as they guided them safely through this strange new world. Enda remembered Jack's caution, and doing exactly as he was told, he never let their chaperones get more than a few metres ahead. However, encouraging Quinn to keep pace after continually falling behind was becoming a significant encumbrance.

Even though most of the track was well-trodden by the tribespeople, some parts became almost impassable. Brandishing machetes, the hunters would tirelessly slash pathways through barriers of Napier grass. Then, before dusk, weaving strong frames from branches and layering them with thick rubbery leaves, the firm platforms created safe places to nest above the forest floor. Nonetheless, the hunter's most cherished gift to the foreigners was a mustard-coloured, mud-like paste prepared from plants and herbs, which, when spread thinly over the skin, deterred most flesh-eating insects.

"With a smell like that, I hope it will deter much bigger flesh-eating animals as well." Quinn's unintentional humour made Enda double up with laughter.

It was late afternoon, and with spirits raised on hearing a light aircraft engine, they hurried to the river's edge, only to have their hopes dashed as the distant spot in the sky grew smaller. Knowing it would be nightfall before they would reach Mossaka, and with an arduous trek ahead of them, they decided to make camp early.

The food offerings from the hunters were varied and usually entirely edible. As the pygmies prepared the meal, Enda keenly monitored the process, wanting to take in everything. Quinn didn't. Then, passing the time, while their minders roasted a Colobus monkey over the open fire, the white men talked about home and a career change.

"So, what do you think will happen when we reach Mossaka? You know something, I never heard of the place before now. Fuck it, I wish Fergie was here with us," said Quinn, his voice shallow and hoarse from the worsening fever.

"Well, me auld flower, we've done well to make it this far,

so don't go getting sick on me now. Come on, lad; we can do this. Things can only get better. Did ya know the hunters kind of speak French, and I've even managed to learn a few words of their lingo? If I understood right, tomorrow, they'll only guide us to the edge of the village. From there, we're on our own."

"I didn't know you spoke French?"

"Ah, now, Quinn, there's a lot you don't know about me. For example, I'll bet ya never knew I adore barbequed monkeys."

It had been a while since humour seemed even remotely appropriate, yet it found a way back into the conversation, bringing wistful smiles to their jaundiced faces. By the following morning, Quinn's condition had worsened. As the day passed, the energy was quickly sapped from his weak body. Then, about three hours north of the village, unable to take another step, Quinn dropped to his knees on the wet ground. They considered carrying him, but, unlike the captain, he was no lightweight and plighted by the quagmire ahead; they halted to evaluate the predicament. Enda had earlier learned from the tribespeople that all along the riverbank were canoes concealed in the undergrowth. After many failed attempts, he patiently managed to communicate his wishes to the hunters. Leaving one of their guides to care for Quinn, Enda planned to head down to the river's edge and paddle a canoe to the village. Even though Jack had warned them to stay off the river, he believed this would be the quickest way for him to return with help before dark.

Within minutes of commencing the search, they were sliding the long narrow dugout down the embankment and paddling hard with the fast-flowing water; it wasn't long before the village came into sight. Concentrating not to lose his balance, Enda stepped ankle-deep into the swampy grass verge and waved as the canoe departed back upstream.

It was evident from the few colonial buildings still standing that the village had seen better days. However, the moment he entered the busy street, he could sense eyes on him. So, keeping his head lowered, the engineer walked quickly, as if with purpose, like a person would in New York City after turning down a wrong street late at night. Enda needed to find a doctor quickly, and the least risky route back to Quinn would be by boat. Slipping down a quiet alley, he walked quickly until reaching the end. His feeling of being watched began to fade as the fishermen in dugouts went about their trade in the bustling port. Enda glanced left and right, searching, as he paced along yet another wooden jetty until the name on an old ten-metre cabin boat caught his attention. TitanicV appeared to be in good shape, and the young woman with the Basenji dog looked approachable. So, pulling a polite smile, he called out in French.

"Bonsoir, madame. I was passing and stopped to admire your beautiful boat. May I speak with your husband? Do you speak English?"

With hands on hips, the young woman stopped what she was doing and looked up at the inquisitive foreigner with the strange-coloured skin.

"Yes, I speak English, and no, there isn't a husband. So, what is it you want? Are you lost?"

Enda wasn't expecting such a direct reply, spoken in perfect English, with a soft French African accent.

"Please, madam, I need your help. May I come aboard? Can we talk?"

"If it's about drugs, weapons, or sex, I'm not interested."

"No, please, it's not about anything like that."

Stretching his leg out, and with the support of the woman gripping his wrist, Enda stepped confidently onto the boat. The woman spoke softly, and hurrying him below deck, she whispered.

"Too many eyes."

The forward cabin door was open, and the three electric fans moved the warm moist air across his skin, awakening a sense of familiar comfort. Separated by a small table, they sat facing each other on the convertible bunk seats. Although he quit years earlier, Enda accepted and drew hard on the Gauloises' cigarette.

"My name is Enda. I'm Irish. Please, madam, before I explain everything, can you tell me a little about yourself, because I would truly like to charter your boat. What's your name?"

"For the moment, my name is of no importance. I rarely get the opportunity to practice my English, so why not? I'll give you the shortened version. I was a law student studying in Kinshasa when I heard about the accident. My parents drowned during the extreme flooding a few months ago. They ran a fishing business, and this was their houseboat. Now, it's mine, and as soon as my preparations are completed, I will depart downriver to Kinshasa."

"Please, madam, can I come with you? Please, you might need help, and I will pay well for the passage."

Not waiting for her reply, Enda reached into the duffel bag. Something about the bag wasn't right; it wasn't his, but it did contain one of the envelopes stuffed with cash.

"This five hundred is to get me down river, and here's another five to get my friend down too."

She looked out towards the wheelhouse.

"What friend?"

"We must depart now, upriver. It'll only take about an hour or two to find him. Quinn is very ill, and he needs a doctor. Then, we have to get to Brazzaville, and I'll pay you an extra thousand dollars when we get there."

Her close-set amber eyes searched his face with suspicion.

"I would be alone on my boat with two white men, strangers. Maybe you're just like all the others who pillaged my country. Why should I trust you?"

"I need your help, but I understand your concerns. So, if you wish, I can leave right now. Keep the damn money. I only ask that you direct me to a doctor and forget we ever met."

The woman began to feel oddly at ease with her unexpected guest, and as she scooped the money from the table, she pointed towards the front of the boat.

"My name is Tshala, and that is my cabin. Keep out. Wash. You smell like the jungle. We leave at daybreak."

Not content with the departure plan, Enda pleaded with her to leave without delay, but she insisted it would be too dangerous in the dark.

"The village doctor is upriver. He might not return for days. Please, you must listen to me or leave."

"Okay, you're right. Is there an airstrip close by?" asked Enda.

"Yes, it's about eight kilometres inland. However, I think you should forget about that idea as well. I heard it's flooded, over four feet deep. Is someone searching for you? I hope you're not a criminal."

"No, Tshala, I'm not a criminal. Now, if you don't mind, I'd like to rest."

CHAPTER TWENTY-SIX

At the police station, after using his sat phone to call his people in Langley, Pepe was advised that when they re-evaluated the situation, they would call him back on the landline. About thirty minutes later, the phone rang and pausing the call, Pepe ordered one of the policemen to fetch the prisoner and handcuff him to a chair. Then, checking Jack's restraints, the agent requested the officers to leave. Then, flicking a switch, he placed the phone on speaker.

"Okay, sir, go ahead. It's just the two of us."

The distant voice was clear and American.

"Doctor Reilly, or is it Kavanagh? Let me introduce myself. I am a senior ranking officer assigned to the Special Operations Division. It would appear you have become involved in one of our enterprises, a venture of great importance to our national security. I urge you to cooperate if you wish to return to your wonderful humanitarian work. Answer our questions truthfully."

"I've nothing to hide, so go ahead, ask away."

"We have become anxious about recovering two small metal canisters. Please, tell us what you know."

"Two? I only know about one. I lied a little to your boy

here, Pepe. When your people collared me at the freighter, that was, in truth, a return visit, as I'd been there the day before. There were four crew, one dead and one seriously wounded. The injured one, I believe, was the captain. Well, he'd lost a lot of blood. I could do nothing for him."

Pepe pressed his thumb to his temple, running his fingers back and forth across his sweaty forehead, guilt weighing heavily on his conscience.

"Even though they were fellow countrymen, my first impression was these fellas are up to no good, maybe smugglers. So, with very sick people onboard my Cessna, I didn't have time to chat. Before departing, they gave me a load of medicines, and a strange object was tucked away in one of the cartons. It looked like a metal cigar tube. When I returned the following day, except for the dead fella, they were all gone. My guess is rebels or mercenaries took them, hostage."

"So, what became of the metal tube?"

"Well, here's the real strange bit. That night, I accidentally broke the inner glass tube. I can't be sure, but I think it resulted in the deaths of more than half of my patients. It's weird, though. Only the ones infected with that new immune deficiency virus died."

Listening from his research centre in Florida, Deckleshine put the phone down and stopped writing, burying his face in the palms of his hands.

"Fascinating, now enlighten us with all the gruesome details?"

After Jack had delivered a sketchy recollection, Pepe picked up the receiver and, switching off the speaker, continued the conversation for a short while before hanging up and homing in on his prisoner.

"Doctor Reilly, while my suspicions remain, it would appear that you have fortuitously done us a great service.

Now, listen up. My superiors have asked me to relay this caution. Do not try to investigate this event any further. We know all about you and the family you left behind. Get back to your charitable work, and forget this ever happened."

At the mention of his family, Jack was surprised by the sudden awakening of his parental instinct, wanting to strike out at the messenger delivering the implied threat. However, holding his nerve, Jack remained poker-faced.

"Yes, I understand."

Eyes red and puffy, Pepe called out to the officers waiting outside in the jeep before turning to face Jack for the last time.

"Okay, you listen to me, Reilly. You'll never understand the depth of the pain I'm suffering. Don't ever try to judge me again. Officer, my work here is done, so you may release your Priest. Now, drive me to the Antonov. I want to be airborne without delay."

Jack sat waiting in the police station for the officers to return. This perilous episode in his life should have been at an end, but he knew it wasn't, and as the racket from the Antonov's out-of-sync engines began to fade away, the ecstatic officers arrived back.

"Priest, please forgive us. An evil people, they leave us with very little choice."

"Don't fret, fellas. Hopefully, they won't be back. But, unfortunately, it's going to be dark in a few hours, so I'll also have to be on my way soon. Can you see that my fuel tanks are topped up? Also, I need a favour, please. I must make an important international call, so may I use your phone?"

On hearing the ringing tone, Jack couldn't believe his luck, as the line connected to the penthouse in Antwerp.

"Jack Kavanagh, of course, operator, yes, of course, I'll accept charges. Jack, is that you? Hello Jack."

He missed his soul mate. Feeling a tightness in his throat, Jack became overwhelmed by nostalgia.

"Yes, my dear friend, Arno, it's me, Jack."

Arno Beulen wanted to know everything about the flying doctor's exploits since the evacuation, and with every yarn he told, Jack could sense the envy from his friend the adventurer, now confined to a wheelchair after a stroke. Although Jack was enjoying the catch-up, reluctantly, he had to steer the conversation back to the reason for his call.

"Arno, you already did so much for me, which makes this even more difficult. I need your help, or to be more precise, I know some desperate people who need help. I don't want to get you heavily involved, so I'll only say what's necessary. Arno, since you left, I get the feeling this country is slipping deeper into entropy. Exploitation and corruption are even more rampant. At least when your people colonised, there was some order."

Jack hesitated for a moment, wishing he could erase his last sentence.

"Arno, I'm sorry. I didn't mean to offend. Forgive me."

"Nothing to forgive, Jack. You're perfectly right. Now, how can I help?"

After Jack explained the quandary, Arno repeated the important parts aloud, which helped him to formulate his thinking.

"Okay, if I understand correctly, you need my help to extract two of your friends from Congo. Well, they might be in luck, as we still run a weekly freight service between Ostend and Brazzaville. In fact, one just departed a couple of days ago, so give me a little time to make the arrangements."

Arno interrupted, becoming embarrassed by Jack's benevolence.

"I know, I know, sure you would do the same for me,

although there is one thing. I hope these men are not wanted by the police. Are they on the run?"

"Well, Arno, they're wanted all right. I don't believe the crew did anything wrong. Consider them victims of circumstance."

Drenched to the skin, the officers drove Jack to his Cessna and, exchanging hugs in the warm, drizzly rain, Jack smiled, his finger poking the officer's belly through a gap in his bulging shirt.

"You need more exercise."

"I need another wife," replied the giggling officer, unable to contain a mischievous grin.

Jack departed, taking the reciprocal route. Darting in and out of the low clouds, he tracked south, flying low above the snaking river. Even though it wasn't unusual, when suddenly the Cessna's engine began to run rough, he couldn't help but suspect sabotage. Then, after a few tweaks of the air-fuel mixture, the engine's smooth note returned, and satisfied that it must have been a little water contamination in the fuel, Jack cried out above the noise.

"Fuck, don't do that to me. I've had enough adventure for one day,"

CHAPTER TWENTY-SEVEN

S tretched out on the bench seat, Enda couldn't rest easy. Burdened with worry about Quinn, he knew he must abandon the niggling temptation to go back on foot and search for him in the dark. So, fidgeting about the boat to stop himself from brooding, he tried to familiarise himself with the ageing little ship, a sturdy Rampart 32, built in the fifties, with a powerful Parsons diesel engine.

Inspecting below deck, he moved levers back and forth, hatches in and out, although mostly, he checked for leaks. Then, sidestepping on her way to her cabin, Enda clumsily asked Tshala a question.

"I've been thinking. Isn't it a bit odd? Here you are, an attractive young woman, alone with this wonderful boat, yet no one seems to bother you. Are you not afraid?"

Flicking the hair from her forehead, she sat opposite him, subconsciously tapping a beat with her long skinny finger on the wooden table.

"I'll try to keep this brief. From the colour of my skin, you can tell I am multicultural. That used to be quite fashionable around these parts. I am an only child. My father was a businessman from Brazzaville, and my mother was

French. She came from a well-to-do family in Marseille. We moved here from the city when I was young, because my father dreamed of building a fishing empire. Within a short time, although not an empire, the business became quite successful. He was even appointed village mayor."

She stopped talking, stopped tapping, and straightened her back. "Am I boring you?"

"No, not at all. Please, continue. I really would like to hear more."

"Earlier today, as you passed through the village, you must have noticed the ramshackle colonial villas. Well, one of those was ours. I wanted for nothing except maybe a brother or sister, but that didn't happen. All too soon, it was time for me to leave for the big city and begin my studies. Almost every summer, I would return to help out with the business. Then, as the years passed, it became obvious that things were beginning to change, and it was not changing for the better. After the accident, I returned to bury my parents and claim my inheritance. Unfortunately, for me, it wasn't that simple. Greed and corruption had poisoned my people. Our new mayor made an offer, insisting it would be unwise of me to refuse—fifty dollars for my parents' villa and business. I got to keep the boat, my dog, and a letter, signed by the bastard, giving me unrestricted passage on the rivers. By the way, those one-hundred-dollar bills are about as useful as an umbrella around here. Haven't you anything smaller?"

Enda rummaged through every pocket until a small pile of mainly single greenbacks decorated the table. Ironing each bill with the palm of her hand, Tshala rolled them tightly together, stuffing the wad into the deep pocket of her plum-coloured culottes. Before departing, like a mother to her child, she felt the need to instil her authority.

"We'll be having fish for dinner. Do not venture above deck while I'm away, and remember, keep out of my cabin."

Enda could not recall having a better plate of food. Then, after tidying up the dishes, under cover of darkness, they moved the conversation to the small wheelhouse, puffing Gauloises until late into the night.

Awakened by the spluttering sound of an outboard motor, the neatly folded bundle of colourful men's clothing, spread along the bench opposite, created a short escape from reality for the young man. He was surprised at how well he had slept on the cushioned bench, putting it down to exhaustion. She had been awake long before him, busily making the final preparations for their long voyage, and now ready to depart, firing up the boat's engine, Tshala called down to her passenger.

"Remember to keep your head down. I'll have a strong black coffee, no sugar, please."

With renewed energy and hope, Enda was eager to face whatever the coming days might throw at him. Keeping himself low in the wheelhouse, he watched as his new captain executed a well-rehearsed routine. Slipping the mooring lines off the cleats, her dog howled with excitement. Then, applying gentle reverse, Tshala eased the vessel astern, fenders compressing, protecting the boat's wooden hull until they cleared the packed jetty.

The fast-flowing river began to take them with it until she shoved the throttle full forward, and spinning the helm hard right, the little ship swung around to slowly motor upstream. Then, checking over her shoulder, content that the port was out of sight, Tshala teased as she grabbed hold of Enda's hand.

"It's okay now, come. Enjoy the morning sun while you can. It'll be raining soon."

Captivated, he wanted the beauty of the moment to last

forever. The forest's wildlife chattered busily, greeting, or scoffing the morning as night gave way to the day's ritual for survival, which was already well underway. Then, once again playing a trick on his senses, breaking cover, the sun glistened in a heat haze above the jungle, on the wrong side of the patchy blue sky. Suddenly overcome with guilt, his joy was short-lived as his thoughts refocused on the friend he'd left behind.

Before departing downriver in the canoe, Enda memorised some features along the embankment, which were beginning to reappear when the dog raised the alarm. The animal's head jerked wildly, paws scratching at the wooden deck, trying to make the humans understand.

After easing back on the throttle, applying just enough power to hold the boat stationary in the flowing water, Tshala waved at Enda to join her.

"I don't like this. I'll try to hold the boat steady while you call out to your friend. We must be sure it's safe before going ashore."

Enda's voice was becoming hoarse from roaring, answered only by the jeering monkeys hiding in the trees. Realising they were getting nowhere, Tshala decided to share her thoughts with her new shipmate.

"I'm going to let the boat drift back to that sheltered section of river, it is almost calm there, and the boarding plank on the deck should be long enough to reach the embankment. I'll keep the engine running in case we need to make a hasty departure. Take the dog with you. If you want, there's a revolver below, in the compartment next to the blue locker."

While she manoeuvred the boat, Enda returned with the revolver tucked into his trouser belt.

Positioning the plank carefully, with one hard shove, it shot out from the transom onto the soft ground and had it been a foot shorter, it would never have bridged the nine-foot gap. Then, braving the narrow wooden bridge with ease, even though he stepped down gently, his shoes sank into the muddy earth with a squish. The dog raced ahead while Enda stepped awkwardly away from the embankment. Straining not to leave his shoes behind, he finally gained better footing, now hurrying to catch up with the Basenjis yodels. The dog began whining and pawing the ground next to the young kapok tree trunk, its long hanging vines swaying in the light breeze, brushing to and fro over the green duffel bag.

Dropping to his knees, Enda cried out in sorrow at the sight of the decapitated bodies of his pygmy companions. The muscular black man sprawled out next to them was almost naked. Wearing only a green string vest and underpants, the head of the arrow that killed him protruded from the side of his neck. After having its fill of human flesh, the unseen predator must have retreated when the dog arrived, leaving the smaller insects to continue with the clean-up. Enda raised himself wearily to his feet, his tearful eyes hopelessly scanning the undergrowth for his friend.

Battling to contain her own emotions, Tshala could hear his cries of desperation, each howl sending shivers down her spine. Anxious about her own safety, somehow, she resisted betrayal and the urge to leave her new shipmate behind.

Enda began to broaden his search, relieved that the dog didn't follow, as it continued to direct its attention towards the dead men. Suddenly, the sight of an enormous crocodile made him tense, conjuring up horrific images in his imagination of Quinn's probable demise. But, behaving like most large predators with a full stomach, it didn't appear to be aroused by Enda's presence. Instead, belly dragging in the mud, it slithered down the embankment, tail thrashing the high grass before vanishing beneath the dark river. Squeezing his eyes shut, trying to grab hold of anything plausible that might offer a glimmer of hope, Enda whispered, "He's been taken. That's it; he's been taken by the rebels."

Feeling hopelessly inadequate, and with the pistol offering no solace, he slung the duffel over his shoulder. Then, calling the dog to heal, Enda headed back towards the boat. After he'd described the bloody scene, which only upset Tshala even more, he asked if she had a shovel to bury the bodies.

"Are you crazy? Bury headless pygmies? They weren't killed by animals, were they? Humans did this, evil humans, so let's go. We're getting the hell out of here."

Before abandoning the search, Enda persuaded Tshala to continue for a while longer upriver. Standing at the bow on an upturned timber orange box, he scanned the water's edge with the binoculars, calling Quinn's name aloud while the dog remained quiet.

The earlier hazy blue sky was gone, wadded by expansive saturated clouds that lashed down, and when the first wave of warm fat droplets splattered off everything, it drowned out the forest's song. No longer calling out his friend's name, signalling the time was right, the captain swung the boat around while the tortured man sat drenched, head lowered, legs dangling over the bow next to the sleeping dog.

Choosing to give her shipmate some space, Tshala decided to let him be, until the river once again began to bustle with small fishing craft, scurrying in every direction.

"Hey, Enda, it's time you get below deck. We'll shortly be passing Mossaka port."

Nearing the village, the river had many small islands and channels. Manoeuvring along the main one, she kept as far from the port as possible. Motoring abeam her usual mooring spot, she was close enough to see that the uniformed men on the jetty were not dressed like government troops. As they viciously battered some unfortunate soul, she could hear them scream the word Mzungu with each blow to his body. Easing back on the throttle, as the boat drifted past, she couldn't resist one last glance towards her old home, its slated roof protruding above the village centre. Tshala, momentarily becoming stricken with panic, felt sure that eyes from the jetty were upon her. Contemplating surrender, with a plea for mercy, she persevered, hoping her world wouldn't drift deeper into uncertainty. Then, rapidly feeding the helm through her fingers to avoid a mudbank, the boat lurched forward as she advanced the throttle.

"Please, Enda, I told you before, keep your head down."

CHAPTER TWENTY-EIGHT

Gerry flopped into his swivel chair, staring at the shoebox-sized package the courier had just delivered. Unable to touch it, he'd asked the delivery man to carry it inside and place it on his desk. Then, leaning forward, Gerry pushed a button on the interphone.

"It's arrived."

Moments later, the airline boss entered and stood gaping at the box.

"Aren't you going to open it?"

"I can't," replied Gerry, handing him the Stanley knife.

After carefully guiding the blade along the brown tape, he removed each item one by one until a line of bubble-wrapped objects lay spread out on the desk. Then, reaching in, he picked up the final article, a large white sealed envelope. The pieces of scorched memorabilia were easily recognisable through the clear plastic wrapping, and the word 'Classified' was printed in large letters across the envelope.

Gerry saw Tumper step out of his minibus in the carpark. Watching through the security monitor, he pressed the lock release button for the outer door. The taxi driver turned down the offer of a seat, and leaning, arms folded against the wall, he listened while the men discussed company strategy.

"Okay, Gerry," said his boss, "I know you're upset. We're all upset. However, this is the way I see it. They're gone, it's over, and nothing will bring them back. The authorities and the insurance company will ask questions, so we must be on the same page. If they accept it was a straightforward accident, we're covered, but if they get a sniff of sabotage or the like, we're fucked. If you want to see the lad's dependants get decent compensation, you have to follow my advice."

Tumper stepped forward and opened the envelope, eyes fixated on the first print.

"Tell me something, you bollox. Do you think they'll ever get compensated for this?"

Spreading the six photos across the desk, only Tumper could stomach looking at the images as the shaken company man hurried to the open office window and sucked hard on the cold morning air.

"I've booked a room in the Stags Head for tonight. We'll make the funeral arrangements, and I'll hand over their stuff. Are you two coming?" asked Tumper.

Gerry replied for them both. "I'll go. I think you should stay away, at least until the funeral. Also, you can start looking for my replacement. I'm leaving after the insurance company coughs up. Now, what was it you want me to agree to lie about?"

Ignoring the brief objection from the company boss, who wanted to keep the photos, Tumper placed everything back into the box. Then, on arriving home, like a true detective, he scrutinised, searching for any inconsistencies, but there weren't any.

· · ·

The musty smell and the dimly lit basement cast a gloomy shadow over the already emotionally charged occasion. Tumper apologised about his choice of venue and suggested they move somewhere else, but as they had already ordered a round of drinks, they all insisted on staying. Although anxious to see what was recovered, no one minded delaying a bit until the alcohol kicked in and properly anaesthetised their senses. Aoife called out to the lone Green Bird representative.

"Gerry, we're ready."

After carrying the box to a well-lit corner of the room, the Operations Manager emptied everything onto a table, and Tumper reached for the envelope in his pocket. Then, one by one, the women stepped forward to claim the scorched memorabilia until nothing remained, except for Berko's unclaimed Breguet watch. Gerry tensed as Tumper placed a single photo on the table, showing the exterior of the ill-fated aircraft. The three women huddled together, almost mesmerised by the image, each making unique snivelling sounds of misery.

"Is that it?" Jenny asked.

Gerry and Tumper replied together. "Yes, that's it."

Except for Aoife, it seemed as if the tears were all used up. The mourners left to share the only things that remained, companionship and sorrow. Heartened by the plan to have the funerals of the four friends take place as a single gathering, they continued to reminisce into the night and, in fits and starts, the weeping once again stung sore, glazed eyes.

CHAPTER TWENTY-NINE

Our Lady Queen of Heaven Chapel, adjacent to the airport terminal, was packed to capacity long before the service began. Some clergymen weren't pleased about aspects of the Catholic service, deeming it less than a proper funeral. Although after reconsidering the unusual circumstances, they reluctantly agreed to proceed.

On top of the closed half section of the coffin in front of the altar, one of the four framed photos reflected colours of the rainbow, shimmering through the chapel's stained-glass windows. The whispers faded, and the congregation fell silent when the priest with his band of helpers appeared at the altar to address the faithful. Most of those present gained little comfort from the priest's pledge of resurrection and the mysteries it would bring. However, the twins did, squeezing hard on their mother's soft hands, trying to imagine their father's rebirth with all their might.

Each speaker stepped forward in turn to the microphone, delivering their scripts with style and grace. Going against their own better judgement, some even ventured to include a little bit of harmless humour. Aoife volunteered to take care of the music and made the selection with the young female organist, her talented recitals permeating every piece of empty space. Before leaving the apartment that morning, Aoife had searched through Enda's music collection. A cassette tape caught her notice—Demo First Twilight, hand-written by him on the label. So, Aoife brought the tape with her and requested that it be played over the chapel's sound system near the end of the service. The queue slowly shuffled along, everyone taking a few moments beside the coffin to adore the lad's photographs. Some leaned over to kiss the glass, while others gently caressed the cold aluminium frames. Berko's sister had managed to make it for the service and laid her brother's photo faceup in the coffin, followed by Fergie's wife and Aoife. Then, huddling them by her side, with some tender motherly persuasion, the twins released their tight grip on their dad's smiling face. Tumper was last in line, and after muttering something under his breath, he gently closed the lid.

CHAPTER THIRTY

After days of news coverage, the media had milked the story dry. Motorists caught up by the slow-moving procession must have had enough of the drama. However, they still showed calm and respect while patiently waiting for the motorcade to pass. At Glasnevin Cemetery, the solitary coffin, with the four brass nameplates screwed to its side, was lowered carefully into the grave. The grief-stricken inner circle wept as they linked arms around the deep trench, and the large crowd of mourners created a natural barrier against the stiff late September breeze.

When the priest performed the final ritual, the flock slowly made their way through the bleak graveyard, regrouping beside the long and high Columbarium Wall. Finally, the ash-less urns were placed in an open niche, and, as the stainless-steel door was locked shut by Jenny, the burial service was over.

The Coachman's Inn was filling fast, and knowing what to expect; most decided to take the day off work; some even took two. Tumper had reserved the front snug for family and helped the floor staff distribute the pyramids of assorted sandwiches stacked on every second table.

Everyone just wanted to forget or even pretend it never happened. Beads of sweat ran down the foreheads of the bartenders as the overfilled glasses lined up along the beer-soaked counter. Small groups of like-minded people gathered to chat about airline stuff until, as the pints took effect, the polite chats began to steer to the question on everyone's mind: what actually happened over there? The sober ones lowered their voices, being aware of choosing their words carefully to avoid causing more upset. But, as the evening progressed, the raised, nagging voices of the clueless reverberated around the pub.

"He wasn't the best of handlers."

"It was only a matter of time, drug runners."

"Always pushing it to the limit."

"Green Bird, lots of very dodgy customers."

Becoming perturbed, Tumper could see the distress growing on the women's faces, so he offered to drive them and the children home. But, before leaving, he put his hand on Aoife's shoulder, having to raise his voice over the chatter to be heard.

"I'll be back soon to collect you."

Aoife shook her head, telling him not to worry, as she had already made plans to stay with friends.

During the long drive, Tumper tactfully tried to explain away the earlier discourtesy at the pub.

"They're all a bit confused back there. Even frightened. They don't know how to handle the loss. I suppose they need to blow off a little steam, and rightly so. Your lads would have understood."

CHAPTER THIRTY-ONE

The insurance company couldn't find any reason to withhold the compensation payments. The only unusual factor being that Enda's would be paid to Tumper, his next of kin. However, they did query the claim for the two hundred thousand dollars loss before finally accepting the company accountant's certified documentation. Tumper and Aoife had agreed during the funeral that he would call over to the apartment in a few days for breakfast. Arriving mid-morning, his preferred disabled parking space was available. He pulled on the handbrake and leaned over the steering wheel, deep in thought. Then, unable to contain his laughter, he recalled that crazy wet day when she tried to drown him and Enda in the minibus.

Aoife was still in her dressing gown and greeted him with a big hug and a forced smile. The apartment was in a mess, and the anticipated smell of a fry-up wasn't happening. Nevertheless, he knew she needed to talk, so he let her take the lead as they sat at the kitchen table.

"I can't handle it. I think I'm going mad. I'm not familiar with all this death shit. It's the first time I've had to confront losing someone, and I'm scared. My friends tell me it'll pass, and what I feel is normal. Tell me, Tumper, is it normal that I want to throw myself out through a window?"

For a few long seconds, Aoife held her gaze on the glass terrace door in the corner of the kitchen.

"My family want me to stay with them, take some time out. Can you imagine, me in West Donegal, in the middle of winter? The isolation would definitely finish me off. Also, I must move out of here before the end of October, as I can't afford it alone, and I'm certainly not sharing. I'm not letting a stranger move in."

Tumper was waiting for the right moment, searching for those elusive magic words, a sentence or two that might ease her suffering.

"Aoife, no one can fix what you're feeling. Listen, I know about death and loss, and it will not go away anytime soon. But you will learn how to live with it. If it helps, I'm also sick inside, just like you."

The friends stood and hugged, and although it was a long time coming, no matter how hard he tried, Tumper couldn't hide his moist eyes as a single tear trickled down his cheek. Aoife felt terrible, not wanting to drag him down as well and spoil the day, so she tried to introduce a little humour, to act a bit.

"I've fucked up your breakfast. Sure, there's not even a sausage in the fridge, so here's what we'll do. I'll get dressed, and we'll stroll down to the deli. I'm buying."

After the bacon and eggs fry-up, Tumper made excuses about having to rush away over some business matter. When Aoife returned home, lying across the toast rack on the kitchen table was the envelope he told her about over breakfast.

Aoife, I don't want any arguments. They paid this compensa-

tion, and I certainly don't need it, so I signed it over to you. It's yours. Use it as you see fit. Please do stick around, and if you don't, then call me before you leave. Also, if it's okay, I'd like to drop in next week to collect a few bits of Enda's stuff as keepsakes. Your pal Tumper.

CHAPTER THIRTY-TWO

R elieved that the recent dramatic events appeared to have calmed down, Jack wanted to settle back into his daily routine, but on receiving news about the murdered tribespeople and hostage-taking, it appeared that the drama wasn't quite over yet. And, even though the new patient might attract more grief, he was determined to shelter him. So, in order to keep a close eye on the wounded pilot, Jack moved Fergus to his cabin. Then, after returning from doing his rounds, he pulled a chair up next to him.

"Well, how are you feeling today?"

"Except for a thumping headache, I'm not too bad, don't even feel much pain," replied Fergus.

"Yeah, that's normal. Morphine is a wonderful drug. However, I want to keep the dosage to a minimum, so you can expect to feel some discomfort. It's all part of the healing process."

"Any news about the lads, doctor?"

Jack brought the captain up to date, explaining that it would be a waiting game, although he was expecting to hear back from the local villagers soon. Not wanting to distress him more, he didn't mention the latest news about the murdered hunters and hostages.

"You must be taking a major risk. If the soldiers come and find me here, I don't think that'll be good for either of us."

"Don't worry about me. What else was I supposed to do? All we need is time. You're badly injured, and I can't risk flying you out of here yet. Don't worry; they're not going to find you. I have my own early warning radar system. I've already arranged for the hunters to take you to a safe place should those maniacs return. Fergus, you might find what I'm about to say hard to understand. If necessary, your newly appointed guardians will give their lives to protect you. Now, enough of this what-if stuff. Maybe you should get some rest."

"I don't want to rest. I want to talk some more with you, doc."

"Hey, you should have seen the state of the control tower's roof. I still can't figure out how you managed to land the DC8 on that airstrip, and with an engine missing."

"We only had two," replied Fergus.

Jack eased his patient's head off the pillow and pressed a damp cloth to his forehead.

"Here, drink this. Don't mind the taste; it'll keep you hydrated. So, what would you like to talk about?"

"You, this place, the Cessna. I can't get my head around it. It's a lot to take in."

"Okay, I'm going to tell you a bedtime story. No questions, though. I want you to rest. You'll probably be asleep by the time I've finished."

After Jack poured himself a cup of palm wine, he moved his chair closer to the bed.

"Surprisingly, one of your crew recognised me at the crash site. It was the older one, Quinn. When you see him again, ask him to tell you the first bit of my story. Anyway, I was a doctor working in the UK when I fucked it all up. I lost my profession, my family, the whole works. Arriving at Charles De Gaulle airport, I went to the British Airways information desk and told the elderly gentleman working there that I was planning to relocate to Africa. When I explained that I wasn't sure which Congo to emigrate to, he suggested I'd have a better life expectancy resettling in The Republic of the Congo. So, I bought a one-way ticket to Brazzaville, and thanked him for his counsel.

"I'd never been beyond Europe, and in the beginning, I found it challenging to comprehend the squalor and poverty in the bustling city. For the first week, I wandered aimlessly, hoping to gain some street sense while avoiding the dodgy areas. Often, I would visit the city's more opulent establishments to drink a beer and pass the time. I particularly enjoyed eavesdropping on both English and French conversations.

"During one of these earwigging intrusions, I heard a few fellas discussing mining opportunities, east of the Odzala National Park. Eventually, I built up enough courage to introduce myself to the opportunists. After that, it wasn't long before I was mixing with the elite, the politically powerful, and the wealthy.

"They all knew me as Jack Kavanagh, the biology teacher from Maynooth University. Everyone was saddened by my yarn about the loss of my family in a horrific motorway accident while holidaying in England, so I took advantage of their pity. Although, afterwards, I felt terrible about using such an awful deception. Anyway, they even invited me to a lavish New Year's Eve party at Denis Nguesso's pad.

"You won't believe this. The President gave me his card after we discussed the possibility of developing educational ties between our countries. But, as time drifted by, I became more disillusioned and less fulfilled. I'd even become paranoid about getting tied up in a relationship, always being the first with an excuse to break it up. It was becoming clear that this was not the Africa I had hoped to find. So, as part of a small exploration group, I headed north to Pikounda.

"As the months passed, I just became more introverted. Realising I had little in common with the rest of the group, I preferred to spend my time with the local Bayaka pygmy tribes. It wasn't long before they accepted me. They even let me live alongside them in their villages. We communicated using a jumble of French words and hand gestures, yet it never felt like a barrier as our friendship grew stronger.

"When I applied my medical skills, they regarded me as a treasure, a good spirit, and even gave me a new name, Priest. I felt I'd served my old sentence. As a doctor, I could offer the tribespeople much-needed help. Up and down the rivers and across the interior, I was made welcome, even by the bloody rebel warlords. Will I go on?" asked Jack.

"Yes, of course. Please do."

"I lived in a small Mongulu shack at the edge of the rainforest. My new family helped me build a large shelter, using branches and dried palm leaves. Although they'd never seen one, we decided to call it La Clinique. The sick and injured would track for days to receive whatever medical treatment was available. I even managed to train some female pygmies in basic nursing skills. However, the lack of medicines usually determined their faith, although many had contracted a new western disease, with no hope of a cure."

"Were you not lonely?"

"The isolation sometimes bothered me, living like a Benedictine Monk. Although, that bit improved after I developed a friendship with a Belgian family called Beulen, whose camp was nearby. Arno Beulen was in charge of a mining project about a two-hour drive away, or if the track became flooded, almost a full day's hike through the forest. The Beulen's invited me to sleep over with them every other weekend. On most occasions, they would dispatch one of the Land Rovers to fetch me, or sometimes I would hike through the forest to get there, kept safe by a band of local Pygmy hunters.

The Beulen camp housed about fifty workers and had its own airstrip, complete with a Cessna. The wine would flow as we dined late into the night, and not wanting the party to end, later, we would gather around the veranda to sing our hearts out or chat until dawn.

One day, this native fella arrived unexpectedly and handed me a purse with keys. The note inside simply read: *We'll miss you, my friend.*

It didn't make any sense, so I decided to trek over to the compound and investigate. When I arrived, the camp was intact but deserted. So, I went to the hangar, and inside were a Land Rover Defender and a Cessna Skyhawk aeroplane. I noticed a large envelope with my name, sellotaped to the planes windshield. There was a letter inside."

Jack stood and, from a book on the shelf over his bed, he unfolded the letter.

"This is it. Will I read it to you?"

My Dearest friend Jack.

Headquarters in Belgium have instructed me that due to threats from a rebel group, we are to cease operations and evacuate the camp immediately. However, before we departed, my boss agreed to my special request.

The jeep and aircraft are yours. You'll find the documentation and keys inside the filing cabinet in the hangar. There is a large quantity of fuel remaining in the storage tanks. You can also use the camp's facilities for as long as you wish.

Jack, do you recall the night when you risked your life in the middle of that wicked storm to attend to my sick wife? Well, I do. Our antivenom didn't work, she was going to die, and you saved her life. Maybe you don't like me saying this, but we will never be able to repay this debt. So, if I can ever be of assistance, or if you have the time, please visit us in Flanders. My contact details are below.

Your grateful friends, Dominique, and Arno.

"Jesus," said Fergus.

Jack ran a hand towel across his face, wiping the sweat or a tear.

"I suppose you're still wondering about the Cessna?"

"Yes, I am."

"Well, when I lived in the UK, I took several flying lessons. Also, I used to practice on trips with Arno, who was a great pilot, and although I did have a few scary moments, it didn't take long to put it all together. I guess you saw the movie Murphy's War? Well, it was a bit like that. I know you'll understand when I say, it's the weather that keeps trying to kill me. So, that's about it. With the help of my faithful followers, it only took a couple of weeks to settle in here. We converted the large dormer that used to house the workers into our new clinic. I couldn't resist choosing this place. It was the Beulen hut. However, the best bit is the corrugated steel roofing on every building. We're never dry from the humidity, but it keeps the rain off. I've just one complaint, though. I can't get the tribespeople to stop their subservient ways. They treat me like I'm some sort of feckin god."

"Maybe you are a god," replied Fergus, before drifting into a deep sleep.

.   .   .

Postal deliveries to the compound would usually take forever. So, Jack was surprised to receive the envelope from Owando so soon, containing news from Arno about the flight out of Brazzaville. He had left Fergus resting, and on the veranda from the comfort of his favourite, Dirk van Sliedregt, vintage Rattan easy chair, he pondered the instructions until his gaze settled on some gently swaying tree branches in the distance. Tapping the small metal tube against his lap, he recalled the recent ugly encounter with the Americans. Jack didn't want his life to end prematurely, aware that the tribespeople living in the surrounding rainforest would also benefit significantly from his staying alive. After the threat towards his family, he decided to do nothing for the moment. Instead, he would wait for news from local tribes to filter back through the forest about the fate of the Irish men on the run.

CHAPTER THIRTY-THREE

From his office on the eleventh floor of the Special Operations Division, the newly appointed, homophobic Director of Operations, watched through binoculars as the latest batch of recruits trained in unarmed combat on the nearby exercise grounds. He muttered to himself repeatedly, like someone rehearsing the script for a movie.

"Flush the fuckers out..."

Distracted and trying hard to ignore the buzzing telephone on his desk, the director finally gave in, snatching the receiver from the cradle.

"Yes, send them in."

Special Agents Bluey and Sable entered with feverish haste. After striding across the room in unison, they stood to attention as the director leaned back in his chair.

"Please, that's not necessary, relax and take a seat."

On his desk lay an amber-coloured folder with an over-sized printed label, Restricted-Prof Deckleshine.

"I believe we recently found it necessary to visit our friend. What did you learn about the professor? Tell me, what do you know about this great man?"

Bluey was the first to offer his observations. "Well, sir, in fact, it was your predecessor who ordered us to interrogate Deckleshine, because we were beginning to have doubts about his patriotism."

The director looked at agent Sable. "So, after your visit, what did you think then?"

"Our orders were clear, sir; his contract would be terminated unless..."

The director interrupted, now turning his attention back to her colleague.

"Suicide, am I right?"

Bluey nodded as he continued, "Correct, sir, but only if we believed he had become a liability."

"He's still alive, isn't he? Which leaves me to assume he is a true patriot. I want to meet the professor. Have him here in my office tomorrow midday. You're both dismissed."

CHAPTER THIRTY-FOUR

"Professor Deckleshine, line five."

The professor could hear his voice being called over the tannoy and walked hastily to the wall-mounted phone with the flashing white light next to the canteen.

"Deckleshine here."

"Good evening, professor. I hope I'm not disturbing you. This is agent Bluey."

On realising who the caller was, Deckleshine became distressed. Feeling his heart racing, he could not imagine what he'd done wrong this time, so he went on the defensive.

"No, sir, you're not disturbing me. Although, I understood we had concluded our business. Let's hope I haven't created another complication."

"On the contrary, professor, our new Director of Operations has singled you out for your contribution towards the security of our great country and wants to meet you personally."

"Agent Bluey, can you please relay my appreciation to the director? Unfortunately, I am at a critical research stage and don't have any time to spare."

"Doc, I truly admire your work ethic, but he wants to see you tomorrow. Your flight departs Miami at 07:00, so be on it. Agent Sable will be waiting for you at Dulles."

Deckleshine leaned back in his chair in the corner of the near-empty canteen, sipping his cup of Earl Grey. Desperate, he tried to understand what could have triggered the need for a meeting, and Bluey's reassurance was doing nothing to help calm his stomach.

Waiting in the black Dodge Diplomat at the restricted parking area outside Dulles International, Sable sat watching with amusement, unable to stop herself from giggling as Deckleshine approached the car.

"Jesus, I can see where they got the expression, nutty professor."

Wearing heavy-rimmed, thick-lensed spectacles and weighed down by the brown leather doctor's bag, made him lean to one side as he walked. His hair and dress were scruffy, and a scrap of dark, blood-stained tissue paper was stuck below his left ear. Sable stepped from the car, beaming a broad smile, and offered him her hand, the soft hand. Then, after opening the back door, she was surprised when he requested to sit in the passenger seat next to her.

"Well, professor, we meet again and under more favourable conditions. It's going to be a short journey, about thirty minutes."

"Do you know why he called the meeting, or who will be present?"

"Just you, me, Bluey, and the director. I've no idea what it's about, although it would appear that the boss is very impressed by your achievements."

The seating arrangement in the director's office made Deckleshine feel as if he was about to be interviewed for an important job. The agents sat on either side of their boss's desk while the interviewee faced the trio and the flags. The director was a Vietnam War veteran, and although he had high hopes of making General, he only managed to achieve the rank of Colonel. Much to his delight, his retirement didn't last for long, after being approached by the CIA on a matter of national security. When it came to jungle warfare, he'd attained a reputation for his ability to deploy troops in unfavourable terrain conditions strategically. To his men, he was affectionately known as Flush. His politics were far right, and he had a deep suspicion, or plain hatred, for anyone who didn't appear normal. This trait must have suited the people who appointed him, because had there been the usual psychometric evaluation, he would have failed miserably.

Even though he knew the director looked upon him favourably, it didn't help to calm the doctor's sensitive stomach. So, as he ran the sleeve of his brown tweed jacket across his sweaty forehead, Deckleshine nervously waited for the discussions to begin.

"My dear professor, I am honoured that you could spare the time to come and converse with me today. I truly do appreciate it. I've been studying your profile, and I believe you are suitably qualified to offer direction on a pressing and difficult matter of state."

The director tapped his finger erratically on the visitor's amber folder, amused to see Deckleshine shuffle uncomfortably in the hard wooden chair.

"I've decided to dedicate a considerable amount of my time for us to explore some of the possibilities of your latest research project, ShineOn. Are you aware, doctor, on the other side of the world, a mission related to this research has already cost the lives of three of our finest?"

Not having an inkling how to reply, Deckleshine sat

motionless, glancing left and right at the agents, and waited for the director to continue.

"We need to be ready, ready to flush the fuckers out from their hiding places."

Sable and Bluey nodded in agreement, but were disappointed when the director ordered them to leave the room —pointing out that the two men had some matters to discuss in private.

"Okay, professor, it's just me and you now, so please, let us be forthright. As you know, the ShineOn field trials in Africa were a great success, although, at times, it did get a bit messy, and we still have a few loose ends to tidy up. But don't worry; we're working on that. Now, tell me, what additional research would be required to scale up the effectiveness of ShineOn? Can you create a more potent variant?"

"I don't understand, sir. Scale up in what way?"

"Okay, let's assume we needed to; how should I put this...? Let's say we wanted to dust a city the size of San Francisco, to medicate the population. Would that be possible? Would the device have to be bomb-like and dropped from an aircraft?"

The director spread his arms above his head, attempting to mimic size.

"No, sir, not at all. It would be a relatively simple process. We'd only need to increase the volume a little, although increasing the concentration level would be the main tweak. Might this be what you're after? Am I on the right track?"

The director leaned back in his brown leather Chesterfield chair and looked directly into the professor's eyes with admiration. Finally, recognising a man after his own heart, a man who could get the job done. Deckleshine probed further, pretending to be puzzled.

"Sir, we already have powerful weapons that could take

out big cities. So, I can't see how ShineOn could be beneficial in that respect."

Before continuing, he tried to interpret the director's facial expression, searching to see if he was saying the right things.

"We would eradicate thousands of our people while unavoidably priming the rest of the population. Anyway, I think this is an appropriate time to give you some wonderful news. We believe we've almost cracked it."

Deckleshine was sure he heard the sound of grinding teeth.

"It seems we've managed to iron out the earlier negative issues with ShineOn. As a result, it will soon be an effective treatment and no longer harm those infected with the new virus."

Deckleshine was lying; he wasn't even close to cracking it, and without taking his eyes off the professor, the solemn-faced director leaned forward and pressed a button on his desk phone.

"Send in agents Bluey and Sable."

When the pair re-entered the office, the director pointed towards them.

"Professor Deckleshine, these are our people, god-fearing people."

Feeling exhausted, it was late when Deckleshine arrived at the air base. Even so, he decided to make a short detour to his office at the research centre. After his false revelation during the meeting, the anticipated telex had arrived from Langley.

Special Operations Division---With immediate effect---cease all development work on project ShineOn---await further instructions---Director of Operations.

Deckleshine removed the Panasonic dictaphone from his doctor's bag. Placing it on his desk, he spoke softly to himself.

"Can't understand why they let it through security at Langley, unbelievable."

When asked, he'd informed the guard that he needed it for his work, expecting him to retain the recorder until after the meeting with the director, but the security guard didn't.

CHAPTER THIRTY-FIVE

The old motor yacht felt roomy, with all the basic facilities to make a long voyage comfortable, including a well-equipped galley, flush toilet, wash cubicle, and the light-coloured teak interior below deck gave it a cheerful feel. The boat's captain mostly stood resting her fingers on the helm, scanning the river for traffic or hazardous debris floating on the muddy water. Enda would watch when Tshala had to attend to something, becoming amused as she performed a well-practised routine.

Firstly, she would reduce the engine revs. Then, after steadying course, she'd make two twists of a wire coat hanger, locking the helm in position. Leaping up onto the deck, she'd make a graceful pirouette to carry out a final check of the river. On one of these occasions, Enda waited until she returned to the wheel to ask a question.

"Why don't you let me steer while you're busy with other matters?"

"Have you ever handled a big boat?" she replied.

"Nothing like this, but I have experience on sailing boats, and I suppose it handles much the same."

"Okay, I can't see why not. So, go ahead, boat's all yours."

Tshala never stopped nit-picking for the first couple of hours, making him almost regret his offer. However, instead of getting annoyed, he decided to be tactful.

"I've learned a lot of interesting stuff from you today. Have you ever considered becoming an instructor?"

A shy look spread across her face, contented by his willingness to learn, giving her the confidence to let her shipmate handle her most cherished possession. Tshala felt her world was changing, becoming a happy place, content to spend more time on deck with her dog or laze at the bow, observing the planet's beauty as it drifted by.

When the evening light began to fade, it pressured them to focus on finding a safe mooring for the night. After sizing up a suitable spot, she spun the wheel full astern to make a U-turn, pointing the bow into the fast-flowing water. Then, using a skilful combination of rudder and engine power to edge them towards the embankment, Tshala steadied the boat for Enda to secure the mooring ropes. Before settling down for the night, she warned him to be alert, ready to make a quick getaway should rebel soldiers or thieves approach.

"My dog will alert us. But, Enda, do not use the revolver unless absolutely necessary, and here, if you have to, use this machete to cut away the mooring ropes."

After sharing another fine fish meal, it was getting late by the time they had tidied up, and not yet ready to pack it in for the night; they sat up on deck for what had now become the customary smoke. Sometimes, Enda could block out the madness in his mind, and, except for the persistent biting insects, he was beginning to feel an odd sense of belonging on the river. Then, recalling visits he'd made to zoos all over the world, Enda concluded that caged animals couldn't be happy.

"You know something, I've never heard anything like it

before. Don't you just love that confused symphony of magical chatter from the forest? Hey, Tshala, how did you come up with the name for your boat?"

"My father had a great sense of humour. During the wet season, he would often say, if it doesn't stop pouring down, the whole forest will sink. So, insisting she would never sink, he named her TitanicV. The V is for victory."

"Brilliant. I would have liked your dad," replied Enda, with a chuckle.

They would sometimes sit silently in the pitch-black abyss, listening to the sound of the fast-flowing water against the hull, inducing a wonderful illusion that the yacht was moving.

"Hey, you mentioned that you worked as a surveyor?"

Enda was just about to say yes, but hesitated.

"Maybe, was that what I told you? Anyway, I shouldn't say too much. The agreement was you take me down the river, but now I'm worried about involving you deeper in my troubles. That sort of shit isn't worth a few hundred dollars."

"Okay, maybe that's true. Although it's a bit late, I'm already involved. Consider this, Enda. If they take me for questioning, and I tell them the truth or lie, they won't believe me either way. So, go ahead, only tell me what you must, maybe you're right. The less I know, the better."

While he cleverly edited the synopsis, she sat and listened in the blackness of the night, unaware that he had tears trickling down his cheeks. After he stopped talking, she didn't probe. Feeling his pain, Tshala shuffled closer, gently laying a reassuring arm across his shoulders.

Awakened by the sound of the rain pouring down during the night, curled up on the bench seat, believing there must be a leaking roof, Enda realised he was sweating profusely. Then, thinking back, at peace after sharing his burden, Enda was once again overwhelmed by sleep. By daybreak, the rain had stopped, and the warm, saturated air spread out in a thin foggy layer that lay still above the water, making the river disappear. Forced to wait until visibility improved to continue their downstream voyage, they sat on the deck watching as the early morning sun triumphed, dispatching the fog to a patchy mist.

Most of the time, they averaged thirteen knots in the fast-flowing river, making progress much better than expected, and soon they would be almost halfway to Brazzaville. Enda was sitting patiently on the toilet, waiting for the diarrhoea to ease, when the boat suddenly began to shudder. He pulled at his pants, tripping over himself as he fumbled up to the wheelhouse, confused as to why the captain was attempting to stop the boat using full reverse. She screamed at Enda above the engine noise, pointing beyond the dog, who scratched and whined at something in the distance.

"I think it's a naval patrol boat, over there, to the right. Check it out with the binoculars."

"Fuck it, you're right. I'd guess a fifty-footer, stationary next to the embankment. It's hard to make out their uniforms from here. Don't think they've seen us yet."

She was applying too much reverse, motoring backwards in the current, forcing splashing waves against the transom that were now spilling over into the wheelhouse.

"Take it easy, Tshala. Back off a little, or you're going to sink us."

Panic-stricken, she didn't hear a word as Enda eased back the throttle, and with a shove of his hip against hers, he took control of the boat. They knew that if the military saw them making a U-turn, it would look like they were trying to evade detection. So, with the ship almost stationary, he let the flow carry them towards the hanging vines jutting out from the river's edge. Even applying the minimum amount of reverse, Enda also struggled to slow the forward drift and limit the surging water that splashed over the transom. Then, realising what he was attempting to do, Tshala grabbed a rope, balancing herself on the pushpit, ready to loop it over a branch while shouting words of support.

Although not the best hiding place, they were out of sight of the military, at least for the moment. As a team, they quickly reviewed their plan of action, which would see Enda trekking inland to follow the river while she continued alone until passing the patrol boat. Then, once safely clear, she would find somewhere to tie up, allowing her shipmate time to catch up. Tucking the revolver into his duffel bag, Enda swung it over his shoulder, and with the dog by his side, he went ashore, calling out as Tshala headed back out onto the river.

"Take it easy. Smile, don't rush. I'll be seeing ya soon."

Keeping the revs low while steering the boat along the middle of the river, she pretended not to hear the challenge coming over the megaphone. However, the burst of machine gun fire into the water ahead forced Tshala to abandon her bluff and comply immediately with their demand to halt. And with boats starboard to starboard, she tossed a rope from the stern to a waiting soldier. As her confidence dwindled, two more soldiers, brandishing assault rifles, leapt onto the deck to secure the remaining mooring lines.

The commanding officer on the naval boat's bridge looked down proudly over his catch, slowly rubbing the palms of his hands together.

"Madam, are you alone? I wish to inspect your vessel and papers."

The soldiers lowered their Kalashnikovs as the lieutenant, wearing a starched white uniform and peaked cap, stepped onboard to confront the suspect.

"Young lady, you are lucky it's us and not the rebels boarding your vessel. Did you not hear our warning?"

"No, sir, I didn't hear it. You were too far away, but I saw your bullets hit the water."

"As I already said, you're lucky. Had it been the rebels, the bullets would have hit you. Now, tell me why you're here, and show me your papers."

The officer seemed content with her explanation and was even impressed with the certificate guaranteeing her safe passage, until one of his men placed one thousand dollars on the table beside them. Counting the money, the officer coughed to clear his dry throat.

"What else are you hiding? Where did you get this money?"

"I'm not hiding anything. If I wished, I could have concealed the money, and you wouldn't have found it. That cash and this boat were in payment for my parents' house and business. It's legitimately mine."

"My dear lady, I can see receipts for the house, the business, the boat and fifty dollars. I do not see any receipts for one thousand American dollars. And, as you are aware, if there is no receipt, then this money does not exist. Every day we risk our lives for our people. Do you know how long it's been since my men and I were paid? I do not believe everything you told me. However, this money will compensate for the ammunition you wasted. Do we have an understanding, madam?"

After acting out a feeble protest, Tshala backed down, content that the plan would work. She struggled to hold the look of discontentment on her face.

From the bridge of his patrol boat, the smiling lieutenant saluted her. Then, after his men tossed the coiled mooring ropes down onto the deck, she eased forward on the throttle. With the first part successfully executed, Tshala wondered if her shipmate was having the same good luck.

* * *

Enda held the dog on a short leash, keeping him close to his side as they made their way across the soggy earth. Even during his time with the hunters, he had never felt the same sense of security that he was feeling now, watching his new companion sniff out the slightest hint of danger. But on hearing the burst of gunfire coming from the river, Enda feared the worst and began to track towards the evil sound. The patrol boat was partly visible through the tree branches, but he was having difficulty making out the figures standing at the rear of the Rampart.

Hesitating to get closer, he patiently waited until he heard the Rampart's engine. As her boat motored away, the relief left him wanting to scream with joy. Then, tugging hard against the leash, the dog panted heavily, pawing the ground, eager to move along. Dripping sweat as he tried to make haste, Enda had to constantly change direction to navigate the dense undergrowth, hoping he would soon catch sight of the woman with the boat.

Feeling nauseous from the exertion, Enda stopped to rest in a clearing, overjoyed to see the stationary TitanicV a short distance ahead, when suddenly, the sound of heavy hooves and snapping branches made him dive for cover. However, his canine companion had no fear, eager to confront the charging animal. Enda pressed his back against a fallen tree trunk, watching in horror as the fully grown hippopotamus charged past. With jaws wide open, it scooped the dog up, and moments later, there was a weighty splash as they both disappeared below the muddy water. The voracity of the attack sickened him to his soul, and burying his head in his arms, he trembled with sorrow.

Tshala also heard the splash and looked out onto the river from the back of her boat. There was nothing to be seen, except for sizeable ripples fanning out from the embankment, to be prematurely cancelled by the fast-flowing water. Then, suddenly, the dog's head and paws surfaced. Thrashing the water, he spun around several times, trying to regain his bearings, before making a beeline towards his home. Leaping to his feet, with revolver in hand, Enda ran to the river's edge, ready to ward off any further attacks on the little warrior.

She could now see them both, and while screaming words of encouragement towards her dog, she shouted towards Enda to put the gun down. The dog seemed to have used up all of his luck, as predators became alerted to blood and thrashing water. Then, leaning over the side of the boat, on the first attempt, Tshala caught the animal's collar, dragging the splashing, whining dog to safety.

Enda was also in a hurry to get on board. Tripping over a fallen tree branch, he fell hard, tumbling awkwardly into the wheelhouse, and lying face down, moaning from the pain, the shivering dog feverishly licked his face. Although the Basenji had a few deep cuts, after they had bandaged him up, he appeared content to limp to his favourite place at the bow to sleep it off.

Trying to lessen the seriousness of the encounters, the happy couple sat cross-legged on the deck, excited to share their part of the stratagem that outwitted the military. With his face bruised like a boxer's, Enda released a few ouches as he spoke, suspecting he'd broken ribs from the heavy fall.

"Jesus, you would not have believed the speed of that

hippo. He was as big as a feckin car; can't understand how the little fella survived."

"Hippos not only kill animals. Every year, they also kill a lot of people. So, you must keep your distance and treat them with caution. But, hey, you were right about the cash; they went straight for it. Although, on the other hand, it wasn't yours to lose."

Eyes lowered, she made her disappointment clear, and brushing his hand gently across her head, Enda made a brief visit below deck. On his return, he asked Tshala to close her eyes and open her hands, and when she looked again, one thousand dollars lay in the palm of her hands.

"Are you some kind of magician? I thought the soldiers took it."

"They did, and yes, maybe I am a magician."

Before continuing the voyage, the adventurers spread the navigation chart on the deck to study the next leg of the journey. Ngabe was a small fishing village along the river bank and ideally located for the next night stop, after which they planned to make an early morning departure for the final stage of the journey to Brazzaville.

"Do you think there might be a telephone in the village?"

"I doubt it, unless you want to ask at the local police station if it's okay to use their phone. Or even better, you could conjure up more cash and buy the police station."

Laughing heartily at her funny taunts, he grabbed her, and as Tshala giggled, struggling to break free, her shipmate relaxed his gentle squeeze around her waist.

They couldn't have planned their arrival time better, slipping in while most of the boats fished the river. They tied up at a quiet spot a few hundred meters south of the village.

"Besides a phone, is there anything else I can get you?"

Pulling a broad smile, he shook his head, then changed his mind.

"How about some cold beer?"

"I'll try, but it certainly won't be cold. Now, keep out of sight till I get back."

By the time he'd finished tidying below deck, and after a long overdue shower, the boat's water tank was almost empty. Enda watched her return from the village through a porthole, pushing a wheelbarrow. When she laid the bags along the deck, it looked like she'd bought enough food to feed a large family for a week.

Tshala knew he was watching, so she kept the two cases of Stella beer till last. Then, holding one of the cases over her head, she could hear hands clapping and leaping up and down; unable to contain his excitement, he rocked the boat.

"I hope you left enough water for me?" she said, admiring his tidy appearance.

Enda hadn't. However, fortunately for him, the rubber hose was long enough to reach the water tap near the jetty —the weak flow taking almost an hour to replenish the large storage tank. Before settling in for the night, the Basenji's short tail wagged with delight when Tshala placed the extra-large bowl of food before him. He savaged the lot down in seconds without pausing to take a breath.

Mooring so close to the village created a concern about intruders, so they dimmed the oil lanterns and closed the curtains on the portholes. Then, after tossing their cigarette ends into the river, they decided, on this occasion, it would be unwise to stay on deck, so they retired below. Her shipmate was expecting another fish dish, but was delighted when she set about preparing a traditional meal with chicken in a moambe sauce instead. She added sautéed onions, nutmeg, green chillies, grated ginger, and tomatoes into a large saucepan with lots of hot peanut oil. As it cooked over the kerosene oil stove, she added chicken and peanut butter, stirring it gently, before letting it simmer. After Enda hauled the net bag with the slightly chilled beers from the river, she served the meal, heaped with fresh couscous. They ate slowly, savouring every mouthful, and when they could feast no more, without saying a word, she washed, so he dried, and they tidied the little galley together. Later that evening, when Tshala returned from her cabin, they sat facing each other across the table, just like on the first night they met.

Talking excitably about music while sipping on a dessert of warm beer, Enda became quiet, and moved to sit next to her. Tshala didn't mind and was in the middle of telling him about her favourite album, when he ran his fingers down her soft cheeks. Drawing her close, he gently kissed her lips. After offering only slight resistance, she wrapped her arms around his neck and kissed him back in a passionate embrace. Exploring her body with his hands, Enda slipped under her yellow t-shirt and caressed her small breasts. A surge of passion made their breathing quicken as the kissing intensified. Then, hugging fervently, they lay side by side on the long-cushioned bench seat. Enda lowered his hand beneath her short linen wrap, gently caressing between her thighs, and grabbing hold of his t-shirt, Tshala dragged it over his head with a whisper, "Hey, baby, slow down, slow down."

The night passed as if time had stood still, until their bodies stiffened. She sighed quietly, and he moaned as they climaxed in erotic, fondling pleasure. Then, as the passionate embrace softened, the caresses slowed as they continued to cuddle tightly, and before they slept, she led him forward to share her cabin.

Enda awoke before Tshala did, and listening to her soft breathing in the early morning light, he kissed her forehead. The young engineer knew she had aroused something in him, a feeling far more profound than physical desire.

CHAPTER THIRTY-SIX

J ack reacted badly to the rumours of a local woman with a boat and Mzungu onboard.

"Dammit, I warned them to keep off the feckin river."

He was having doubts about his continued involvement, or at least until he understood more about the men, suspecting they might, in fact, be smugglers after all. Either way, he just wanted the whole episode to end. After giving the matter considerable thought, Jack read over the note he'd just finished writing.

Fellas, I don't know what the fuck you were getting up to over here. However, you indirectly involved my family, and at least two tribespeople are dead. You've upset some very powerful people, and they're searching for you. I warned you to keep off the river, and to be honest, after hearing the rumours, I'm surprised you lasted this long.

I said I'd help, and through a close friend, I've arranged two seats on a Belgian freighter departing Brazza in a few days. I've written the details below. I want to believe you were victims of fate (I've been there!). Anyway, there's little else I can do. Your captain is recovering well at the clinic; that said, it's too soon to move him. There's a lot of tissue damage, but he's a tough auld fecker. Here's a final caution. The authorities monitor almost all international phone calls, so if you plan to phone someone looking for help, forget it. It would be best to wait until you're far away from here. Maybe someday we'll meet up, and we can reminisce over a few pints. In the meantime, all the best and guluck, Jack.

Rolling the note, Jack slid it inside the ShineOn metal tube, then dropped it into an empty five-litre plastic container, screwing the lid tightly closed. He held the container down in a rain barrel to be sure it would float, checking it was watertight. When he let it go, it popped to the surface.

Fergus woke from a light sleep as Jack entered the room.

"I'm heading off to make a delivery. It seems your lads have hitched a ride on a boat, and I've got a good idea where to find them on the river. Also, I've arranged passage on a freighter, so they'll be on their way to Belgium in a couple of days."

"Jesus, that's great news, Jack. Don't know how to thank you."

"Don't thank me yet. I still have to figure out how to get you out of here. See ya soon, won't be long."

After take-off, Jack flew a south-easterly track until passing overhead Mossaka, descending to fly low-level south, chasing the Congo River. Zigzagging along a twisty section of the river, Jack felt his heart miss a beat as his eyes widened at seeing a patrol boat coming the other way. But to his surprise, the enthusiastic waves were from the soldiers' hands and not their weapons. He'd already passed a few small vessels on the river, but nothing matched the boat's description until south of Ngabe, when he saw TitanicV.

On the first pass, Jack could see people looking up from the stern. Rocking the plane's wings, he waved down from the open left window. Before making the drop on his second pass, he waited until the river straightened, extending the flaps to slow to a minimum fly speed. Jack expected three people, but could only see Enda and a woman as he whizzed past about thirty feet above their heads. The dog at the bow growled and jumped until exhausted, becoming agitated by the flying machine. He waved the plastic container from the window before letting it drop to get their attention as he overflew. Then, easing the throttle fully forward, Jack made a left climbing turn, straining as he repeatedly glanced over his shoulder, keeping the boat in sight for as long as possible and wishing he could have done more.

From the little ship, their eyes followed the Cessna until it disappeared below the forest canopy, bringing the air display to an end. Then, almost forgetting, they turned their attention to the plastic container bobbing in the dark water. Enda reached out, trying to steady the boathook with a net attached, while the skipper slowed the boat, steering so that her crewmate could scoop the container from the river. Eager to know what was in the message, Tshala waited as he brushed his fingers across her hair, stepping alone onto the deck to read it. Wondering if the news was good or bad, barely resisting the urge to follow, she stayed put until he was ready to share the communique. Then, returning with a confused expression on his face, he handed over the letter. As she stepped back, Enda took over the helm.

"So, this is the legendary, Priest. You're very fortunate to have him as a friend."

"Yes, but read it again. Can you not see?"

"See what, Enda? What I see is, if all goes to plan, this is your ticket home. Even your captain Fergus is safe."

"It's Quinn. He must be still alive, and I left him. Jack knew about the dead hunters. He only mentions the hunters. He thinks Quinn escaped and is here with us."

She thought about the quandary before replying. "That doesn't mean he's still alive. It just means they haven't found his body. It's a big jungle out there."

Enda began to turn the boat around until Tshala, kicking his shins with her slippered feet, made him release the wheel. Then, straightening the bow, she idled the engine, letting the boat drift quietly down the river.

"I want to go back. I shouldn't have left him. Quinn was like a brother to me, and I deserted him."

Although Tshala knew there was little she could do or say to ease his distress, she also knew he wasn't thinking clearly.

"Enda, in this part of the world, emotions are best kept for the bedroom. If we go back now, we will both die. Priest was right. The longer we stay on this river, the more danger we'll be in."

"But what about the paper from the mayor, giving you safe passage?"

"It cost me more than my home to get that paper. It was either him, or him and his henchmen, so I let him rape me. Do you honestly think I'm going back there to search for a dead man?"

Tshala turned her back on Enda, but stepping forward, wrapping his arms around her waist, he rested his chin on her shoulder, and holding his lips pressed softly against her neck, they gently rocked.

With about four hours remaining until they reached the capital, the captain suggested they stop and rest for a while before departing for what could be the most challenging part of the journey. Studying the navigation chart, Tshala had often sailed the busy waters with her father, so she knew it would be best to approach Brazzaville from the north easterly channel, which would place them about five kilometres east of the airport. Despite having strong feelings towards Enda, especially after what they'd been through over the past days, the young woman was emotionally confused and desperate to understand more about her mystery passenger.

"Enda, you haven't told me the whole story about the crash, so before we go any further, I want to hear it all. I searched your duffel bag while you slept. I found a letter, but I didn't read it. That's a lot of money you're carrying around, and now, another one of those metal things drops from a plane. Please, tell me," insisted Tshala.

Knowing it was pointless to hold back any longer, he told her everything, including details of the horrific carnage at Jack's clinic.

"After me and Quinn wrote our account of what had happened, we swapped notes. The idea was to be able to corroborate our stories, in case we became separated. Somehow, the bags got switched around, and now, no one will believe me. It's only my word. I ended up with my own feckin story. The money was to buy fuel for our return flight home. I didn't realise, till a couple of days ago, that I was carrying one of the canisters. They'll want it back, so it might give me an edge, something to bargain with."

"Okay, at least it's a bit clearer. Although, from now on, let's try work things out together. We're friends, and I intend to keep you to your promise. What was it I had to do? Ah, yes. Guinness doesn't travel well, so I'll have to visit you in Dublin, for the one!"

Hauling in the ropes, her humorous remark helped to lighten the conversation. As the little ship chugged away, spluttering boiling smoky water from the engine's exhaust, the propeller churned up the muddy river bank. Nearing the end of their voyage, the canal became busier, with boats of all sizes hustling for a position. Every vessel respected a simple rule: the bigger boat has right of way. Enda wore a linen wrap and an oversized straw hat to conceal his reddened skin, and perched at the bow; the captain soon regretted asking him to call out if any boats were getting too close.

"Jesus, over there, watch that fecker, and that one there, where the fuck is he going?"

Tshala grew up on the river and was taking it all in her stride, but his nervous shrieks were beginning to make her uneasy.

"Okay, I'm fine, no more. Shut up or go below. You're driving me crazy."

Her shipmate remained on watch, although now, unless absolutely necessary, he kept his observations to himself. Enda would make her laugh out loud when, occasionally, he couldn't contain a fist-waving outburst. Arriving later than planned at Brazzaville, in the twilight, they just about managed to find a suitable mooring, almost directly abeam the international airport. Fitting snugly into the gap, the boats on either side showed no signs of life, so Tshala positioned the Rampart bow to shore, which offered better privacy from prying eyes. Then, with a final tug on the heavy rope, she bent down and stroked her dog.

"If any strangers put a foot on this boat, you have my permission to bite it off."

Deciding not to venture out during the night, they agreed that come morning; she would find a bank to exchange a few hundred-dollar bills for local CFA francs. Tshala had a bank account and was confident that once she explained about the inheritance, there would be no awkward questions about the cash.

"Hey, Tshala, maybe tomorrow it would be best if you

head back home across the river to Kinshasa, and I'll try to make my way to the airport alone."

"Really, Enda, and how long do you think you'll last, handing out hundred-dollar bills for every taxi ride? Are you trying to get rid of me?"

"For fuck's sake, yes, I'm trying to get rid of you, to keep you safe. I left Dublin with my friends a little over a week ago, expecting to return in a few days, but I'm still here. Some crazy people want me dead, and I have no one to trust but you."

"I think you're overreacting. Maybe they're not looking for you anymore. Tomorrow, why don't we go to the American Embassy and ask for their help?"

Enda thought about the suggestion for a moment, until he recalled what Jack had written and the accents of the so-called Red Cross aid workers.

"No embassy. I'm not feckin paranoid, but it's the yanks who are after me. However, I am having a problem figuring out how to get past airport security and onto the cargo ramp to board the aircraft."

"Let me help, and I'll return home to Kinshasa, when you're safely on your way."

Snuggled up in her cabin, the water lapping against the boat's hull created a gently rocking motion, and just before he slept, Enda whispered to his sleeping friend.

"Go raibh maith agat Tshala, mo ghrá."

The following morning, before she left, Enda pointed at the metal canister containing the glass tube.

"I know this might sound odd, and I hate to ask, but can you post it for me? Here's the address. If possible, pack it in one of those bubble-wrap bags, and if you get any shit while trying, dump it and walk away."

"Yes, I can do that, but I want you to keep out of sight

until I return. It will take some time, queues, always queues, and then there's the bureaucracy to deal with."

Without telling Enda, Tshala also planned to take a taxi across town to the airport's cargo office to check on the expected arrival time of the Belgian aircraft.

The bank and post office visits went without any significant hitches. Then, later, as she leaned across the counter in the small cargo office, she flirted with the dispatch agent. Tshala schemed far beyond getting information about the aircraft's arrival time, and accepted the dispatch agent's offer to head across the street to a small corner cafe. As they sat making small talk over a coffee, he placed his hand on her leg beneath the table, smugly confident he would have his way after laying five thousand CFA francs on the table. However, he quickly removed his hand when she made her counteroffer, shoving the money back at him.

"I have a friend who needs to get onto the cargo apron tonight, and we'll pay well for your assistance. However, if you accept to help and cheat me, I have other friends who will cut your balls off and feed them to you."

Tshala placed an envelope with fifty thousand francs on the table.

"Fifty now, and fifty when the aircraft gets airborne, are we agreed?"

The dispatcher looked inside the envelope, tongue licking what remained of the chocolate cake around his mouth, and nodded.

"No nods. I asked you a question, are we agreed?"

"Yes, madam, I will not cheat you. We are agreed."

Before she left the cafe, the dispatcher warned her not to be late, vowing he would meet them at midnight outside the remote staff entry gate that led to the ramp.

Enda didn't mind having some time to himself on the boat.

The demented man brushed his teeth at an extra slow pace, trying to make his thoughts follow suit, but they wouldn't. His aching ribs and doubts about the future were beginning to blur his thinking, and although the ibuprofen helped to ease the pain, his concentration faltered. Grabbing hold of the duffel bag, he emptied it onto the table. And after reading back over the note that he'd just finished writing, together with the cash, Enda rolled it up in a pillowcase, placed it in the compartment next to the blue locker, and put the revolver on top of it.

The long, refreshing cold shower made him feel good. Returning to the cabin, Enda grinned, having not earlier noticed the laundered tourist outfit he wore the day they first met, neatly laid out beside the bed. Then, lacing up his polished shoes, dressing again in his clothes felt odd, and as the smile faded, he spoke to himself.

"Yeah, if only I were dressing up for a night on the town."

Awakened at seven o'clock from a light sleep by hailstones dancing on the boat's roof, Tshala had not yet returned. Moving outside to wait in the wheelhouse, the noisy traffic and bustling city nearby glistened in the pouring rain, and when eventually the green taxi stopped alongside, overjoyed, he cried out.

"Jesus, at last."

Before getting out of the taxi, Tshala asked the driver to return at eleven to take them to the airport. Then, safely back onboard, pulling him down to sit beside her, and thrilled with excitement, she hurriedly gave her shipmate all the great news.

"You're a gem. Do you think we can trust our new friend?"

"Enda, I'm not sure how it works in Europe, but corruption is a way of life here. You could have your enemies killed for the money you're paying, and the cargo agent knows it."

Overacting, sniffing the air playfully, he already had the answer to the question.

"What's that smell?"

Before lifting the bag up onto the table, childlike, Tshala clapped her hands with delight.

"Look what I bought, fresh juicy beefburgers and fries."

The couple giggled, wolfing the food down, unashamedly behaving like starved naughty children. But, as the hours slowly passed, and with the rain pouring down, Enda became impatient, continually checking the time.

"Relax, will you? He'll be here. I told him I'd pay double."

Seeking distraction, Tshala wandered around in a half-daze. Retrieving the torn pieces of paper from the bin, and joining them together on her cabin bed, she reread his terrifying story, often pausing to clear her wet eyes. Then, reaching into a drawer, she opened a notebook; it was a good time to write words from the heart to her new friend. When she returned from her cabin, Enda appeared eager to talk about their future, but when he raised the subject, she pressed a finger to his lips.

"You must go home tonight, and later; if you still want to talk about that, this is how you can find me."

Tshala crammed the folded letter she had just finished writing into his shirt pocket and hugged him tightly.

By ten-thirty, Enda couldn't wait any longer, convincing her it would be best if they went to the street and try to wave down any taxi. Earlier that day, when she was in the city market, Tshala bought two long green ex-army capes. Although the capes worked well against the rain, they sweated so much that their clothes were already wet as they stood waving at every car that passed. Then, as agreed, a taxi pulled up just before eleven, and the driver leaned over to shove open the back door.

"Why are you waiting in the rain? I said I would beep my horn?"

In the back seat, the couple pulled the hoods of their drenched capes down, and as she squeezed Enda's hand, the car rattled and rolled over the rough potholed surface. The single wiper blade kept a beat like a piano metronome, and, as if trying to self-destruct, it slammed left and right against the windscreens frame. Arriving before midnight at the gate, they anxiously peered through the half-open window for any movement on the ramp. In case she forgot, Enda again reminded Tshala to check the revolver, explaining he wasn't sure if he'd put the safety on. Then, a loud thump on the car's roof suddenly made everyone flinch.

"You're early; that's okay, that's good. Please come with me," said the man in the bright yellow jacket.

Enda tried to make Tshala stay in the taxi, but she wouldn't listen. So, holding hands tightly, they slowly took their final steps together, and before he passed through the small gate, the lovers embraced as if it was to be their last. She tried to look one last time into his eyes, but the dark, wet night denied her. Becoming impatient, the cargo agent urged Enda to end the farewell and didn't look up at the distraught woman as he locked the gate behind him.

"Hey, lady, wait for me here. They will depart soon. Please, show me the money."

The raindrops mixed with her tears, and gripping the chain-link fence like a frightened caged tarsier, Tshala's fingers ached, as she watched the ghostlike image on the waterlogged ramp fade into the night.

Sitting on the rear steps of the Boeing 727 freighter, a man stood up, pointing his powerful torch in their direction, prompting the cargo agent to make a hasty farewell. Enda continued walking, and dazzled by the bright light; he tried to shade his eyes with his hands.

"Hey, can you lower the flashlight?"

The loadmaster switched off the torch and shouted an invitation for the passenger to board the aircraft. Then, without speaking a word, they walked the passageway between the stacked freight, and just before reaching the flight deck, the loadmaster sidestepped, waving Enda past. Just as it was on the DC8, the three crew members sat at their stations, and were about to commence the before-start checklist.

Speaking in a monotone, the captain turned to face the distrusted guest.

"I would like you to please pay attention to what I have to say, and as you claim to work for an airline, you should understand the extent of my authority. However, before I begin, I have a question. Do good cigars come in a tube?"

Enda understood, and reaching into his duffel, he held the empty metal canister out in front of him.

"Excellent. Now, once again, heed my words. I was not pleased when my boss asked me to cooperate, to permit a person without identity papers onboard my aircraft. I told him my conditions, now I'm telling you. First, my loadmaster will search you for weapons. There will be no social interaction with my crew, and you must not enter this cockpit again, unless I permit it. On arrival at Ostend, we will claim you were a stowaway. You'll be handed over to the Belgian authorities for them to determine your fate. Help yourself to food and drink; you will find dry clothing in one of the lockers. I expected two people."

"Just me. My friend, Quinn, didn't make it."

"Fine, now please excuse us, and close the door behind you."

Enda understood the risk the crew were taking, and before he left, he wanted to have his say.

"I am as innocent as you, and maybe, someday, you will realise you made the right decision by helping me. I had no option but to leave my crew behind, and, for all I know, I might never see them again. Anyway, thank you."

It had been a long while since Enda buckled into a jump seat, and as he sat listening to the familiar sounds of hatches slamming shut and the high pitch whizzing of hydraulic motors, he felt an emptiness. Then, the whine of the first engine start drifted through the cabin and into his soul. Closing his eyes, he tried to visualise every stage of the departure until the positive g-force launched him with a heavy heart into the night sky.

The taxi window was slightly open, and when the cargo agent returned, he called out from the locked gate.

"That's them. They're taking off now."

Tshala leapt out, staring to where the driver pointed. The noise was like thunder, and its strobe lights twinkled a few times before the plane vanished, consumed by a blanket of low-lying clouds.

After returning to the boat, her dog yodelled and wagged its tail as she led it to the shelter of the wheelhouse. Tshala's life had changed, and instead of the independence she once cherished, she felt an awakening, a need to share her life again. Below deck, after opening the compartment, the revolver's safety was on, although under the gun was something that wasn't there before. Emptying the pillow-case stuffed with cash onto the bed, she found a hand-written letter, and sitting below the oil lantern, she began reading in the dim light.

Tshala, I don't know how it came to be, but I've fallen in love with you. In the beginning, I thought I was just reaching out for comfort, trying to escape the mayhem. But that was only a tiny part of it. I'm in a relationship, so when I get home, I plan to talk with my girlfriend, Aoife. Not sure how well that will go; I doubt if she'll understand. It won't be long before I find out how much shit I'm in, so please, until then, you must not try to make contact until this is over. Phone my godfather if you haven't heard from me in a few weeks. I'll tell him to expect your call and, should anything bad happen to me, he will know how to find you.

As for the money, maybe you should invest in a bigger boat, and when I return, who knows, perhaps we can start a little charter business. Tshala, my contact details are written below. Stay safe, see ya soon—Enda xxx.

The loadmaster came and sat next to the young engineer.

"Well, son, you're quite a mystery man. We don't usually carry live cargo, and what's with the pharmacy in your bag?"

By the accent, Enda correctly guessed Glaswegian.

"I think it best we keep our distance. Don't you remember? Your skipper laid down the law when I boarded."

"Ahh, don't mind yer man; he's harmless. Ex-Belgian Air Force, god's gift to aviation, takes himself a bit too seriously."

"What's your name? Which airline do you work for? What's your job? Which aircraft?"

"Listen, I don't mean to be rude, but can you leave it? I've got a whole load of shit coming down, and to be honest, the less any of you know about me, the better."

"Nae bother, sounds very serious, but I can live with that. Did ya find a change of clothes?"

"I did. I like the jumpsuit; gonna change later. Are you permitted to tell me about tonight's flight schedule?"

"Aye, well, we're going to make a fuel stop at Tiska in Algeria, and after that, it'll be a straight run home. Should arrive in Belgium around ten-ish in the morning. I hear there will be a welcoming party waiting to greet ya."

Enda wasn't sure how to take the remark, deciding to dismiss it for a touch of Scottish black humour.

"Believe me; I'll be pleased to meet the welcoming party."

"Listen, buddy. I'm not trying to pry. You know it's a small world in the freight game, so maybe ya know some of me, loadmaster mates."

The Scotsman watched Enda's facial expression as he spoke their names.

"Johnny Reed, he's a Scot like me. Peter Hurly, a paddy flying the pond, and Berko, ex RAF, I think he's also on the...."

Enda flinched, stopping the questioning in mid-sentence.

"No, I don't know any of them. I didn't do much airfreight."

"Nae problem, I'll give ya a bit of peace now. Oh, by the way, the old man said I was to tell ya not to leave the aircraft during the refuelling at Tiska."

After landing, they taxied to the ramp, and as the doors began to open, a flood of chilled, fresh night desert air rushed in. With little else to do, Enda walked to the rear of the aircraft and sat midway down the rear steps, watching as the colossal fuel bowser arrived to replenish the tanks. Enda quickly stood, leaning to one side, making way for the captain coming up the narrow steps.

"I see you preferred the jumpsuit. You may keep it. Is everything else okay? Did you get enough to eat?"

"Yes, captain, everything is fine, thanks."

Within forty minutes, they were airborne again, tracking

northwest towards the Mediterranean Sea and, for the Irishman, closer to safety. When the beautiful ancient city of Constantine passed thirty-eight thousand feet below, Enda was in a deep sleep, and not even the intense rays from the sublime sunrise could wake him. However, a short time later, he slowly regained awareness when the seatbelt sign lit up with a loud chime as the aircraft entered an area of turbulence. The loadmaster strapped himself into the adjacent seat, and gazing out through the window, he tried to get his bearings.

"Ya were away with the fairies, so I didn't disturb. That's Marseilles down there. It won't be long now."

During the descent, the French controller transferred them to Brussels ATC, and the captain keyed the microphone.

"Control, this is Freight Line Six, inbound Ostend. Please be advised we have a stowaway onboard, requesting police assistance upon arrival."

After the controller had acknowledged the unusual request, the captain gave the twenty minutes to landing call over the interphone. It was a bright, cold morning, and touching gently down on the easterly runway, they taxied slowly to the cargo apron. One of the two officers leaning against the police car stomped his half-smoked cigarette. Watching for the marshaller to signal engine shutdown, they scrambled up the rear steps the moment they were lowered. Then, hurrying from the flight deck to confront the policemen, the captain held his hands above his head.

"Whoa, take it easy; he's not a murderer. This man was mugged and slipped aboard our aircraft to escape the assailants. Please, treat him well."

One of the officers stood tall in front of Enda.

"Sir, you have entered Belgium illegally. Therefore, we

must place you under arrest, and, apologies, we must hand-cuff you."

Silently watching as the prisoner was escorted from the aircraft, the crew pondered the mystery of the young man's true identity.

In the interrogation room at the city's central police station, Enda sat opposite two plain-clothes detectives.

"Sir, we must establish the facts and would like your cooperation. Firstly, you will be fingerprinted, and then we'll take a few photographs. But, for now, please state your full name, date of birth, and nationality."

After giving the officers the information, the prisoner felt oddly liberated, as his battered confidence began to grow.

"Well, Enda, that's a nasty-looking bruise on your fore-head, so after you answer a few more questions, we'll transfer you to our local hospital for medical assessment. Please, tell us how you ended up here in Flanders?"

"Thank you, officer. I understand you're doing your job, but before I say anything more, I have a few questions of my own. To begin, I'd like to make a phone call, and secondly, I've already told you enough. Now, I would like you to tell me who I am."

"Very well, you may return to your cell, or if you wish, wait here while we process the information. We'll discuss the phone call, after we see the hospital report."

Enda accepted the cigarettes, coffee, and biscuits. It wasn't long before the detective returned and laid the newly prepared file on the table.

"Well, sir, may I be the first to welcome you back from the dead. According to our colleagues in Ireland, you, and your crew, were killed in a plane crash in Congo several days ago."

Enda had no reply, as the surreal words reverberated in his head.

* * *

Outside his hospital room, a uniformed officer stood on guard. Enda was pacing up and down when two doctors and a nurse entered. While one of the doctors read through the single page on a clipboard, the other spoke in a matter-of-fact voice.

"Sir, you are very welcome. Please be seated. The x-rays show two cracked ribs. However, besides mild concussion, you appear to be in good physical health. We have spoken with the police, and please do not take this the wrong way, but we are more concerned about your mental health."

Enda suppressed the urge to scream.

"It is not unusual after a traumatic event and, especially after a concussion, the mind can become confused and play tricks with reality. Therefore, for your well-being, we think it best to confine you for a few days, while we carry out some more tests."

The engineer could no longer contain himself. "I thank you all for your concern. However, please listen carefully to me. I am not confused, and I am no longer a prisoner. I want to speak with an official from my embassy, immediately."

Although the medical staff tried to reason, they were cut short.

"You heard what I said, doctor. Jesus, I'm not even permitted to make a phone call, and there's an armed guard at my door. I've had enough. The embassy, now."

It was late evening, and Enda was listening to classical music on the radio when there was a knock on his door. A moment later, a tall, elderly man, dressed in a dark suit and carrying a leather attaché case entered.

"Hello, young man. I've been sent by the embassy to assist."

After a short greeting, Enda laid down his wishes plainly, while the elderly man took notes.

"Okay, sir, this is what I'm going to do. The police gave me one of the photos they took of you. It has a dated stamp on the back, so I'll attach it to the temporary papers permitting you to travel home. I think it best we use an ambulance flight out of Ostend, and with a little luck, you'll be on your way by tomorrow."

Before the consul left, Enda squeezed his hand and pleaded with him to get his bedside phone reconnected. It was almost midnight when he turned the radio's volume down. About to try to get some sleep, he noticed the green light above the phone's keypad. Enda moved the receiver close to his ear, and on hearing the dial tone, his hand shook. Then, overwhelmed by a rush of emotion, he hung up and spoke aloud.

"Oh, sweet Jesus, what am I going to say? They'll never believe me."

CHAPTER THIRTY-SEVEN

Tumper was stretched out on the sofa when the phone rang. As his fingers ran gentle strokes along the dog's shiny coat, he began to doze off again. It was late, and he wasn't interested in making any more taxi runs, so he just let it ring out until, a minute later, it rang again.

"For fuck's sake, it's after midnight. What do you want?"

"Tumper, it's me, Enda."

From earlier activities, Tumper had learned the art of self-discipline. However, as every tendon in his body stiffened, that control was slipping away.

"I'm sorry to do it like this. It's not a joke. It's me. I survived."

Tumper was confused, and when he finally spoke, his voice trembled, and everything became blurry through his watery eyes.

"Where are you, son? You're going to have to help me out here. I don't frighten easily, but you've just managed to scare me half to death."

Enda hesitated, words in his head tripping over themselves.

"Listen to me, can't say much now. I'm okay. I'm in

Belgium. Don't tell anyone I phoned, at least not yet. I'll call again tomorrow, when I have the flight details. Can you collect me from the airport?"

"Of course, I can, but..."

"I'll say no more for the moment except, trust me. I'll see you tomorrow."

Tumper hung up the phone and, deep in thought, began stroking his dog again, until suddenly, the animal leapt off the sofa, misinterpreting the shaking hand as a command from his master.

It was just past midday when the man from the embassy returned.

"Right then, young Enda, it's all arranged. However, you'll have to go along with a tad of protocol. We don't want this to become a diplomatic shambles, at least not for us at the Irish embassy. So, in about an hour, you'll be taken by ambulance to the airport, where you will board a privately chartered plane. Then, on your arrival in Dublin, you'll be taken by ambulance to the hospital, under Garda escort."

Enda accepted the gifted three-quarter-length Helly Hansen jacket and, not ready to discard the rest of his clothes, he turned down the offer of the new two-piece suit. Before getting dressed, he removed the elasticated bandage from around his chest. There would be more pain, but at least now, he could breathe.

Tumper had cancelled his bookings for the day, and waited restlessly for the phone to ring.

"It's me again, still in Belgium. Although they said, we should be on our way shortly. Expecting to land around four o'clock, and then to the hospital, so can you follow us."

He immediately regretted mentioning hospital. The

word set alarm bells ringing in Tumper's head, and it took Enda a while to calm him down, before he could continue.

"The ambulance will be parked outside the old terminal building, and don't go getting upset about the Garda escort; they said it's just protocol."

From the moment they collected him from his room, Enda was impressed by how the authorities dealt with his repatriation. The young Irish man received the royal treatment from his Belgian liberators, each performing their tasks with total efficiency, until he reached Dublin.

CHAPTER THIRTY-EIGHT

As Enda stepped down from the Cessna Citation, the detective Garda with the rough Dublin accent, introduced himself.

"Jaysis, fella, you've caused a bit of a commotion. C'mere til I tell ya, I hope you weren't getting up to any divilment?"

Enda dug deep, resisting the strong urge to go on the defensive.

"Thanks very much, Garda. Yes, it's good to be home."

On duty outside his hospital room, the smiley-faced policewoman got up from her chair and knocked before entering.

"There's a man here who wants to see you."

Tumper didn't wait for an invite and walked in behind the Garda, who reacted by grabbing hold of her wooden baton.

"Garda, it's okay. He's my friend. Leave us, please?"

His godfather felt awkward, keeping his distance from the bed.

"Fuck, did someone beat you up?"

The response was immediate, and half expected.

"Should have seen the other fella."

Enda absorbed the pain with ease, as the men rushed to embrace in the small room of the Mater Hospital. After much objecting, the patient eventually agreed to get back into bed. Then, dragging an easy chair alongside, Tumper had a lot on his mind.

"Ya know, son, this will be all over the media by morning, and I'm struggling to take it in. Can we expect to see any more resurrections?"

"There might still be hope for Quinn and Fergie, although Berko... Berko isn't coming back. As for the two yanks, fuck knows. So, brace yourself, Tumper. I'm going to tell you a little about what happened over there."

The godfather listened without interrupting, while Enda struggled to recall the horror of the previous days.

"Then, last night, I finally got to use a phone. You were the only one I could trust to call. I'm frightened, Tumper. I don't know how to handle this. I can't figure out how it's all going to end."

"Son, I know you're not lying. I'm trying to make sense of what you've just told me. Parts of it sound plausible. Even so, I still can't get my head around it. You've been through some serious trauma and need time to heal. You understand what I mean, time to recover. But, please, promise you won't repeat what you told me to anyone. Instead, offer the media jackals another version, and keep Quinn and Fergie in the grave, just for now. Tell them what they expect to hear."

Enda wasn't surprised by the reaction. Every time he recalled what happened, he also had difficulty believing it himself.

"Okay, I'll do as you say. But first, we have to make contact with Jack Reilly. If it weren't for him, I wouldn't be here today. Jack helped us escape and said he would take care of Fergie. Here, check this out, Tumper. When have you ever seen a cigar tube made of titanium? And this? How did I get Berko's insignia ring? Also, what about the woman who helped me escape, and while I'm on the subject, can you please give Aoife the news?"

"Jesus, no, what am I supposed to tell her?"

"Tumper, as you already said, this will soon be all over the media. She will find out anyway. At least coming from you, it should be a bit easier for her to handle. She trusts you."

Enda slid the photo from the paper-clipped travel documents and handed it to Tumper.

"If she doesn't believe you, give her this. On the back of the photo, the time and date were rubberstamped by the police."

Before leaving the hospital, Tumper phoned Aoife and asked if he could drop by for a chat.

CHAPTER THIRTY-NINE

A t Langley headquarters, the Director of Special Operations summoned agents Sable and Bluey to his office.

"There has been a serious development. It would appear that I, or to put it more correctly, we, have a situation. Damnit, ShineOn was showing such promise, but matters are getting out of hand, becoming messy and volatile, if you get my drift. We thought we had that little calamity in the jungle under wraps. But now it seems that one of the crew hitched a ride on a Belgian freighter out of Brazzaville. Also, we're certain he couldn't have managed it without help. Even worse, he might have one of the canisters, and now, according to intelligence, he's back in Ireland. More than likely shouting his mouth off. On the other hand, even if he does, who will listen to him? As I understand it, the doctors consider him delusional and unbalanced. And as for the pilot in Congo, we haven't decided what to do with him yet. He could become useful—an opportunity to apply pressure on his friend in Dublin, or even for some good old-fashioned propaganda. Then, there's the frigging captain. Not sure where he got to."

Bluey glanced at Sable, before focusing his attention on his boss.

"This is indeed unfortunate news, sir. How may we assist?"

"I think it has to be you, agent Bluey. Isn't it true you served as LRRP in Vietnam? Weren't you credited with the highest number of enemy officer terminations, correct?"

Bluey stiffened and, scarcely able to contain his emotions, he saluted.

"Affirm, sir, I do concur."

"Right then. Unfortunately, agent Sable, this will be a solo mission, and agent Bluey will have the honours. You leave for Dublin tomorrow, dismissed. Sable, please remain seated."

She waited anxiously while the director jotted down notes before clearing his desk.

"Okay, Sable, I want you to visit Deckleshine at the research centre. I only have a few agents left entrusted with this mission, and you're one of them. I'm sure you read or heard the news about the immune deficiency epidemic, a frigging national disaster. Could be over a million people infected. Those cocksuckers have even infected our nation's blood stockpiles. We have to end this, and we're going to flush them out. Deckleshine has inadvertently come up with a solution, and tests have shown how effective it can be. The crucial thing is it only targets the filthy enemy. In Congo, we recently carried out a very successful field trial. But, unfortunately, during the mission, it cost us three of our finest agents."

"Yes, Sir, I'm already aware of the situation, but may I inquire, which Congo?"

"What do you mean, which Congo? Denis Nguesso's Congo, the one in Africa, of course. Anyway, I instructed our friend, the professor, to develop a souped-up version. It's now ready, and I want you to go down and fetch it, then bring it to me in person."

Agent Sable nodded in agreement.

"Sable, I hope you understand; the stakes could not be higher. We're dealing with a national menace. We may have to go on the offensive, so I will need strong, loyal soldiers if we are to triumph. Can I depend on you, agent Sable?"

"I'm aware of the danger our great nation faces. So yes, sir, you can depend on my loyalty."

"Good. I've instructed the professor to cease further development of ShineOn. It's perfect as it is. He was ordered to prepare four individual canisters of the concentrated, more potent version of this outstanding protective shield, and it appears it should be ready for collection very soon. Make your arrangements. You may use the Gulfstream. Dismissed."

CHAPTER FORTY

By the time Tumper arrived, Aoife had the table set with tea and his favourite chocolate biscuits, determined to show how well she was coping.

"Thanks for calling. It's great to see you, but what could be so important at this hour of the night?"

"Ahh, nothing much. I was just passing. How are things?"

Deep in his jacket pocket, Tumper rubbed the photo between his fingers before placing it on the table, covering it with his hand.

"Well, I've some great news. The agency accepted my offer on the apartment. So, it looks like I'll be staying right where I am. Isn't that brilliant?"

Tumper didn't reply as he slid his hand away from the photo, waiting for Aoife to pick it up.

"I don't remember seeing this picture before; who took it? Is it from one of your albums?"

As she examined it, her curiosity grew. After a glance at the back, she ran her finger across the face she still loved.

"It's not very flattering, is it? Looks more like a police mugshot."

Aoife was handing the photo back to Tumper, when he leaned away.

"Aoife, take another look at the back, please."

Dumbstruck with fright, she repeatedly turned the photo from front to back.

"Are you trying to tell me he's alive? Is that what you're trying to say?"

"Yes, he's alive, Aoife. The lad survived."

* * *

Enda was going through his belongings, and was about to bin his tourist clothes, when he remembered that Tshala had stuffed a letter into the shirt pocket.

"Well, my dear cheeky monkey, just kidding. I've been thinking, did my parents spirit you into my life? I remember them giving me advice on how to recognise the right man; he never sounded anything like you. You're probably back home by now with your loved ones, and distance has a way of making memories fade. So, don't forget about me when you get your life back. But try to hurry up, because you owe me a pint. Love and miss you, Tshala.

Oh, by the way, I recovered the torn paper from the bin and patched it up with Sellotape. You might regret throwing your story away someday, so I'll keep it safe until you return."

After reading the letter, in a near panic, Enda grabbed at the bedside phone. He'd begun dialling the international country code for Kinshasa, when suddenly he stopped, fearful that someone would be listening in—not wishing to imagine what would happen if the wrong people found her with that letter.

"Fuck, the calls are monitored. It'll only draw attention to her."

The nurse with the freckled face entered his room, holding a pen and notebook.

"You should be asleep young man. Is this what you need? Don't make it too late. Here, take this; it'll help you to rest. I'll check back on you later."

Enda tried to blot out the growing worry about Tshala as he prepared to write the significantly modified version of the events for the press.

It started out as a routine flight, until we developed problems with a fuel leak. By the time we reached Ouésso, the weather had deteriorated, so we diverted. However, we didn't have enough fuel to make our alternate airport. We had no option but to put her down on a small airstrip near the rainforest. The captain and co-pilot did everything possible, but the runway was too short. After landing, there was a huge bang. I think the wing must have caught something, and suddenly there was a lot of smoke. It was dense and toxic. I could hardly see anything. However, I managed to open an exit door. Next thing, the blast blew me down the escape slide, and the aircraft burst into flames. No one could have survived. After the fire died down, I managed to recover some supplies from the bellyhold, and waited for help at the edge of the forest. When I first saw the tribe of pygmy hunters, I thought it was over, but they were friendly and took me with them. We must have been tracking south for days. When we eventually reached a small village, I managed to get passage on a fishing boat downstream to Braz-zaville. The rest is history. You probably heard rumours or other versions of the event. Well, I'm sorry if it disappoints; this is the only real one. Now, I wish to be left alone. I need space to rebuild my life.

Enda lay back on the pillow, and everything felt calm as the Valium filtered through his blood and into his weary brain.

CHAPTER FORTY-ONE

At the military base in Owando, the former sergeant was surprised, and proudly accepted his promotion to lieutenant for his handling of the American calamity. In particular, his superiors were especially impressed when he didn't hesitate to sacrifice his men in the line of duty. And although he was the only person in the room, he stood to attention, listening carefully, as orders were read out over the phone from Brazzaville.

"There's a yank; you met him before. He will arrive by road from Brazza. You must greet him warmly, and you will be his willing servant. One other thing, the American made a request; well, it was more of a demand. He wants the interior of the BTR, and your men, scrubbed clean for the mission."

CHAPTER FORTY-TWO

Jack was sitting on his veranda, when two hunters came running from the forest.

"Priest, soldiers are coming, maybe two hours."

Jack couldn't imagine what they might want, but he wasn't surprised.

"Government or rebels?" he asked.

He knew it would be easier dealing with government troops, so he relaxed a little, figuring that maybe one of them was injured and needed medical attention.

"Okay, Captain Fergus. Your leg is still a mess, and I didn't want to move you, but we've no choice. Soldiers will be here soon."

"Where am I going?" asked Fergus.

"Don't you worry about that? I've been expecting a visit, so it's all prepared. Four of the hunters will carry you by stretcher. They might be small, but they're as strong as horses. Anyway, you can't weigh more than a flea; you're not exactly a heavyweight. Here, take these with you. I have written the dosage on the bottles. Go easy on the morphine. They know how to change your dressing, so just let them get on with it. You'll be safe enough. They'll take you to a village, not too far away."

"Jesus, Jack, I'm sorry for bringing this shit down on you."

"It'll be fine. I'll catch up with ya later."

Not long after arriving in Congo, Jack had learnt how futile it was to try and stay dry. If it wasn't rain, it was the humidity that left him in wet clothes for most of the day, and he'd gotten used to it. But even now, years later, he still found trying to smoke a cigarette the most challenging pleasure. Under the shelter of the corrugated roof, the chair creaked as Jack leaned back and marvelled at how the Belgians had constructed the mining camp. The entire area beneath the Laterite had an elaborate water drainage system. There wasn't a single puddle on the surface, even after a heavy downpour. Then, lighting up again, his thoughts drifted to Ireland.

"I'll bet they could teach us a thing or two about road building," thought Jack, beginning to tense on hearing the approaching engines.

The troop carrier came to a halt in the middle of the small square in front of Jack's cabin. Heavily armed soldiers clambered out through the hatches and spread out, creating a cordon, while the lieutenant, his torso protruding up through the forward hatch, shouted down orders. In the middle of the action, a couple of lean Teke tribesmen, scantily dressed in loincloth, with AK47 rifles slung around their necks, leapt off the armoured roof and trotted towards the forest. Jack remained seated and was surprised to see Pepe emerge from a side hatch. The American sauntered over with his head down, glancing left and right as he strutted up the steps and sat opposite Jack.

"I didn't think I'd be seeing you again. Would you like a

dry towel?" asked Jack, hoping to be considered the perfect host by the intruder.

While Pepe made himself comfortable in the bamboo chair, he ran the towel across his face and shoulders before massaging his short black hair.

"Well, Jack, to be honest, nor did I reckon we'd be getting together this soon. Hey, because of you, my colleagues stateside cancelled my compassionate leave so that we could have this little reunion."

"What can I do for you, Pepe?"

"The first thing you can do is tell your little band of miniature gladiators to stand down, before they get hurt."

Stern-faced, Jack shouted a few words, and, without hesitation, the tribespeople retreated, lowering their spears.

"I see you brought that thieving sergeant along with you," Jack snarled.

"Who? You mean our newly promoted lieutenant?"

"So, that's how they reward thieves. He stole a large sum of cash from me. It was in my Cessna at the crash site."

After Pepe bellowed at the lieutenant, he hurried over and stood soaked to the skin, facing the seated foreigners.

"My friend, Priest, accuses you of stealing money from him."

"He lies American. I would not steal from Priest."

"Well, I don't believe you, lieutenant. This matter will be investigated with your commanding officer when we return to base. Dismissed."

Before the reprimanded soldier retreated to the troop carrier, he paused, brazenly glaring contemptuously towards his accuser.

There was a period of quiet, as Pepe appeared to be deep in thought, before he spoke again, this time in earnest.

"I suppose being isolated out here, it's hard to keep up with the latest news, so let me update you. Do you recall our chat at Ouésso? You were given a caution. It went something like this. Do not try to investigate this event further; we know all about you…et cetera, et cetera. Well, we now know where one of the pilots is being held, and someone helped him. It's a place called Mossaka, you must know it, the small fishing village where the Shanga and Congo Rivers converge. A group of Angolan mercenaries are holding him captive in the village, demanding a ransom for his release. We've been trading messages back and forth with them. These dickheads seem to be well informed. They think they've been negotiating with the airline boss. In fact, it was us, and shortly we're going to pay them a surprise visit. However, I don't understand why we're getting involved at all. My boss mentioned leverage and propaganda. Jesus, they want one million US dollars, the cheeky bastards."

Jack tried to act surprised by the revelations.

"That will be great news for his family, especially if he manages to avoid getting himself accidentally killed during his liberation. Hey, and what about the other one?"

"Ah, Jack. We also know where he is, in Dublin. However, we can't figure out how he got there. Any ideas? Then, of course, there's the captain. I could have killed him. But, instead, I was merciful. Now, look where that's gotten me. Have you any suggestion where he might be?"

"You told me to keep out of it, so I did."

"Your Cessna was spotted by a naval patrol buzzing a riverboat near Ngabe. Who was on that boat, and why were you there? They said you were flying so low; they thought you were going to crash."

"Okay, yes, I was in the area and heard they might be on the river, so I dropped down to take a look. It wasn't them, just another fishing boat."

The lieutenant ambled back to the veranda, and whispered to Pepe.

"Our loyal Teke trackers found the trail. They say about one, maybe two hours, direction southeast."

"Tell them to take the captain alive. We'll rendezvous at Mossaka," ordered the American.

Suddenly, Pepe stood and, hand raised high, made a circling motion with his index finger. The soldiers ran to the clinic and dragged two of the tribes' women, gripping them by the hair. They held machete blades against their throats, forcing them to kneel facing the veranda.

"What the fuck are you doing?" said Jack. "Are you mad? Have you taken leave of your senses?"

"You were warned, yet you continue with your bullshit."

Pepe signalled the first soldier to move closer.

"You have ten seconds. Was he on the boat?"

"Why should it matter now? For fucks sake, he's in Dublin, and yes, he was on the fucking boat. Now, release her."

The woman sobbed with fear as the soldier lowered the blade, and when he released his grip on her hair, she fell to the ground.

"So, what was the name of the boat?"

Jack hesitated. He knew the agent was bluffing, but by the count of seven, he shouted aloud the word Titanic. As the soldier released the second nurse, Pepe grinned.

"You've got to be making that up, Jack. Anyway, before we depart, there's just one last matter. I've been ordered to check the papers of your aircraft and Land Rover."

Jack returned with an air of confidence from his cabin, carrying two separate wallets.

"It's all in order. This is for the Cessna, and this one is for the jeep."

After flicking through the documents, Pepe handed the wallets to the nearest soldier.

"Mister Priest, you are suspected of using these

machines for illegal activities, and, in such matters, I am authorised by Brazza to confiscate or destroy them."

Jack's protest was silenced as Pepe stepped forward. Pushing the barrel of his pistol into his stomach, he roared at the lieutenant in the BTR, and after making the victory sign above his head, Pepe pointed towards the airstrip.

The soldiers' actions were swift. In a concurrent manoeuvre, they lobbed hand grenades into the aeroplane and jeep, slamming the doors shut before diving to the ground. Then, on hearing the explosions, Pepe holstered his pistol, lit a cigarette, and sat back down.

"Well, Priest, it looks like you're all the way back to where you started. Be grateful, because if it weren't for your special friend in Brazzaville, you would have ended up in one of them, dead."

Jack was frozen in deep thought before raising his head.

"It's over for me. I only bring death, misery, and false hope to these gentle tribespeople. A long time ago, I made an impulsive decision to come here. Now, I'm making a calculated one to leave. Let me travel back to Brazzaville with you. From there, I can catch a flight away from this place. Also, my Irish accent could be useful when dealing with the hostage-takers."

"Jesus, you're full of surprises. Are you frigging serious?"

Pepe removed the sat phone from his pocket to call in the request, and, to his astonishment, it was granted.

"You know something Jack, you're a proper pain in the ass. Yet, oddly, I do enjoy your company. How much time do you need?"

CHAPTER FORTY-THREE

The sneeze that woke Enda from a deep sleep sent him curling up into the foetal position, moaning from the pain darting across his chest.

"Fuck, that hurt."

The breakfast tray was on the over-bed table, and the coffee pot was still hot to the touch. It was just after 7am, and with the pain lingering, he moved carefully to sit upright, wedging a pillow against his back. Sipping the warm coffee, he began reading over his press statement and was surprised at how convincing it sounded. Then, sliding his feet across the linen sheets to the cold tiled floor, the phone rang. Aoife spoke apologetically.

"Enda, it's me."

She thought how ridiculous the words must sound, talking to a ghost, so, raising her voice, she tried again.

"Enda, you can't imagine what it's like making this phone call. I'm sorry, I tried to prepare, but now I hardly know what to say."

"You're right, Aoife. I can't imagine."

"Tumper was over. He said you'd need some time, so I won't bother you for long. One of my pals is a nurse at the hospital; that's how I got your number. I'm sorry, I just wanted to hear your voice."

"You're not bothering me at all. Can you come over around lunchtime? We'll talk then?"

After the call, he hurried to the bathroom, and looking at his image in the mirror; he wondered if she would see the guilt on his face. Then, while Enda pondered the meaning of guilt, leaning back against the wall for support, Aoife slid down and sat cross-legged on the kitchen floor, hugging the receiver between her breasts as she wept.

Tumper arrived at the hospital around eleven and handed Enda a small package, along with the freshly baked pastries.

"Ah, my favourite, but what's this?"

He removed the scorched watch with the melted plastic face, and held it up.

"Isn't that your watch, lad? And here, take a look at that photo. You're still in your engineer's seat on the aircraft, a cinder. Do you know who took that photo?"

Enda shook his head while handing his godfather the press statement. Then, after rereading it, Tumper took his time, trying to weigh up the pros and cons of the subterfuge.

"Well, from what you told me yesterday, we know this isn't what happened, but I get it."

"So, we agree then, that's all they're getting for now. I was going to ask you to hand it over to the press fellas, but Aoife is calling soon. If you don't mind, I'll ask her to do it. Also, some good news. I'm gonna be discharged in a couple of days, and I was wondering if I could use your spare bedroom, just until I get sorted. It'll only be for a short while."

"You don't have to ask. Of course, you can stay as long as you like. I'm not going to push the issue now. However, we must have a serious chat soon about all of this. Did you hear from the company yet?"

"Nope, nada."

Deciding a change of subject was in order, the men had settled into a diverting catch-up chat, when there was a knock on the door.

"There's a lady called Aoife to see you," said the nurse.

Tumper checked his watch, and muttering excuses, he hurried away, as Aoife, glowing with joy, ran across the room about to wrap her arms around her man, but he stopped her, arms outstretched, his hands firmly against her shoulders.

"Jesus, I'm sorry, Aoife. They're still running tests, in case I caught something in the jungle. So, be careful. I could be infected."

Brushing his hands aside with a dampened smile, Aoife grabbed hold, and hugged him passionately.

"I don't care if you're carrying the plague. We're together again, you're alive."

As the twosome sat chatting, fingers entwined on the bed, Enda felt nervously clumsy. Then, not wishing to cause her more pain, he became uncertain about how much he should say.

"Aoife, a lot has happened, and I'm all fucked up. I'm going to stay with Tumper for a few days, and then I think I'll head to the cottage. I need some time to myself."

"I understand, Enda. Take all the time you need. You know I'm here for you, day, or night. Did Tumper tell you I changed my mind about moving away?"

The young couple became reacquainted, even managing a few hearty laughs, although, for Aoife, something was missing. Her man was damaged.

CHAPTER FORTY-FOUR

Unable to move a muscle, the captain lay cradled in a hammock-like stretcher made from animal skins, with leather straps at each end, lashed to a long thick bamboo pole. Briskly, the hunters trotted from the compound in perfect unison, and looking up at the grey sky, Fergus was drenched by the warm rain. Then, in an instant, it stopped, as the enormous trees gave shelter, turning the forest into near darkness, with creatures high up in the canopy chirping or screaming warnings of approaching danger. One of the hunters led the way, followed by the stretcher-bearers, while the fourth kept guard at the rear, and zigzagging along narrow tracks for an age, they never seemed to tire. Fergus had no way to communicate, yet instinctively his minders seemed to know when he was getting distressed, and they would rest. On the damp forest floor, Fergus managed to sit upright to drink from his canteen while the hunters squatted together nearby.

Suddenly, they all leapt to their feet, gesturing towards Fergus to be still. Then, when the stretcher-bearers then raised the bamboo pole onto their shoulders, the captain was forced to lay back as they began to sprint, running even faster than before. The other two hunters remained behind, disappearing into the underbrush. With every stride, the wet leather straps snapped hard against the flexing bamboo shaft, causing Fergus to grimace with pain. Thin patches of mist hovered in the late evening light as they entered the small settlement, encircled by half a dozen straw-roofed huts. After gently lowering him on a patch of soggy ground, the tribespeople gathered around to greet the new arrivals, and the captain called out in distress.

"Help me stand. Please, help me up."

One of the hunters leaned over. Easing Fergus's shoulders back onto the stretcher, he spoke quietly, placing a finger to the captain's lips.

"Silencieux."

In an instant, the tribespeople and hunters scattered, vanishing into the forest without a sound. Fergus was searching his pocket for the morphine pills when the Teke trackers arrived and stood with the barrels of their AK47s pointing down at him. One of the trackers began cautiously checking each of the huts, each time poking his rifle in, before entering. Then, becoming aware of shadowy movement in the thicket, he was about to shoot, when several arrows sped out of the undergrowth, emitting sharp thudding sounds as they found their target, killing him instantly. The other tracker pulled back the slide on his rifle and, firing from the hip, sprayed the huts with bullets until the magazine was empty. Fergus was sure he was going to die. He held his hands to his ears from the deafening racket, staring up at the panicking man struggling to reload his weapon. Suddenly, in the still air, there was a swift, faint whistling sound as the first poison dart struck. A split second later, as the tracker began to fall, a handful more slammed into his flesh. The tribespeople reappeared from the forest and gathered around the suffering antagonist.

Devoid of emotion, one of the hunters leaned like a man on a garden spade, easing his spear through the dying man's neck.

The captain squeezed his eyes shut, struggling to comprehend what he had just witnessed.

"Oh, holy god."

* * *

Jack knew they didn't understand, and as he walked amongst his tribe, they reached out to touch him. Then, chanting something sad, they waved their hands above their heads and called on Ejengi, the spirit, to protect and return him safely from his travels. For once, he needed them to obey. After all, he was their leader. So, stern-faced, he commanded his people to leave and make their homes deep into the rainforest. He reminded them of the white man's greed, warning that they would come in greater numbers, and hugging one of his closest companions for the last time, pleading, Jack dropped to his knees, gripping the hunter's spear.

"Prévenir les autres."

With a rucksack over his shoulder, Jack stood in the pouring rain, spellbound by the black smoke beyond the rooftops billowing up into the sky. His stomach was sick with grief, and lowering his eyes to the ground, without a glance back, Priest walked away from his people.

As the troop carrier menaced along the narrow muddy track, Pepe came below and sat next to Jack.

"You've probably done them a favour, buddy. Hey, I've spoken with HQ, and this is how my boss wants me to proceed. They were going to send in the Frogmen. However, we've been reliably informed that there are only three opportunists, so it wasn't necessary. With our firepower and the element of surprise, they won't offer much of a challenge. Anyway, they're holed up in a single-storey shack on the outskirts of the village. We'll camp nearby tonight. I want to be in position by dawn, and then you'll get your wish."

"What wish might that be, Pepe?"

"You're going to do the talking, after you stroll up to the front door and introduce yourself as the airline negotiator. You can give some bullshit story about how you flew into Brazza a couple of days ago, then came upriver in a chartered power boat. Tell them you could only raise $600K, sounds more realistic, and when the hostage is released unharmed, you'll take them to the boat to hand over the money."

"I'm not going to piss them off by saying six hundred, and anyway, what will you be doing, Pepe?"

"Don't you worry about me? I'll have one of these in my ear, listening for the right moment to strike. I recommend you get your head down fast when the shooting starts. We won't be taking prisoners."

That night, after setting up camp beside a narrow stretch of river about four kilometres from the village, unable to sleep, and trying to relieve a cramp, Jack became aware of the young private reading his pocket bible by candlelight, and attracted by the naked flame, orbiting erratically, one of the brightly coloured moths wings caught fire. It was an hour to daybreak, and the soldiers gathered around Pepe, transfixed, as he briefed the ambush by torchlight. First, he sketched the attack plans on the side of the BRT's armour using a piece of white chalk. Then, when he opened the well-used carrying case, the American ran his fingers along the Remington M24 barrel before securing the telescopic sight.

Pepe rested the wooden stock on his hip, and focused on the admiring lieutenant.

"This is the newest addition to our peacekeeping kit, and when I fire this beauty, that will be your signal to move in. I should be able to drop a couple of the fuckers before your lot finish it. But, be careful. Priest, and the hostage will be in the line of fire. Pass around a few of these thunder-flash grenades, and tell your men this will be close-quarter combat, so no assault rifles. I'll be doing most of the shooting. Hand pistols only."

The more Jack listened, the more agitated he became.

"Seems to me you're keener to kill a few scumbags than safely secure the release of the pilot."

"You offered your help, and are lucky to be here, so keep your opinions to yourself."

Just before daybreak, the assault party was fully prepared to advance towards the village, and the BRT's infrared lights didn't help much as they mowed their way through the undergrowth to the river's edge.

"You know, Pepe, in the darkness, I could almost imagine we're in a city bus. Listen to the engines, and look at the way he drives."

Jack's remark brought a smile to the American's tense face, as he watched the driver, hunched forward, constantly slipping the wheel left, right, then left again, through his fat, sweaty fingers. He was struggling to see ahead through the tiny armoured window. Then, suddenly, the machine reduced speed, and edging towards the embankment, the shimmering, flooded river, shrouded by a silky mist, was beginning to materialise in the dawn light.

Pushing and pulling on levers, the driver swung the amphibian around before gently reversing from the forest floor into the muddy water. Then, nearing the middle of the river, he swung it back around to face forward. As the colossal propeller trashed the water, the eight massive tyres found grip as they edged up the steep embankment on the other side. For fear of raising the alarm from the noisy engine, the lieutenant ordered the driver to halt and remain with the troop carrier while the assailants continued on foot to the edge of the treeline, which was a few hundred meters from the village.

Then, with everyone in position, scanning through the telescopic gunsight, Pepe focused on the most likely building.

"Yep, I'm sure that's it. I wish the blinds weren't down. Can't make out any movement. Are you ready?"

Jack tapped on his shirt pocket.

"What's the range of this thing?"

"You'll be fine, so when you're ready, chop-chop," goaded Pepe, fiddling with his wireless earpiece.

CHAPTER FORTY-FIVE

Tumper arranged to collect Enda from the hospital at 4am, hoping to avoid the press, and the drive back across the sleeping city created a surreal moment for the young engineer.

"Fuck it, Tumper, this feels familiar. Like I'm heading to work or home after a party."

In the top-floor bedroom, Enda slid the wardrobe door open, and it looked like someone had been shopping. His godfather had followed him up the stairs and stood in the doorway.

"Ahh, for fuck's sake, you shouldn't have. It looks like you've dressed me for a year. It must have cost a fortune. Do ya accept credit cards?"

As they headed back down the stairs to the kitchen, Tumper ruffled the young man's hair, teasing him about getting it cut.

"I'll put the kettle on and make some breakfast. We'll talk about my reimbursement later."

After the traditional fry-up, Enda cleared the table while Tumper made a fresh pot of tea.

"Well, son, I've been thinking a lot, and now I'll do some talking. Firstly, I gave away your insurance cheque."

"What insurance cheque?"

Tumper explained what he had done with the compensation money from Green Bird, and as expected, Enda agreed it was the right thing to do.

"Now, I get it. So that's what Aoife meant about staying," said Enda.

"But more importantly, son, as you know, I lived a turbulent life and am pretty good at sniffing out the truth. When you arrived back from Congo, everyone reckoned you were delusional from a few knocks to the head. You never did tell me the whole story about what happened, but now you seem content to fob me off with that nonsense you wrote for the press."

Enda broke eye contact, shuffling uneasily.

"I'm hoping that when they print the story, it'll buy me some time. However, I must be cautious about what I say. The safety of the others depends on how I handle this."

"Yep, I already figured that. So, when are you going to let me in? I know I can help."

"Give me a couple of days. Hey Tumper, there is something you can do. I mentioned it before. Find Jack Reilly."

* * *

With a Washington Post press badge draped around his neck, agent Bluey mingled with the other reporters, hoping to catch a glimpse of his target, as he waited outside the hospital entrance. Instead, the frustrated concierge came storming out, clapping his hands above his head.

"Right, ladies and gentlemen, the show is over; he's gone home. You're causing an obstruction. Please, move along."

Bluey homed in on one of the independent reporters,

and after a promise of some steamy stateside gossip, she accepted his invitation for coffee across the street. Ravenous, she lapped up his creative, fictional yarns, while he skilfully kept returning the conversation to what she knew about the lone survivor. By the time they parted company, the assassin felt he knew Enda personally, and whispered to himself, "What a kind, gullible lady. Had she asked, we would have paid $100K for that information."

Except for when he slept, Bluey became a part of Enda's shadow. In public, he followed him everywhere, and using simple disguises, together with the latest surveillance technology, he didn't have to get too close to eavesdrop on his target's conversations.

After driving to the airport, Enda sat in the carpark, watching from his jeep until only Gerry remained in the Green Bird office. When the Operations Manager answered the intercom, the voice from the dead frightened him, sending a cold chill down his spine. When the electric lock buzzed again, Enda entered and walked to where Gerry sat on the other side of the high counter.

"You don't look too pleased to see me, Gerry."

"That's fucking ridiculous, Enda. Feckin typical. It seems you haven't lost that bad attitude."

"Speaking of losing, where do you think we should start?"

Gerry shrugged his shoulders. Then, after lifting the countertop, the engineer followed him down the narrow corridor to the scantily furnished coffee room.

"Gerry, we all know accidents happen. That said, I think you and that prick of a boss could have prevented this. You knew a lot more than you said during the pre-flight briefing."

"You're right. There were a couple of unusual bits that I should have mentioned. Believe me; I tried to reason with the boss. We all know what he's like. In the end, he convinced me that it was just another routine humanitarian flight. Enda, I saw the photos and read your press statement, and they don't tally. Anyway, I really can't see how any of those initial concerns would have added in any way to the accident."

"Accident! Gerry, you saw the photos and read my press crap, so which do you think tells the real story? You bollox, you're still holding back. You know a lot more than you're saying, and there are only two reasons why I'm playing along with this. The real version of events would have made the insurance claim invalid, and the families would have got fuck-all. Also, I don't think I'm safely out of the woods yet."

"Well, Enda, you could be right. But what the fuck can I do about it now? It's over. How much time will you need to recover? We're short of crew, and I'm working on next month's roster?"

The punch sent Gerry's spectacles flying as he went backwards over the stool, with blood streaming from his nose. Falling hard to the floor, he made no effort to get up and retaliate.

"Gerry, sorry about my bad attitude. Now, listen carefully. You can consider that punch my resignation? Also, I heard the insurance company coughed up $200K for the loss of the cash. Which is odd, because you knew we were only carrying one hundred and twenty thousand. You have my bank details, so tell the robbing bean counters not to delay. Transfer eighty grand. Let's call it my redundancy pay. I'll let myself out."

CHAPTER FORTY-SIX

Outside Miami International, Sable stepped from the Gulfstream II into the waiting black Dodge Diplomat. Then, after a longer-than-expected drive, she arrived at the research centre. Deckleshine didn't greet her as before. Instead, he left his office door slightly ajar, leaving her to wait after she'd repeatedly knocked. When she entered, the professor stood with his arms folded, ignoring her outstretched hand, which made her feel even more unwelcome.

"I was expecting you. Please, take a seat, madam."

The aluminium case, with the four metal canisters tucked into dark foam lining, lay open on his untidy desk.

"So, that's it," she said, pointing at the case.

"Yes, that's it. However, I've already voiced my opinion. Not going to be very useful, is it?"

"Well, professor, it would all depend on your perspective. Aren't you aware there's the genuine hazard facing our country? What if the Soviets instigated it? What if they intentionally spread the disease?"

"But that doesn't make sense. They would only be targeting a minority."

"Not so. Even our people in Atlanta are calling it a contagious form of cancer. We're all vulnerable."

Deckleshine was playing her well. He wanted Sable to feel safe, and to express her rationale fully.

"I see; you could be right. But what more does your boss want me to do?"

"You're aware that San Francisco is the epicentre? Some of our most senior officials believe we should not delay, and that we should go on the offensive. Will one of those canisters be sufficient?"

"Yes, madam. One will be sufficient."

Sable leaned over, closed the case, and snapped the handcuff on the carry handle around her wrist. Without warning, two men with FBI printed across their bulletproof vests held their badges high as they burst through the office door. Grabbing Sable by the arm, one of the men removed her pistol from the holster, and after unlocking the handcuff from the case, snapping it shut on the woman's other wrist, his colleague cautioned her.

"Agent Sable, you're under arrest for conspiracy to commit murder."

When Deckleshine removed the tiny wireless microphone from his jacket pocket, he handed it to one of the FBI agents. Looking up at the CCTV camera, the professor wondered if the director was watching.

CHAPTER FORTY-SEVEN

Jack left the treeline and walked briskly across the two hundred metres of level ground to the shack. He was just about to tap on the solid wooden door, when it squeaked slowly open to a soldier dressed in tatty jungle combats, with bloodshot dark grey eyes, holding a Smith and Wesson 38 revolver. Straightening the black badge-less beret on his head, and with an air of confidence, the soldier stepped outside onto the rotting timber platform, pulling the door behind him.

"Good morning, sir. How may I be of assistance?"

Jack was surprised by his calm, mannerly demeanour, and tried to match it with his own.

"And a very good morning to you, Colonel. I am the representative from the airline. I believe we have business matters to discuss."

After the soldier patted Jack down, he holstered his revolver, and, carefully stepping along the planks, he eased himself into the rusting swing chair in front of the window. Jack followed the mercenary, who appeared to be deep in thought. Jerking his razor-sharp flick-knife open, he sliced away the tip of a matchstick, and began scraping the dirt from under his fingernails. Then, without looking up, he replied.

"You're too kind, sir. I'm not a Colonel. I'm just a simple soldier, who got lucky, a soldier of fortune, so to speak. While proceeding downriver, we stumbled upon your colleague, who was in a distressed state. Some nasty native savages were holding him captive. But don't worry; we punished them."

Jack longed for a bullet to arrive.

"Well, that's very interesting. So, it would appear my colleague, Quinn, was fortunate you happened to be in the neighbourhood. Now, please allow me to explain my company's position."

Pepe had the crosshairs on his target's forehead, but listening through his earpiece, he found the conversation entertaining and held fire.

"I flew into Brazzaville a couple of days ago, then made my way upriver to be with you today, Colonel. Please, allow me to be plain-spoken. We felt your demand for one million was reasonable. Anyway, it's the insurance company who are footing the bill. Although, given the short notice, we could only accumulate $800K in cash, I hope you will find this an acceptable reward for your efforts."

The soldier licked his lips, and slowly dragged the back of his hand across his sweating brow.

"Yes, I find it most acceptable. However, there is a little problem. Your colleague is very ill. We tried to find the doctor, but alas, he won't be back until tomorrow at the earliest. I think your friend will be dead by then. I'm sorry. We did everything we could to help. Still not sure which disease got him."

Jack stood speechless, with a puzzled look on his face. He'd had enough of the masquerade, but the soldier continued.

"We didn't harm him. On the contrary, we would have honoured our arrangement. So, let us conclude our business, or maybe you would like to take his place."

Pepe was about to squeeze off a shot, when a stubby tree branch whacked him on the back of the head. The lieutenant was wondering what the delay was, and had lobbed the tree branch towards the American, trying to attract his attention. The start caused Pepe to jerk the trigger, and instead of seeing his victim's face explode through the rifle telescope, the bullet struck the wall, a metre from the target's head. Jack dived to the ground, and as he crawled on his belly to the side of the shack, the unnerved soldier clambered to his feet, fumbling at his holstered revolver.

Dumfounded, Pepe swung around and screamed at the lieutenant.

"What the fuck, you idiot?"

Then, quickly composing himself, Pepe aimed again. This time, holding the crosshairs steady on his man, he fired a second round. The bullet hit square between the target's shoulders, instantly dropping him dead on the wooden planks with a thud.

On hearing the first shot, the platoon, as ordered, broke cover from the treeline and ran, pistols in hand, towards the shack. One of the soldiers became over-excited, and instead of drawing his gun, he slid his machete from its sheath, swinging it in circular motions above his head. No one expected two heavily armed men to appear on the shack's rooftop.

The attacking soldiers realised they were in trouble when the enemy opened fire with RPK Kalashnikov machine guns, and finding themselves trapped in the middle of the clearing, it was too late for the troops to turn back. So, in desperation, they fired their handguns, which were uselessly inaccurate, hitting everything except their intended targets. Pepe let off a few more rounds, but, in the mayhem, he missed. Then, discarding his sniper rifle, he rearmed with one of the soldier's assault rifles. The sound of the heavy gunfire made the driver disregard his orders and, slamming the BTR into gear, it lunged forward towards the battlefield.

From the rooftop, the mercenaries rained down hundreds of bullets on the advancing vulnerable soldiers. Riddled with holes, they fell, until not a single one remained standing. Pepe selected automatic, and from hip level, holding the trigger, he sprayed an arc of bullets in the general direction of the shack, emptying his magazine in seconds. The enemy's RPKs replied, sending tracer-guided bullets to his position, forcing him to dive for cover.

When the gunfire eased, hearing the throaty rumble, Pepe ran back under cover of the treeline towards the approaching BTR, waving his hands frantically until it came to a halt. Scrambling inside, to reappear through a roof hatch, he pulled back on the cocking handle of the pintle-mounted KPV-T heavy machine gun, and screamed at the driver to advance. Jack lay motionless against the sidewall of the shack, with his hands covering his ears. Then, tilting his head back, he saw the eight-wheeler accelerate from the treeline. The men on the roof fired a salvo at the advancing troop carrier, but their bullets were ineffective against its heavy armour.

The cannonade retaliation from the heavy machine gun was immediate and frantic, causing Pepe's face to distort with screams of rage. The shack began to disintegrate from the heavy calibre armour-piercing bullets ripping through everything in their path. The walls offered no protection against the powerful weapon, and as the enemy also disintegrated, their mutilated, bloodied limbs lay strewn across the rooftop. The gunfire finally ceased when the BTR rumbled to a halt a short distance from the shack. Unsure about the battle's outcome, Jack kept himself low until a familiar voice called out his name.

"Jack, it's over. You can get up now. I got the bastards."

Shell-shocked, Jack staggered to his feet. Gazing at the carnage, his lungs filled with the pungent smell of the fire-fight lingering in the morning air. When Pepe clambered out from behind the pintle, he stood tall, with his legs apart, proud to emerge victorious. He was climbing off the roof, when one of the soldiers lying nearby called out Mzungu, before firing a single shot from his pistol. The bullet struck Pepe in the stomach, causing him to lose balance and tumble to the ground.

Keeping his head low, Jack edged over to where Pepe lay, and dragging him by his arms, he propped him up against one of the massive tyres. Then, cautiously, he approached the lieutenant lying motionless, face down in the dirt, arm outstretched, still holding his pistol. Jack paced the battle-field, stepping over the bullet-riddled bodies, finding no reason to check for signs of life before returning to the BTR.

"Who shot me?" asked Pepe, in a frail voice, as he pressed his bloodied hands against his belly.

"It was your friend, the lieutenant. He's dead. Satisfied? You managed to kill them all."

After Jack checked the American's bullet wound, he delivered his prognosis with a tone of despair.

"Pepe, you've got a serious gut wound, and I'm sure you understand how this will end. Although it's uncanny, had we been here with my Cessna, you would have had a sporting chance. We can wait around. I believe the village doctor is expected to return soon, or we can take you to Oyo. It's about twelve hours west of here. But I reckon you'll be long dead before we get there."

"I don't want to die in this shit hole. Please, help me. I

need morphine. Call ops; they'll arrange everything. The sat phone is in my jacket pocket."

After patching up the wound, Jack returned to the battered shack and kicked the door open. Inside, a different stench filled the air, and in the dim light of the back room, Quinn's swollen, blistered head lay on a dirty white pillow. Jack went back outside. After fetching a stretcher from the driver, they carried Quinn, laying him down on a wooden bench at the side of the shack. Jack was surprised that the bullets had missed the sick man, and even though he wasn't responsive, Jack spoke aloud as he checked his vitals.

"Well, you poor bastard, it looks like you missed your flight."

Although he couldn't be sure, Jack reckoned it was Ebola, and if so, he also knew how contagious it was. The villagers that had gathered moved aside as the old man with a cane hastily limped over to where Jack stood.

"Priest, my friend, it's so good to see you," bellowed the chubby village doctor, almost crushing Jack's chest with a bear hug.

"Doctor Banza, been a long time. You look well."

"Yes, it's been far too long. I was a few kilometres upstream when I heard the rumpus. I came as quickly as I could. What's going on?"

When Jack finished the narrative, doctor Banza thought for a while before asking the question he knew there was no answer to.

"Is this insane bloodletting ever going to end?"

"Listen, doctor. I can deal with the wounded American. Can you to please see what you can do to help this man? His name is Quinn; he's a pilot. Unfortunately, I think Ebola, so we can't risk taking him with us."

"Of course, I will. I'll get word to your clinic when there's news."

"There is no clinic, my friend. I'll find a way to contact you in a couple of weeks, but for now, I have a few urgent matters to attend to."

The weary old doctor didn't understand what he meant, as Jack smothered his questions with a lengthy embrace.

After the driver gathered his comrades' dog tags and weapons, he began to stack them next to the troop carrier. Initially, he protested, then finally doing as Jack ordered, he moved the weapons inside the shack. The villagers were overjoyed to accept the American dollars, and using makeshift wheelbarrows, they ferried the bodies from the battlefield. Jack stood watching, and wondered if they would bury them as agreed, or toss the corpses in the river. With the engines rumbling and the wounded American onboard, before departing, Jack returned to the shack, and cried out softly as he lobbed the phosphorus grenade through the broken window.

"Destroying these weapons will probably save more lives than my medicines ever did."

The morphine hadn't fully taken effect, and with every judder of the machine over the rough terrain, Pepe groaned in agony; stubbornly ignoring the doctor's advice to rest, he insisted on sitting upright as the slow-moving troop carrier began its long journey west.

CHAPTER FORTY-EIGHT

Alone in his office, the director was delighted to hear Deckleshine's voice.

"Are you aware there's been a new development?" asked Deckleshine.

"No, my friend. I've been away from my desk. Tell me."

"The FBI has arrested your agent Sable, and charged her with conspiracy to commit murder."

"What the fuck are you saying, man? Those frigging feds have their heads up their asses."

Deckleshine couldn't wait to get the words from his mouth. "I helped to bring her down, and I will do the same to you."

The director tried to take control of the conversation, but the professor cut him short.

"No, you listen to me. The ShineOn project is over; it's finished. You will gracefully accept my resignation. Then, you will approve my new appointment as senior physician at the Biomedical Research Agency. From the knowledge I've already gained, I can offer them invaluable support to help fight this appalling disease."

Flabbergasted, once again, the director tried to have his say.

"Do not interrupt," insisted Deckleshine. "You must pay attention. Listen carefully. I will destroy all files and physical forms of ShineOn, retaining only the positive aspects of the research. The FBI will investigate you, and although at this moment they might not have enough evidence to bring charges, if you ever cross my path, or should I be involved in an unfortunate accident, certain tape recordings and restricted documents will reappear. I'll put you behind bars for a long time. Director, allow me to offer some final counsel. Accept my proposal."

"I overestimated you, professor. You were never a patriot. Although it would appear you do have me by the balls, so without prejudice, I accept."

CHAPTER FORTY-NINE

Tumper arranged to meet Enda downtown, in the Stags Head pub, and arriving early, they'd managed to secure two stools at the end of the busy bar. Tumper never liked Gerry, and relished the story, especially the bit about the redundancy pay and the punch.

"Did he get back up before you left?"

"Nope, he just lay there, staring up at me in amazement."

Initially, the conversation was light-hearted until Enda became more serious, raising his voice to be heard above the bustling trade.

"Tumper, you know people. Can you try to find out what happened to Quinn and Fergie? I need to know, because it's playing a lot on my mind. I'm heading up to the cottage for a few days. I have to get my head clear, and when I return, we'll go have a beer, and I'll tell you everything, the full story."

"Okay, but the cottage, is that a good idea, Enda? The press people are under the impression you live there, and they've made it very public. This city's full of heartless reporters. I'm sure they'd love the fame, at your expense. Anyway, I'll see what I can find out about the lads."

"It'll be grand, and hey, I've been meaning to ask, how did my funeral go?"

Tumper placed a friendly hand on Enda's shoulder. "Trust me, son. You don't want to know."

"Thanks. It was a stupid question anyway."

A stranger stood next to them, leaning against the bar, watching as the men left. Then, in a salute, he raised his Guinness to the stag's head, hanging above the antique wall clock, while outside on the street, pulling up their coat collars against the cold drizzle twirling erratically in a light breeze, Enda and Tumper waved goodbye.

CHAPTER FIFTY

"Fuck," the assassin winced. It wasn't the pain that vexed him, but rather the rip in his new beige cotton trousers, as blood began to ooze through. Bluey had stepped clumsily back over the barbed wire fence, brushing his thigh against one of the jagged metal tips. Sitting back in the Ford rental, he eased his trousers down to inspect the damage. It was only a scratch. After swabbing the wound, he applied light pressure with tissue paper until the bleeding stopped.

As Bluey continued to drive up the gorse-lined laneway that led from the main road, looking for a suitable spot to park the rental out of sight, he quickly dismissed the possibility of his target arriving ahead of him. Then, stepping from the car, the assassin zipped and tightened the hood of his hunter-green anorak, seeking comfort against the miserable weather, as whirling scuds of misty drizzle clung to his already damp clothing.

It had taken some time to settle on the method of the kill, until he concluded that under the circumstances, assisted suicide would be most appropriate. Leaning into the boot, Bluey unwrapped the Glock semi-automatic from a muslin cloth, grabbed the thick coiled rope, and tossed it over his shoulder. The cable ties were already in his jacket pocket as he set off up the narrow track that led to the cottage gate.

On the first attempt, the rear bedroom window didn't break, but completely shattered from the heavier clout from the edge of the pistol's handgrip. It would have been possible to climb straight through, but to avoid the chance of shedding more blood on the jutting glass edges, he undid the catch and jiggled the sash window open. Then, wiping away the glass fragments, the assassin rested his backside on the windowsill. Swinging his legs up and over, he ducked a little to ease his torso through the wooden frame.

Cautiously checking each of the four rooms, and sensing the cosiness that seemed to radiate from the oak wood-panelled interior, Bluey's voice echoed a little in the sparsely furnished room.

"Shit, man, this place reminds me of my hunting lodge back home in Colorado."

CHAPTER FIFTY-ONE

E nda paid no attention to the poorly positioned road
sign.

CAUTION LOOSE CHIPPINGS 20 MPH

"Fuck you and your chippings."

The loud music muted his words as he increased his grip
on the jeep's steering wheel. The vocal outburst helped to
focus his mind while struggling to regain control after the
tyres briefly lost grip on the unstable surface. The shot of
adrenaline seemed to sharpen his reactions, and instead of
slowing, he eased down further on the accelerator. Knowing
the route well, he instinctively navigated the twisty moun-
tain road that would soon lead him to Securo, a small
thatched cottage hidden deep in the Dublin Mountains.
Almost a year had passed since the last visit to his place of
sanctuary, although, this time, he wasn't expecting to find
much sanctum. With the unlikelihood of the package being
delivered, his thoughts still remained fixated on it.

As the jeep bounced along the uneven surface, Enda
caught a glimpse of himself in the rear-view mirror. Glazed,

dark blue eyes, set deep in his unshaven, bruised face, gave him the look of a troubled man possessed by demons. Pulling hard on the handbrake, the tyres made a short skid on the gravel outside the rusting steel gate.

Enda sat motionless, gazing through the drizzle and intermittent swipes of the wiper blades, the uneasy anticipation replaced by a sense of urgency. The soft rain was stimulating as he walked up the gravel path, and it felt good on his face. But when he turned the key in the door lock and pushed, it didn't budge. So, he put a shoulder to the swollen timber door, releasing a controlled moan as he forcefully prised it open. Then, stepping inside, a cold draught rushed through the cottage, intensifying the musty smell. Usually, he would linger in the hallway to admire the panorama of cherished framed photographs, awaking memories stretching back to his childhood. But not today.

Being mindful to avoid more pain, with a shove of his backside, the hall door slammed shut, leaving a mound of junk mail heaped against the wall.

Enda was about to bend down when the assassin, Glock in hand, stepped from the sitting room, surprised by the young man's composure.

"So, that's why there was a draught."

"I guess so. Now, follow me. Sit yourself down over there, buddy. That's a comfortable-looking sofa."

Bluey spun the wooden chair around, slipped it between his legs, and sat with his elbows leaning on the backrest.

"I must say, I'm very impressed by your survival instincts. You would have done well in the military. Are you aware that according to the last count, we've lost three of our best agents in that African shithole? Yet here you are, the celebrated survivor!"

Bluey looked up, eyeing the oak wooden beams that spanned the raised roof.

"Unfortunately for you, your luck has run out. However, if you cooperate, I'll do my utmost to make it painless. So, here's the deal. Because of your fragile state of mind, you're going to hang yourself. Now, I could slide the chair away, and you would slowly choke to death, or I could let you fall from a height, then it'll be quick. The drop will break your neck."

Enda recalled Haily's behaviour, fearful of being at the mercy of another professional psychopath.

"I suppose your handlers would like to have the ShineOn canister?"

Bluey tensed. "Yes, they would. I was about to get to that. So, as you've mentioned it first, where is it?"

"I suppose it's pointless for me to try to negotiate. Would you accept it in exchange for my freedom?"

"Correct, pointless. The best I can do is offer a painless exit for the return of our priceless merchandise."

Enda tossed his keys on the floor.

"It's in the jeep's glove compartment."

"Okay then, we'll see. However, remember what I said. If you're dicking with me, I'll have to slow it all down, until you lose your sense of humour."

To be sure his prisoner stayed put, Bluey fastened his hands and legs to a chair with thick cable ties, and went to the hall door. However, he couldn't get a proper grip to pull it open, so he returned to the broken window. Sitting on the ledge, with a pivoting movement, Bluey swung his legs out, then ducked a little to exit through the frame.

Like a player taking a swing at the slither for the winning goal, the base of Tumper's hurley caught the assassin flat on his face. The force drove him tumbling back through the window, with Tumper scrambling behind. Had Bluey not reached for his weapon, Tumper might have spared him. The agent's skull split wide open to a loud snap as Tumper brought the heel of the hurley crashing down. Then, stepping over the swelling puddle of blood, he removed the gun from the assassin's hand and hurried to the sitting room. Stunned to see his godchild strapped to the chair, he began frantically pulling at the cable ties, trying to set him free.

"Are you okay? Are you hurt? Jesus Christ."

"Fuck, that won't work, Tumper. There's a knife in the kitchen drawer."

Leaning against the wall, the stunned young man could hardly stand up from the shock. Tumper rushed back to the bedroom, and removing the dead man's wallet, he grabbed a blanket and hurried to where Enda now sat, shivering at the kitchen table. After draping the blanket across the lad's shoulders and quickly searching the wallet, he found what he was looking for.

"Special Agent Bluey Gardner, he worked for the Americans, CIA."

The young man was unresponsive as the stillness of the evening was adjourned by the squawk of a startled pheasant taking flight.

"Enda, snap out of it. I'm going to need your help."

"We must be fast; there's some tidying up to do. I'll get the minibus from down the lane, and later we'll stuff him in the back. Move your jeep a bit? I want to park beside the gate."

"Okay, I'll move it," replied Enda, his sad eyes radiating surrender.

After climbing through the window, Tumper came to the front of the cottage and, leaning against the hall door, the second heavier shove burst it open. Together they hurried along the weed-strewn garden path, and while Tumper continued down the laneway, Enda's hand shook as he tried to put the key in the ignition. Then, returning to execute the rest of the master plan, wrapping the body in bed linen with the remaining cable ties, they tightly secured the ends.

The men trudged their way towards the side door of the minibus, but the load was too heavy and painful for Enda to bear. Tumper could see his godson was struggling, repeatedly lowering his end, until it brushed along the wet gravel path.

"I'll take it from here. Go on back to the kitchen and wait for me there. Maybe you can make a cup of tea, and listen; I need a mop, rags, and a bucket of water."

As Enda leaned down to pick up the jiffy bag in the hallway, he looked outside, expecting to see Tumper grappling to get the body into the taxi, but the job was already done. It was getting dark by the time they were ready to leave, and after drawing the curtain, it took a few attempts before Tumper finally managed to pull the hall door shut. Then, with drizzly rain matting his grey curly hair, the guardian offered words of comfort to the wasted man sitting in the jeep.

"I've friends who owe me a few favours. They'll put us up in a safe house for as long as it takes."

Driving slowly down the laneway, the minibus stopped just before the main road, and after shading his eyes from the jeep's headlights, Tumper leaned through the driver's window.

"Here's the address. Stay close. We're heading to the north inner city. If we get separated, or the cops stop me, drive on, and I'll see ya at the house."

CHAPTER FIFTY-TWO

Weighing up the moral dilemma, Jack knew that if he applied all of his skills, Pepe would have a good chance of recovery, although he wasn't sure if he deserved that chance. Approaching the halfway point, the troop carrier's three occupants were exhausted from the torturous journey, and stopping to rest under cover of the forest; Jack administered another shot of morphine.

"Tell me something, mister. Back at the compound, would you have played out your threat to murder the women?"

"I don't know. By answering my questions, it gave me a way out. Hey, when I asked you the name of the boat, I knew it couldn't be Titanic, yet I spared her. So, let's be clear; I never murdered anyone. I obey orders, and sometimes that means having to kill. In your profession, you save lives directly. I save lives indirectly."

"You know something, Pepe? You're right. I did lie. The boat's name wasn't Titanic. Also, you know what else? I can only feel pity. You disgust me. That said, I am a doctor, so if you follow my instructions, there's a good chance I'll be able to save your life. Your wound is not as bad as I led you to believe, but you'll be dead within hours if I don't continue to treat that wound."

"Hey, and what about your pilot friend in the shack?"

"Had one of your bullets hit him, you might have done him a favour. I don't think he will make it," replied Jack.

As the men mulled over the quandary of who held the high ground to pass judgment, reaching out with both arms, Pepe grabbed hold and squeezed his adversary's hand weakly.

The road surface began to improve as they approached Oyo, and after a few kilometres further, government troops waved them to a stop. The soldiers were expecting the men. Then after being transferred from the BTR to the waiting military ambulance, it sped away, sirens blazing, towards the hospital. Jack knew his patient would live, so he didn't wait around to visit after the surgery, and when the driver dropped him at his hotel room, even though all he wanted was to sleep, he couldn't. Lots of cold beers, a long hot shower and a slow shave appeared to be the remedy. Jack was strutting around naked in his luxury suite, taking time to select from the gifted new clothing spread across the bed, when the phone rang.

"Doctor Reilly, I'm agent Pepe's boss, calling from Langley. I hope your room is satisfactory, along with our little offerings of thanks. I thought we'd lost another good man. However, the surgeon informed me you saved his life, and I'm very grateful for that. Now, is there anything else I can do for you?"

"Yes, do not punish the tribespeople. They had no part in this."

When the director finished speaking with Jack, he immediately made another phone call, his earlier appreciative tone becoming menacing.

"I don't give a shit if he's in intensive care. Put the phone to his ear. I want to speak with him."

"Please hold," replied the rattled nurse, trying to get the attention of her superior before handing him the phone.

"Now, listen up, doctor, whoever you are. I want you to give my man, agent Pepe, some sort of stimulant. Then, when he's awake, call me back. Do you understand? I just need two minutes. This is a matter of national security importance. Call me when he comes to."

The Naloxone worked better than expected, and as Pepe lay semi-conscious on the hospital bed, a young doctor held the phone to his ear.

"Agent Pepe, you hang in there, buddy. I'm proud of you. But listen, I have a very, very important question, and I need an answer. Have you managed to retain any of the ShineOn canisters? If so, are they in a secure place? I need them; I have some unfinished business to attend to. Speak up, agent Pepe, say again."

"Affirmative."

The following morning, Jack sat in the back seat of the chauffeur-driven Landcruiser as it sped along the N2 towards Brazzaville's international airport. Gliding past another roadside shanty village, savouring the comfort of the air-conditioning and the smell of the leather interior, left the doctor struggling with the paradox. Resetting his thoughts, holding a spellbound gaze through the dark tinted window, as the lush green forest swished by, Jack pondered the how's and what ifs, eager to rekindle the better parts of the life he once had. But, again, burdened with grief, his thoughts drifted back to the life he was leaving behind, and the madness that brought it to an end.

CHAPTER FIFTY-THREE

Enda followed Tumper through the maze of narrow streets until they stopped outside the two-storey end of terrace, in a gloomy council estate.

"It's that house. Wait here until I call you."

Stepping over the waste high garden gate, and before knocking, the hall door edged open. Moments later, frantically waving, trying to hurry Enda, the two men scampered inside to the welcome of a strong northern Irish accent.

"Boys, close and bolt the door behind you."

In the sitting room, after adding a shovel full of coal to the fire, the man with the accent spoke in a slow, matter-of-fact timbre, admiringly looking towards his close comrade.

"Meself and your godfather go back a long way, so you can rest easy. You're safe here. You're under my protection now. This neighbourhood is special. You won't find any informers around here, although, for the moment, stay inside, and stay away from the windows. Well, go ahead, lad, sit down and tell us what happened."

Faced with recalling the ordeal again, Enda tested his troubled mind while the men listened intently, regularly trading concerned glances as if in disbelief, until the man with the accent lit a cigarette and took a deep drag.

"Son, would you mind making a pot of tea? You'll find all you need in the kitchen. I want to have a chat with this auld fella."

The men waited until Enda was out of earshot.

"Right then, Tumper, I first need to bring you up to date. We were never short of sympathisers, and, as a result, the movement has expanded greatly since your time, reaching right across the pond. So, I'm going to make a few phone calls. It shouldn't be difficult to find out exactly why they want him dead. I'll be back as soon as I can."

After bolting the hall door, Tumper returned and sat beside Enda in the kitchen.

"So then, what about that woman who helped you? What are you going to do about her?"

"I don't understand how it happened. Even in the middle of all the shit, Tshala made me want to survive, and I can't get her out of my head."

Feeling awkward, and not wishing to delve into matters of the heart, Tumper was sorry he'd brought it up.

"Let's pack it in and have an early night, could be another very long day tomorrow."

CHAPTER FIFTY-FOUR

The director was on a stopover when the phone in his hotel room buzzed.

"Sorry to bother you, sir. We have some important intel from the Irish. I know it's late, but may I come over?"

When the director came down from his room, the agent was already seated in a quiet corner of the busy hotel bar.

"Well, sir, they would like to do some trading, from what I understand."

"Trading? What sort of trading?"

"Sir, before I begin, another matter needs urgent attention. They want to know what they should do with agent Bluey's body, and the rental. It seems he's gotten himself killed. They said they'll deliver him to us, or if we wish, they can dispose of the remains."

"How the fuck, not Gardner as well? Anyway, that's for later. We don't want the authorities involved. Get them to hand over the body to our people and return the rental. Extend my gratitude for their assistance. Now, tell me the rest."

Beady-eyed, while listening intently, the director sipped

his Jameson whisky, pondering the pros and cons, before interrupting.

"How many agents have we stationed in Ireland?"

* * *

Although regular meetings between the IRA and American intelligence occurred both stateside and at home, this one was different. The atmosphere was relaxed as the four men sat around the polished oval-shaped desk in a meeting room at the Shelbourne Hotel, Dublin. The Irish tried to reason, making a plea on behalf of the hunted man.

"He's only a frightened kid. You read his statement to the press. He's no longer a risk to anyone. The lad is of no value to you, so we think you should let it go."

The Americans detected a disagreeable tone.

"We've always cooperated in the past, and continue to offer strategic guidance for your cause. However, this is a national security matter, our national security, and it's got nothing to do with your political goals."

"Is there anything we can say that might help you change your mind?" asked the Irish man.

"I'm afraid not. We still consider him and his buddy's a hazard. So, the hit remains valid."

When the meeting ended, the men stood and shook hands before departing. First to leave the room, the American's Pan Am smiles quickly faded to looks of displeasure and, descending in the hotel lift, the senior agent couldn't contain himself.

"Can you believe those cheeky cocksuckers?"

. . .

The man with the strong Belfast accent arrived back at the house with two large shopping bags, and handed Tumper a piece of paper with a UK phone number written on it.

"Well, boys, I hope you had a decent night's sleep. Here's some fresh food. I'll join ya for breakfast."

Enda and Tumper were eager to know how the meeting went. However, sipping his tea, the man with the accent voiced his concern about finding a solution.

"We could set you up with a new identity. You could even choose the country, but, to be honest, it would only be a matter of time. They'll find you."

Returning after an extended visit to the bathroom, Tumper had come up with an idea which would require a second meeting with the Americans.

"I'll be back shortly, lads. I have to make a few phone calls."

* * *

"Hello, who's this?"

"It's Tumper, Enda's godfather."

"How the fuck did you get this number?"

"That doesn't matter. What matters is I know you risked everything to help the crew. Enda is here with me. He's safe, for now. It's Quinn and Fergie I'm concerned about?"

Before Jack said what he knew, he received assurances from Tumper that he wouldn't reveal his whereabouts to anyone or try to involve him further.

* * *

Deciding to wait until the photos were developed before requesting a second meeting at the Shelbourne, this time, the atmosphere was cooler and less friendly than before, with the Americans at one end, and Tumper standing next to his Ulster friend at the other end of the desk.

"We thought we made our position clear during our last meeting."

"Well, I wasn't at that meeting. So, for all our sakes, let's try again," replied Tumper.

His curt manner grabbed their attention. Sliding the A4 envelope across the polished wooden desk, the Americans took their time to examine the photos, unable to recognise which of their colleagues had been targeted through a telescopic gunsight.

"What is this? Are you insane? Are you seriously attempting to intimidate us?"

"No, never, on the contrary. One of our operatives acquired those photos, and we believe we know the identity of the insurgents. A bunch of Middle Eastern psychotics, based in the UK. Nonetheless, it appears to be a bona fide threat, and we can alleviate it."

Before they could reply, Tumper slid the jiffy bag with force, sending it flying off the far end of the desk. One of the Americans picked it up from the floor and removed the ShineOn canister. Then, after shifting back out of earshot to discuss the new development, they stepped back to the desk.

"Okay, under normal circumstances, I wouldn't bother the director, but this ain't normal."

The American spoke for some time, shading his mouth with his hand. Then, switching his satellite phone to speaker, he placed it on the desk.

"Gentlemen, I truly admire your Irish innovation. However, on this occasion, you're behaving like amateurs. Goddammit, don't you ever attempt to undermine my people? I'm having a Jameson, and, fortunately for you, it's helping to calm me down. One of your compatriots, Jack Reilly, recently did us a great service, and now, with your surprise offering, we have the last missing piece of this fucked up mission. So, here's what I propose. Tell your young man to move on and forget about the past couple of weeks. Tell him to believe the story he told the press. If he can do that, he can have his life back. Hey, before I sign off, who killed Bluey Gardner?"

Tumper took a few steps along the desk and leaned over the phone.

"I did. I killed him in self-defence, and if you want to know where I live, just ask. And there's one more thing. About the pilots, Quinn, and Fergus. We just got word there's a chance they're still alive. One of them is very ill, but if they survive, I'd like you to include them in the deal; let them all be?"

"You've got some real cojones. Now listen carefully to what I'm about to say. You lot better come up with another compelling story for the press, and we better not be included in it. Okay, same deal for them."

Before returning to give Enda the surprising news, Tumper made a detour. Jenny was alone in the cottage, and her face lit up with a smile on seeing her old friend at the hall door.

"Come in; please come in. I'll put the kettle on."

Jenny knew it wasn't a social visit, but she went along with the small talk as they sipped tea in the living room, until she could wait no longer.

"Tumper, please tell me, what's the real reason for your visit?"

Sitting paralysed, with a distant look on her face as he delivered the news about her husband, Tumper leapt to his feet, managing to grab her before she collapsed in the chair. However, it wasn't very long before she recovered, and with tears filling her eyes, her close friend held her, wrapped safely in his arms.

"I'm sorry, Jenny, I only got the news a short time ago, and another matter had to be dealt with before I could say anything. Enda doesn't even know. I'm going to write a letter explaining what I've just told you, but Enda won't be reading it for some time, because if I tell him now, he'll be on the first available flight back to Congo. Either way, I don't think he will ever forgive himself. He truly believed Quinn was dead. You must be strong and keep this information to yourself, until I can find out more. It will take time. Both Quinn and Fergie's lives might depend on it. Also, let's not be getting our hopes up too much."

Jenny sat sobbing uncontrollably, while slowly nodding her head.

CHAPTER FIFTY-FIVE

Enda knew his world was damaged, but he didn't want to repair it; he wanted a new one. After he told Aoife about Tshala, they agreed to live apart and try to continue as friends. However, secretly, she hoped it was only an infatuation that time would heal. Not ready to let go, Aoife would often phone Enda, trying to persuade him to ask for his job back, and although well meant, he didn't like her persistence. Tumper wanted to keep a close eye on his godchild, and was delighted when he agreed to extend his stay, at least until he was sure the danger had indeed passed.

It was early one evening, and while having a pint in their local, Enda suddenly changed the subject.

"I bought a sailing boat."

He expected Tumper to be surprised, but he wasn't.

"Sure, that's great news. Tell me more?"

Enda beamed with joy, and spoke excitely.

"Do you remember the story I told you about my farewell to Gerry? Well, I couldn't believe it. They actually coughed up the eighty grand. I had savings, and with the surprise bonus, I bought a five-year-old Malo116. She's an absolute beauty; would take us safely around the world. For the moment, she's moored in Malahide. I hope you don't mind; I've already moved most of my stuff. She's so roomy, I've decided to liveaboard."

"And why not? Sounds like a great plan. When are you going to take me out for a spin?"

Enda was relieved. He respected his godfather's opinion. If Tumper had disapproved, it would have spoiled everything.

"I'm considering a long solo voyage, so I am. I'll tell ya more when I've figured out the details. Did you hear that Aoife and some lads have organised a flight for my birthday? Although, to be honest, I'm not too pushed. They keep going on about my damn career, and when will I return to work. Anyway, I'll go along with their little celebration; they're just trying to get me back into the saddle."

CHAPTER FIFTY-SIX

Unable to wait any longer, Tshala phoned Tumper.

"Please, please forgive me for phoning. Enda told me to wait. I'm so sorry."

Tumper could hear the distress in her voice.

"You must be Tshala? I'm Tumper. I was half expecting to hear from you."

"Please, I need to know if he's safe. Is he okay?"

"There's nothing to be sorry about. Now, calm down, and let's have a chat."

After talking for much longer than expected, Tumper tried to be tactful before ending the call.

"Well, Tshala, the way I see it, I only know of one person who wouldn't be very pleased to see you."

* * *

It was a crisp, clear morning, and the trio met at Iona Flying Club on the perimeter of Dublin Airport. The instructor informed them that he had filed a flight plan for a low-level jolly, which would take them south along the coast.

"My pal couldn't make it, although for you, Aoife, that

will work out well. You'll have the whole back seat to your-self. Enda, it's your birthday, so you'll be doing all the work, me lad. I'll only interfere, if you're about to fuck things up."

There was plenty of humour and a few hearty laughs as Enda taxied the little aeroplane towards the runway. However, the birthday boy wasn't enjoying himself. It had been a long time since he had flown a Cessna, so he manoeuvred slowly, while trying to retune his ear to the pilot jargon over the radio. Then, while waiting on the taxiway for their turn to launch, the Boeing ahead of them received its departure clearance over the radio.

"Shamrock 1703, you are cleared to destination, via Liffy One Alpha."

The words struck like lightning at his soul. Quickly undoing his seatbelt, Enda reached forward to remove the ignition key, and as the propeller swung to a stop, a heavy shudder ran through the airframe. Enda, almost tripping over, leapt down from the Cessna. Then, ducking under the wing, with all his strength, he threw the key as far as he could, watching it tumble through the air before disappearing into the high grass.

CHAPTER FIFTY-SEVEN

Tumper arrived with his dog to have lunch with his godchild.

"Jaysis, Enda, she's a fine vessel, and I know you've got a Yachtmaster's, but are you sure ya can handle her on your own?"

"She's a doddle. The only thing I need to be cautious about is the weather. I've got every conceivable safety gismo, so I'll be grand, as long as I don't rush or become over-ambitious. Will we head out for a spin?"

Tumper shuffled uneasily as he sat in front of the wheel, gently brushing the tips of his fingers across the chamois leather covered helm, like a baby discovering touch.

"To be honest, son, I'm quite happy here in the marina. I never had great sea legs, but maybe, when you return. What's the plan anyway?"

"If I set off early in the morning, I should have no problem making Kilmore Quay before dark. I might hang around there for a day or two before continuing to Kinsale. I really like Kinsale, so I'll stay there while planning the big trip. I'll be heading south for sure. Maybe initially to Galicia in Spain, or I might simply drop a pin on a map."

"Fuck, I'm envious. By the way, what name have you given her?"

"Did you not see it on the transom, when you boarded? I named her, *Lisette Letitia.*"

"Well, I remember your Mam's name was Letitia. Who's Lisette?" asked Tumper.

"That was Tshala's mother's name."

Feeling an unfamiliar sadness drift over him, Tumper made excuses that it was time for him to go. Stepping onto the pontoon, he called his dog, but the dog wouldn't budge. Instead, Semtrick stretched his belly on the deck, mewling like a child, paws against his floppy ears, making them laugh aloud.

"The little fecker looks like he's chosen a new master. Enda, can ya take him with you? He's due a holiday, and do me a favour. Before you bring him back, could you give him a new name? I was very drunk the day I tried to baptise him."

"What if I don't come back?"

"You'll be back. But, listen, before you go, take this, there's a letter from me inside. I need you to promise not to open it until you're well on your way. Give it a month or two."

"Sounds very mysterious. Okay, I promise."

The young man and the old man's dog watched as the godfather strolled away, until, never once looking back, Tumper disappeared from sight. Then, leaning over the steering wheel, unable to see clearly through his watery eyes, Tumper whispered before driving away, "I must be starting to dote."

CHAPTER FIFTY-EIGHT

A lthough the wind was bitterly cold, the stiff morning westerly made sailing conditions perfect. Enda had prepared an equipment checklist, and thrilled to see the boat making seven knots over the water, he ticked off the last item, marvelling at how the yacht flawlessly performed. After spending only one night in Kilmore, he couldn't wait to get back on the water, so he continued to Kinsale. Being off-season meant it wasn't difficult to secure a mooring in the fabulous new marina, and by the time Enda had finished hosing the boat down, the light was beginning to fade. So, feeling his appetite grow, with a perk in his step, he headed up into the town.

Unfortunately, with the tourist season over, there was a shortage of open restaurants, so Enda settled on The White House. Usually, he didn't like dining alone, yet, for some unknown reason, that no longer mattered. After wolfing down a bowl of delicious fish chowder, followed by cod and chips, he moved into the bar. Making himself comfortable on a high stool at the counter, Enda was pleased it wasn't jam-packed. Only a few locals were gathered in their corner, chewing the fat, next to the blazing log fire radiating a homely warmth. The chatty elderly lady across the counter was very engaging, and not only did she tell Enda where he could buy provisions, she even drew a map. He was on his third pint when, straining his vision, he tried to make out the reflection in the faded antique mirror above the bar. Enda rubbed his eyes, and speaking louder than he had planned, he swung around, sliding off the stool.

"Either it's the Guinness, or I'm hallucinating."

Tshala stood motionless, the hood of her soaked, over-sized, bright blue raincoat almost covering her whole face, while her hands appeared to have disappeared up the sleeves. Then, as Tshala ran towards Enda, the hood flew back, her Duchenne smile magnified by the orange glow from the open fire. Reaching out, he caught her as she leapt from the floor, and wrapping legs and arms tightly around him, they kissed and hugged passionately, to the delight of the small adoring audience.

"How did ya know I'd be here?"

Tshala had begun to explain about the phone calls with Tumper when, breaking into a cold sweat, she became apologetic.

"Oh no, I should have asked you before coming."

"Ask? Are ya mad? You're the best surprise ever. Jesus, I can't believe this. When did ya arrive?"

"A few minutes ago. I flew from Kinshasa to London, and then to Cork airport. I just got off the bus."

"Jesus, I can't believe my eyes. You must be worn out from travelling."

"Nope, I'm grand. Hey, Enda, can I have that pint of Guinness, please?"

The young couple were euphoric, and aware that another pint would have them crawling on the floor; the bar lady insisted that the sweethearts let her drive them the short distance down to the marina. When they got out of the car, the driver stood in the middle and, linking arms, guided them safely down the dimly lit gangway. The kind lady offered a steading hand as they boarded, until suddenly, Tshala took a step back, imagining she'd seen her mother's name painted on the yacht's transom. Then, easing down carefully to her knees, Tshala whispered something to Lisette and Letitia, as warm tears of joy trickled down her cheeks.

Had it not been for the dog with no name, whimpering outside the door, the couple would have slept all day. Sprawled out across the bed, stretching her arms, massaging the sleep from her eyes, her radiant smile fused with his to light up the snug cabin. Then, leaning closer, sensing the spiritual awakening, he tenderly kiss her forehead, and gently caressed her long silky hair. Enda had found his new world.

"With a fair wind in our sails, and you as me first mate, I reckon about ninety days. Tshala, can I take ya home?

AFTERWORD

Conceived over two decades ago, my story, *Liffy One Alpha*, is finally in print. Way back in the nineties, employed as a first officer by a legendary Irish freight airline, I flew the DC8 to many remote locations around the world. In fact, there were scenes during the writing when I simply recalled actual events. Flying with so many colourful characters made it easy to reproduce a surreal mix of fact and fiction in this, my debut novel.

To tell a story is one thing; however, to get it down on paper, well, that's another matter altogether. Fortunately for me, and more importantly for you the reader, my friend and mentor, David G Llewelyn, the man with unflappable patience and intuitive editing skills, chaperoned me to the final draft. Forever grateful David. To the beta readers, Eduardi Jurado, Des, Monica, Gerry, and Dave. To Ken Scott, author and ghost-writer. Richard Bradburn, author and editor. Anthony J. Quinn, author and journalist, whose kind endorsement encapsulates the story so well. Thank you all so much. To the missus, Dominique, my daughter, Tanith, and my sister, Carmel, who, over the years, encouraged and enthusiastically reviewed the many rewrites. Love you to bits.

And lastly, there's my dear pal, now crewed by squadrons of mischievous angles, no less. I miss ya, Captain Fergie, me auld flower.

Padric J. Kelly

*My first attempt at copyright protection. Posted to my home and
unopened to this day, the registered letter containing the first draft of*
Liffy One Alpha.

Printed in Poland
by Amazon Fulfillment
Poland Sp. z o.o., Wrocław

25840640R00176